Chosen
by God

JODY MARIE WHITE

Chosen
by God

TALES OF

EXCEPTIONAL

CHARACTER

TATE PUBLISHING
AND ENTERPRISES, LLC

Published by Tate Publishing & Enterprises, LLC
127 E. Trade Center Terrace | Mustang, Oklahoma 73064 USA
1.888.361.9473 | www.tatepublishing.com

Tate Publishing is committed to excellence in the publishing industry. The company reflects the philosophy established by the founders, based on Psalm 68:11,
"The Lord gave the word and great was the company of those who published it."

Published in the United States of America

ISBN: 978-1-61346-934-7
1. Fiction / Christian / Short Stories
2. Fiction / Short Stories
11.11.17

Dedication

To: Erwin, the one God chose to keep me going.

The Chosen Queen

"Yet who knows whether you have come to the kingdom for such a time as this?"

Esther 4:14b (NKJV)

To: LuAnn, who got me started.

Chapter 1

"That is the last time you will embarrass me," King Cortierre said as he stormed into the room where he had sent his son after the banquet. He slammed the heavy wooden door and stalked across the brocade carpet to tower over where his son sat. "You cost me a vital alliance with the country of Janier!" His face turned bright red as he fumed.

"It is still my choice whom I marry, Father," Prince Roygan said with a quiet firmness.

"It is your choice for eight more months," the king reminded his son through clenched teeth. "If you forfeit that choice by your twenty-fifth birthday, the decision becomes mine."

"I know, Father," the young prince said with a slight tone of defeat. Then he added with a hint of humor, "Can you honestly tell me, though, that you would like to have the princess of Janier as your daughter-in-law?"

The king gave way to the father as he physically grimaced. The prince relaxed and allowed himself to chuckle.

King Cortierre sighed. "You did not have to ask her to marry you, son. You could have simply rejected her. The alliance would still have a chance in that scenario. But did you have to offend her in the process?" His voice rose as he remembered the embarrassment anew.

A sly smile played at the corner of Roygan's lips. "You know you were thinking the same thing."

"Thinking is one thing. Speaking is a different matter entirely," the king lectured.

Roygan smiled, knowing his father was amused, though embarrassed.

"Eight months, Roygan," Cortierre said sternly. "You have your freedom for that period of time. I suggest you exercise it." He turned his back, silently dismissing his son.

Roygan quietly stood and exited the room. His mood had now changed from merriment to pensive. The relationship between father and son was genuinely pleasant. They usually were able to get along. However, they did have their disagreements. The closer his twenty-fifth birthday neared, the more heated the disagreements became over the marriage law.

According to the royal law of the country of Groy, to be crowned king, the prince must be married. If the prince was not married by the time he was to be crowned king, the crown would be passed to the closest married male relative.

The prince had the right to choose his bride, if he chose her before his twenty-fifth birthday. If a bride was not found by that date, the choice became the king's in an effort to keep the crown in the family line.

Neither Cortierre nor Roygan wanted the crown passed to the next male relative. They did not get along with Roygan's cousin, Magdorn. He was pompous, sleazy, and incredibly disrespectful of women. He was everything Roygan was not and nothing Roygan was. Despite his radical ideas, Roygan did want to become king. He wanted to do good for the people.

He passed down the long stone hallway to his quarters as he mused over the situation. Arriving at his door, he slowly pushed it open and solemnly entered his room. He was met by his servant and close friend, Arriah.

"Good evening, Your Highness," Arriah said, bowing. He brought over the prince's evening robe. "You don't look your jovial self, Sire. I thought the evening a great success. The look on the princess's face was priceless as she stormed out of the banquet hall."

Roygan smiled as he remembered. "It was quite entertaining."

"Then why the long face, if I may inquire?"

"Of course," Roygan acknowledged. He was extremely lax with his servants, especially Arriah. He did not require the strict adherence to protocol that his parents did. He considered Arriah more a friend than a servant and confided in him regularly. "It's *the law*," he said raising an eyebrow.

Arriah understood completely. The two had had many conversations regarding *the law* over the past years.

"We've been looking for a bride for the past seven years," Roygan lamented, dramatically pacing across the room, "and we're nowhere nearer a solution now than we were then. Now, I only have eight months. Eight months, Arriah! What am I to do? I do not know who my father has in mind for me to marry, but I assure you, I do not want to find out." He flung himself across his bed.

"I've continued thinking on the matter, sire."

"Have you come to any solutions?"

"Just an idea, Your Highness," Arriah said carefully.

"Do tell, please. I'll consider anything." Roygan raised himself up, leaning on his elbow. He listened with hopeful interest.

"What if we simply gathered all of the beautiful, available women your age and brought them to the palace grounds? There are plenty of unused rooms throughout the castle in the guest wings that would hold one hundred or more girls." Arriah suggested simply. "We could send them through beautifying treatments such as facials, hair styling, nail coloring, and makeup techniques, as well as etiquette classes. You would be able to meet them all and then choose for yourself. We could invite all women who qualify, no matter their station."

The prince mulled the idea over. He wasn't sure if it would work. He wasn't sure if his father would agree. "I suppose it would be worth a try," he finally said. "If we didn't find anyone after all of that, we could at least say we did everything we could. Every available woman in the country doesn't leave much to be left behind."

"Precisely, sire"

"It actually might work," Roygan said, becoming excited at the idea. "With all the pampering, surely the true personalities of most of the women will be forthright. We could really weed out the pompous, snooty ones from the lot of them."

"Exactly, sire." Arriah had thought of this, knowing the prince's biggest desire was to have a sensitive, caring, companion for a wife. The biggest challenges he had had with the women his father suggested was their arrogance and inclination toward being pampered.

"I think it is a grand idea, Arriah," Roygan smiled. "You are in charge. I want all beautiful, available women from the age of seventeen to twenty-three brought to the palace. Spare no expense. Give them beautifying treatments and etiquette classes and whatever else you deem necessary. I want to meet the first lot within four weeks."

"Yes, sire. I'll begin at once."

Roygan smiled. "Nice job," he praised his friend.

———

"This is utterly ridiculous!" Katyan Amman laughed as she read the announcement. "Someone out there has more money and time than brains. Can you imagine the king actually placing an advertisement for a wife for his son?"

"It is not a joke, dear," Katyan's Aunt Barria said. "Look, the king's seal is on the announcement."

Katyan looked closer at the paper. She was shocked. The official seal of the king was indeed on the ridiculous publication.

"Not only is it not a joke," Uncle Dadaan joined in, "but you, my dear, have been chosen as a candidate."

Katyan looked at her uncle incredulously. "Surely I don't have to do this," she hoped.

"I'm afraid you do, my dear," Aunt Barria said. "They're not asking for volunteers. You've been conscripted. You're to leave tomorrow morning."

Katyan was speechless. Not only was she going to have to stop working until this ridiculous affair was over, but her freedom had just been stripped away. She had now been told what to do and where to go. She knew she would be told what to do and where to go once she arrived at the palace, as well. She had always been a headstrong girl and had enjoyed her independence. This loss of freedom suddenly left her tired and sad. "I must go inform Lady Odi of my absence," she said quietly as she left the house. Katyan worked as a personal maid to the wife of one of the largest land owners in her town.

Dadaan and Barria knew their niece well and decided to not follow her. She would talk with them when she was ready.

Katyan walked pensively to her employer's house, not sure how to inform the lady of this news or how she would take it, but she knew she needed to get it over with. As she approached the house, her pace slowed, her nerves becoming more tense. Lady Odi had a temper and could be quite prejudiced at times. Katyan reached the door and, using the brass knocker, announced her presence.

The house maid answered the door and went to tell the mistress of Katyan's return.

"Katyan," Lady Odi said with surprise, "I thought you'd left for the day. What are you still doing here?"

"Forgive me, my lady," Katyan bowed to her mistress. "I had indeed left, but I needed to return to inform you that I will not be returning to work for an indefinite period of time." Katyan was embarrassed at the request from the king and hoped this excuse would be sufficient.

"Why not?" Lady Odi asked haughtily.

Katyan took a deep breath. "My presence has been requested at the palace. I am to report tomorrow."

Lady Odi clasped her hands in pleasure. "How wonderful. My daughters have been nominated as candidates for the prince's wife. It will be nice for them to have someone there who knows them. I must be sure to request that you serve them during their stay." Then she winked. "Perhaps they will keep you on when the prince inevitably chooses one of my daughters to be his wife."

"Forgive me, my lady," Katyan corrected, "my presence has not been requested as a servant. I, too, have been nominated as a candidate."

Lady Odi's eyes narrowed. Then she laughed incredulously. "You, a servant, nominated for the future queen. How ridiculous. Oh, this must be so embarrassing for you. Obviously the prince won't choose a servant to be his bride. Well, enjoy your vacation, but I expect your immediate return once the prince has made his decision." She turned and walked away muttering, "Now, who am I going to find to replace that girl while she's gone?"

Katyan stood for a moment outside the door. This interchange served not to embarrass Katyan further, but to embolden her. She turned and walked down the long driveway and back across town to her uncle's cottage. Her pensiveness turned to resolve. She would go to the palace. She would do her best to honor her family. She was under no illusions that the prince would choose her, a servant, but she would do her best nonetheless.

She met her aunt and uncle in the garden and told them of the conversation with Lady Odi and her new resolve. "What advice can you give me?" she asked.

"Be yourself, dear," Aunt Barria said. "You're such a pleasant young lady, just be yourself."

"Listen to the servants," Uncle Dadaan said. "Being a servant, yourself, you know servants usually know the master better than anyone. Seek their council, and do as they say."

"I will," Katyan agreed. "Anything else?"

"Yes, dear," Uncle Dadaan said slowly. "Don't tell them you're Doriian."

Katyan looked confused. "You want me to deny my heritage? Deny my mother? Deny you, Uncle?"

"No dear, not deny us, simply not to divulge anything. The prince has no prejudices, I have heard. However, that is not the case with many on the king's council of advisors. The king, himself, might have some prejudices. Many on the council have an irrational dislike of the people from the country of Dorii. Some of them are descendants of council members of King Patran who ordered the purges of '24. It would be best to keep this secret for now."

Katyan's mother was from the neighboring country of Dorii. She married a man from Groy, Katyan's father, and moved to his country with him. They both had died when Katyan was twelve leaving her to the care of her aunt and uncle. They had kept their heritage secret knowing the prejudices of many against their country. Katyan had an easier time of hiding her heritage since she looked more like her father who was from Groy. She had the same dark hair, eyes, and skin as he. Her uncle had a more difficult time since his features were almost clearly Doriian with light hair, blue eyes, and fair skin. These features made the Doriian people stand out among many countries in the area. Ancient wars had cultivated a modern hatred between the countries, though most prejudices came simply from a dislike of the physical features of the people.

Katyan agreed to keep her heritage secret. She respected her uncle and the advice he gave. She thanked them and went inside to gather her meager belongings.

Chapter 2

Katyan gazed out of the carriage as they approached the palace. She had never been to Sharin, the capital city of Groy, and had never seen the palace. What she saw took her breath away. The castle had been designed to intimidate foes. The architect had done a superb job. Tall spires stretched toward the sky like fingers, challenging anyone who might oppose the king. Sentries stationed behind stone outcroppings watched the people with careful eyes, ready to strike with their arrows. Flags flew atop the spires reminding everyone of the ruling family.

Merchants surrounded the castle wall selling their wares and calling to the passersby. Nobility browsed through the stalls for something worth their money. Peasants scampered around the nobility in hopes of finding something they could afford.

Katyan's carriage approached the moat surrounding the castle. The driver announced himself and his passenger. The drawbridge was lowered and hit the ground with a thud, sending a cloud of dust into the air. The driver clucked the horses on over the bridge. Katyan gazed out the back window of the carriage at her last glimpse of freedom as they rolled across the bridge. Once they were inside the castle walls, the drawbridge was raised and clanged shut eerily.

The driver pulled to a stop outside a side door. He came to help Katyan down from the carriage then turned to carry her bag. She followed him to the door and waited as he knocked.

The door was answered by a severe-looking woman dressed in a plain brown dress. Her hair was pulled straight up into a bun, giving her face a more severe look. The driver announced Katyan, said good-bye to her, and left.

"I am Mrs. Fasi," the woman said. "Follow me." She turned and walked briskly down the hallway.

Katyan grabbed her bag and hurried to catch up. The hallway was as foreboding as the outside of the castle. They were in a long, dark, stone hallway. Every few feet on the walls were mounted candle sconces giving dim light. Heavy wooden doors hid the rooms behind them. The only decorations were large coats of armor giving tribute to past glories. As she passed the armor, Katyan could envision ghosts of the former occupants peering at her through the face guards. She shuddered and tried to stifle her vivid imagination.

Mrs. Fasi stopped abruptly at one of the heavy wooden doors. She grabbed the knocker and knocked three times. The door opened and a young man stood greeting them with a smile.

"Sir, this is Katyan Amman," Mrs. Fasi announced.

"Thank you, Mrs. Fasi," the young man said. "You may come in, Miss Amman."

Katyan thanked Mrs. Fasi and curtsied.

Mrs. Fasi seemed flustered at the act of deference. Only servants curtsied in that manner to those above them.

Katyan turned back to the young man who was smiling in approval and amusement.

"I am Arriah," he said as he showed Katyan into the room. "I am the personal assistant to the prince. This will be your new quarters for the time being. You shall have your personal assistant within a few minutes."

"Thank you," Katyan said and curtsied.

Arriah bowed in response. "I will leave you to get settled. If you need anything, do not hesitate to ask."

Katyan thanked him again and curtsied.

Arriah left the room and closed the door behind him. He smiled to himself as he went to inform Ania who she would be waiting on. He already liked this Katyan Amman.

The knocker sounded, and Katyan went to answer the door. She was met by a lovely young woman about her age. The woman had short brown hair, brown eyes, and tan skin. She looked very Groyan. But then, so did Katyan although her mother's ancestry was not from this country at all. The woman, in fact, had many features the same as Katyan. Katyan had cut her hair in the recent style as well. Her dark eyes and tan skin almost matched the woman facing her.

"Good afternoon, my lady, and welcome to the palace," the woman said. "I am Ania. I will be assisting you during your stay."

Katyan smiled, "Thank you for the welcome. Please, do come in. I am Katyan Amman." She stepped aside for Ania to enter.

"I hope you find your quarters pleasing, Miss Amman," Ania said.

"Very much so," Katyan answered. "Please, though, do not call me 'my lady' or 'Miss Amman.' I know your station is above mine. I am uncomfortable with the titles."

Ania looked pleased but confused. "What shall I call you, then, for I will be waiting on you?"

"I prefer to simply be called by my given name," Katyan pleaded.

Ania looked at her new mistress with appreciation. She nodded and said, "All right, Miss Katyan."

That wasn't what Katyan had hoped for. She smiled slyly at Ania and said, "I can settle for that, *Miss* Ania." Then she curtsied.

Ania giggled knowing she would not win. "I cannot abide that. I will call you Katyan."

Katyan smiled knowing she had made a friend.

Ania then began to show Katyan around the suite that would be her quarters for an indefinite period of time.

Chapter 3

Katyan had been at the palace for three months and had not seen the prince. She had been through the etiquette classes with the other ladies and had seen the beauticians, and besides Ania, that was it. She had tried to talk with the other ladies, however, thanks to Lady Odi's daughters, they all knew her station and treated her as such. She realized Ania was her only friend at the palace. She was becoming restless. The beauty treatments had been fun at first, but now were tiring. She enjoyed learning the fine points of etiquette, but now was becoming annoyed at every little detail. What was the point of all this, if she didn't need to use it? The prince had five months left before he needed to be married. Surely he would pick someone soon. Perhaps he already had and they'd forgotten about her. She didn't mind not being picked; she just wanted to know what was happening. She was fidgety.

She did enjoy her time with Ania. The assistant had become a friend. The two shared long walks along the palace grounds, often being allowed into each other's confidence. Katyan had learned that Ania was engaged to Arriah, the prince's personal assistant. However, they were waiting on their wedding until the prince wed.

They shared about their families. Katyan had met Ania's parents who worked at the palace as well. She had shared about her family, though leaving out the fact that her mother had been Doriian.

This particular morning, Katyan had risen with the sun. She was up and ready for the day before Ania knocked on her door. She sat looking out the window at the beautiful day ahead of her, though she was still sad. It was her twentieth birthday this day and she was not able to share it with her aunt and uncle. She had mentioned only briefly to Ania during the first week of her stay when her birthday was. She did not expect Ania to remember.

"Good morning, Katyan," Ania announced as she entered the suite.

"Good morning, Ania," Katyan smiled at her friend.

"I was thinking perhaps you would enjoy a walk outside today, perhaps to the stables?" Ania asked.

This was where Ania's father worked. Katyan had come to love this part of the palace. She had always loved horses. She found the palace horses magnificent. "I would love that," she said, her face brightening.

"By the way," Ania said smiling, "happy birthday." She brought out a small bouquet of flowers and set it on the table.

"Oh, thank you!" Katyan cried. She hugged her friend, appreciating the gesture immensely.

Breakfast arrived and the two sat down to eat together, as had become their custom since Katyan first arrived at the palace.

"Ania, has the prince found a wife, yet?"

"No, not yet, why would you think that?"

"I've been here for three months and haven't heard a thing. I've immensely enjoyed our friendship, but I'm getting fidgety otherwise. I don't mind not being picked. In fact, I truly expect that, but I would like to know something. How long will I be here before the prince sends me home?"

"Now, Katyan, you have no idea that he will send you home. He's simply seeing each woman one at a time for dinner until he finds the right one. Believe me, Arriah has told me it's not going well. There are one hundred women here. The prince wants to be fair, so he is seeing each woman in the order of when they arrived. He only saw the first ones three weeks ago."

"What number am I?" Katyan asked, dreading the answer.

"Forty-five," Ania said.

"Forty-five! The prince won't be seeing me for another month, then." Katyan sighed, resigning herself to the fact that she would be here for a while. "Ah, well, I will make the most of it."

Ania liked this part of her mistress. Katyan's attitude always seemed to come around to the positive, no matter how down she became.

They finished their breakfast and gathered their wraps to walk outside.

———

"Arriah, this is not going well," Roygan said. "Some of these women are worse than the royalty my father set me up with."

"There is someone out there for you, my Lord, I know it," Arriah said. He was biding his time. He had come to know Katyan almost as well as his fiancé. He believed she was the one, but didn't want to push his master.

"Then where is she?" Roygan asked, exasperated.

Arriah didn't answer, knowing it was a rhetorical question.

Roygan went to the window and gazed out as if looking for something. After a few minutes he said, "There is Ania walking the gardens." Then, after a pause, he asked, "Who is that walking with Ania? The woman looks like her. Ania doesn't have a sister, does she?"

"No, sire," Arriah answered as he walked to the window. He knew full well it would be Katyan walking with his fiancé. He took his time answering. "That is Miss Katyan Amman, sire. She is one of the one hundred. Ania is assisting her."

Roygan cocked an eyebrow at his assistant. He knew Arriah would assign his fiancé to the woman with the most potential. He became exasperated with himself. Why hadn't he thought of that before? His assistant would know just what he was looking for. He should have asked Arriah's opinion first. He looked at Arriah who simply smiled at his master.

"She's beautiful," Roygan said, looking back at the window. He liked the fact that the woman was walking out of doors. The other women he had met would not set foot outside unless to step into a carriage to travel to another place. He also liked that the woman was walking with Ania. It looked as if the two were conversing. That pleased him. "Invite her to dinner tonight, Arriah. I should like to meet her."

"Yes, sir," Arriah said smiling, obviously pleased. He bowed to his master and went to write the invitation.

———

Katyan and Ania arrived back at the suite in time for luncheon. Katyan was in much higher spirits. She always felt invigorated after walking outside. Ania's father had let her groom one of the horses as a birthday present. She enjoyed working with her hands and was especially thrilled with the gift.

As they entered the front room, something on the table caught Katyan's eye. "What is that?" she asked as she began untying her wrap to hang it on the hook.

"What?" Ania asked.

"That on the table," Katyan gestured toward what looked like an envelope. "It was not there before we left."

"Would you like me to open it?" Ania asked.

"Please," Katyan was struggling with the ties on her wrap.

Ania was silent for a few moments as she opened the envelope and read the contents. Then a huge smile spread across her face. "It is an invitation."

"An invitation?" Katyan said innocently. "To what?"

Ania read the contents aloud, "Prince Roygan cordially invites you to dine with him this evening at eight o'clock in the guest dining room."

Katyan stopped trying to figure out her ties and stared unbelieving at Ania. "Tonight? But he's not to get to my number for another month."

"Shall I go to Arriah and inquire about the change?" Ania asked excitedly.

Katyan looked at her friend not knowing what to do. Would the prince want her to know?

Ania understood the silent question. She knew the prince quite well, having spent time with him and Arriah. She appreciated Katyan's confidence in her. "I shall inquire and return quickly." With that she slipped out the door.

Katyan waited impatiently, forgetting about her wrap. Thankfully, Ania was not long in returning.

"The prince saw us walking the grounds this morning," she explained as she helped untie Katyan's wrap. "He was impressed with your beauty as well as what he perceived of our friendship."

Katyan wasn't sure what to say. After a few minutes she found her voice. "What should I do?" she asked.

Ania smiled reassuringly and grasped her friend's hand. "Simply be yourself. The prince does not like anyone to put on airs. He wants someone he can be comfortable with; be himself with. He is a kind, fun, gentle man. I'm sure you will have an extremely pleasant time together."

Katyan took a deep breath and nodded, unable to say anything. She was now extremely nervous. She allowed Ania to fix her hair and clothing and prepare her for the evening.

Chapter 4

Katyan entered the dining room and tried not to let her intimidation show. They weren't having dinner in the palace's grand dining room, but this room was certainly more grand than any Katyan had ever seen. There was a long mahogany dining table down the middle of the room surrounded by ornately carved high-backed chairs. Two matching buffets adorned either side of the expansive table. Colorful tapestries hung on the walls telling stories of ancient folklore. Three large chandeliers full of flickering candles hung from the ceiling lighting the room.

Prince Roygan stood near the head of the table. Two china place settings had been set across from each other at this end of the table separated by a single candlestick. "Good evening, Miss Amman," the prince said.

"Good evening, Your Highness," Katyan replied curtsying.

"Please, come sit down," Roygan invited.

Katyan followed her host, thinking his tone of voice lacked enthusiasm.

A servant brought their dinner and set it before them. Roygan thanked the servant. Katyan thought his voice had softened in his thanks. She eased a little. Then he began talking to her.

"You look somewhat ill at ease, Miss Amman," he said almost snidely, as if he might be enjoying her discomfort.

At his tone, Katyan's temper got the best of her and she responded in kind, "Forgive me, Your Highness, but my limited experience with royalty, albeit low royalty, has not been pleasant."

Roygan was taken aback by her frankness. He was intrigued. No other woman had ever been so frank with him. They all seemed to want to please him and say whatever they thought was most appropriate instead of what was actually on their minds; a fact that thoroughly annoyed him. Therefore, when Katyan was willing to state her mind, he became interested. "Please do elaborate," he said.

"Well, sire," Katyan began unsure how to proceed. Ania had told her to be herself and that the prince wanted someone he could be comfortable with. She wanted to be comfortable with him as well. She decided the best way to do that was to be completely honest. "I work as a house servant for the Lady Odi. Her husband is the largest land owner in the neighboring city of Henai. My main job is to assist her two daughters. Their family is one of great wealth. They are low royalty and have a tempered distain for anyone of lower station than they. To their family and friends, I am nothing but a servant, there to do the bidding of the family."

A slow smile Katyan was unable to define spread across the prince's lips. Now it was Katyan's turn to be intrigued. However, she didn't need to inquire. The prince readily explained his reaction.

"I believe I know the misses Odi of whom you speak," he said still smiling. "I had dinner with each of them on separate evenings last week." His voice held a hint of disgust.

Katyan giggled at his tone. "Were the evenings unpleasant, sire?"

Roygan rolled his eyes and groaned. "One's nostrils were so big, I'm sure I saw a bug fly up her nose during the second course of the meal."

Katyan tried unsuccessfully to stifle a laugh at the description of the eldest Odi daughter.

"The other's lips were so small they could barely contain teeth that should have been in a horse's mouth. I know I saw food fall out of her mouth during dessert."

Katyan laughed outright, thankfully with an empty mouth.

"They were both so hideously boring and arrogant; I had the servants bring the courses out as quickly as I could eat them. I couldn't stand to be in the same room with them any longer than I had to. Dinner lasted a half hour at the most with each one."

"Your Highness did not say as much, did you?" she asked.

"No," he said, "but I have said such things in the past."

"What have you said?" Katyan asked aghast, yet quite interested.

"That is a topic for future conversation," Roygan answered easily.

Katyan tried to ignore the conflicting feelings inside. She was enjoying the prince more than she thought she would. She did not want to get her hopes up at his hint toward future conversation. She knew the prince never saw a woman more than once.

"Your Highness has described the misses Odi quite well," Katyan laughed shaking away her feelings. "With your frank appraisal, though, I'm nervous as to what Your Highness thinks of me."

"Well, we have been conversing for more than a half hour and we're not even finished with the first course," Roygan replied playfully. "I'd say you're in better shape than either of your employers."

Katyan smiled, feeling very relaxed.

The evening progressed with easy conversation. They each felt the other was honestly interested. Katyan had never been given more than a fleeting look by royalty. To be talked with as an equal by the prince was a great feeling. Roygan had never conversed with anyone besides Arriah and Ania who did not want something from him. Katyan seemed to be confident with who she was and seemed not to need him for anything. They both felt at ease with the other.

Conversation drifted from family to childhood to schooling. They were never at a loss for dialogue. Katyan turned the conversation slightly more personal. "What do you like most to do, sire?"

"What do I like most?" he repeated.

"Yes, what makes you most happy?"

Roygan did not have to think about this answer. He answered immediately, "Being out of doors; especially with horses. I love walking or riding the grounds by the lake or in the woods. I enjoy hunting as well." He enjoyed her interest in his personal life. He wanted to know more of hers as well. "What makes you happiest, Miss Amman?"

She smiled. "I, too, enjoy horses, sire. I often spend time in my uncle's barn alone with the horses. It's the only place for privacy in my uncle's small cottage. I enjoy riding the country around Henai. I also enjoy cooking."

"Really? Cooking?"

She smiled at his innocence of the joys of hard work. "Yes, sire. Before my mother died, she taught me to cook. We were often in the kitchen cooking dinner for my father's return from a day's work."

Interested, he asked, "What do you enjoy cooking the most?"

"I don't have as much time to cook now that I must work," she answered with a hint of sadness. "My aunt does the cooking now. My favorite memories of cooking, however, are of cooking anniversary dinner with my mother. My father would hunt a duck for dinner as my mother and I would bake honey bread. Then we would go to the garden and pick potatoes and other vegetables to steam. When my father returned, he would let me help him clean the duck before Mother and I roasted it. It was an entire day affair. We had great fun together."

They continued talking about each other's likes and dislikes. Before either was ready, one-by-one the candles began to flicker out. They had continued talking well into the night, neither noticing the time. Wax dripped onto the table cloth from the chandelier above.

"Forgive me, Miss Amman, I have lost track of the time," he was pleasantly surprised by this fact. "I have enjoyed our evening together."

"As have I, sire."

"Are you fond of horse racing?" he asked.

"I have never had the pleasure of attending a race, sire."

He was shocked. "Really? Would you like to come to the race tomorrow?"

She was surprised at his invitation. "What race?" she asked, trying to calm her nerves.

"Twice a year, my father gives the servants a holiday. Tomorrow is one such day. Each holiday, one of the big events is a horse race given by the stable hands challenging the trainers. It is great fun. Oh, please join us. Arriah, Ania, and I always go."

Her heart had slowed to almost its normal pace now. "I would be delighted, sire."

"Wonderful," he exclaimed. Then, calling Arriah and Ania in, he informed them she would be accompanying them the next day. They both were extremely pleased.

"Tomorrow then, Miss Amman."

"Tomorrow, Your Highness," Katyan curtsied.

Roygan bowed.

———

"Arriah, I'm disappointed," Roygan said gruffly to his friend.

Arriah was suddenly nervous. He thought Katyan Amman would be perfect for the prince. Had something gone wrong? Had he misjudged the situation?

Roygan gave a sly look, "Why did you not bring her sooner? We could have saved a lot of heartache."

Arriah gave an exasperated sigh.

Roygan laughed heartily.

———

"Do not get my hopes up," Katyan said to a smiling Ania as they walked back to her suite.

"Katyan," Ania said, "he has not seen another woman for more than an hour. Tonight he lost track of time. Your dinner lasted over five hours. He has never seen another woman twice. He asked to see you again the next day."

Katyan looked almost fearfully at her friend. "I said do not get my hopes up."

"I'm merely giving a history lesson," Ania said innocently

Katyan relaxed and smiled. All-in-all this had been a good birthday.

Chapter 5

"Ania, Miss Amman, we're over here," Prince Roygan called out as the two women picked their way through the people setting up blankets and picnic baskets in preparation for the day.

"Good afternoon, Your Highness," Katyan said as they reached the prince and his aide. "What a beautiful day."

"It is indeed perfect," Roygan said, meaning it more now that Katyan had joined them.

Arriah and Ania exchanged pleased glances.

"I must say, sire," Katyan began, "I am surprised you chose to sit out on the lawn."

"Oh, I hate sitting in the grand stand," he replied emphatically. "I would much rather sit out among the people."

Katyan was pleased with his answer.

He then proceeded to tell her the names of each family around them, beginning with the children.

"Oh look," Roygan said almost excitedly. "Here comes Siri and Tamu."

Katyan looked around expecting a royal couple to join them. Instead she was surprised when the prince was knocked over by two rambunctious four-year-olds.

"Hello!" Roygan squealed as the children tried to tickle him. "How are you?"

"Good, sire," the little boy said.

"I brought you a flower," the girl said.

"Oh, and what color did you bring me, Siri?" Roygan asked.

The little girl studied the flower for a moment. Then her face brightened. "I brought you a purple flower, sire."

"Yes you did!" Roygan said proudly. "Good job. You are learning your colors well."

Siri then went to Arriah and Ania with flowers. "Mr. Arriah, I brought you a," she paused wanting to get the color right, "a blue one."

"Very good," Arriah praised.

"And Miss Ania gets a pink one."

"Thank you very much," Ania said.

Siri then turned to Katyan. She looked at Roygan waiting to be introduced.

"This is my friend, Miss Amman," Roygan said.

"Hello, Miss Amman," both children chorused.

"Hello," Katyan greeted warmly.

"Would you like a flower?" Siri asked.

"They are beautiful, I would love one," Katyan replied.

Siri beamed proudly that the prince's friend would want one of her flowers. "What color do you want?" she asked as she surveyed her bouquet.

"What color would you like to give me?" Katyan asked giving the girl a chance to further show off her knew knowledge.

Siri studied the flowers then picked one out. "You can have the yellow one. It will match your dress."

"Why, yes it does," Katyan said as she took the flower and put the stem through the lace of her collar. "Thank you very much."

"You're welcome," Siri curtsied.

Roygan smiled appreciatively at Katyan. Then he chatted more with the two children before they ran off to meet their parents.

"You're very good with these children, sire," Katyan said.

"I love children," Roygan answered emphatically. "I hope to have many someday."

Katyan smiled shyly.

"Prince Roygan." A tall man walked up to their group. The man was well dressed. Much more well-dressed than anyone out at the celebration. His dark hair was slicked back with grease. His mustache was thin and also greased. He had a hard look in his eyes that made Katyan uncomfortable. She noticed the others in their small group stiffen at the sight of the man. "I thought I'd find you here."

"I hoped you wouldn't," Roygan said flippantly as he began to spread their picnic lunch on the blanket.

"You're late, sire," the man said.

"For what?" Roygan asked still not looking at the man.

"For the cabinet meeting," the man answered haughtily.

"No, I'm not, Yamur," Roygan said. "Because I'm not going."

"Sire," Yamur said with obvious frustration, "you cannot simply choose which cabinet meeting you want to go to. Your presence is required."

Roygan stopped preparing the food and stared at Yamur with mock confusion. "Yamur, who is prince?" he asked mockingly.

Arriah stifled a chuckle under a cough.

"You are, sire," Yamur answered slightly embarrassed.

"Oh, you do remember who is in charge," Roygan exclaimed. "I was beginning to wonder."

This time Arriah erupted in an actual coughing fit as he tried to hide his laughter. Ania patted him on the back and turned her head away to stifle her grin.

"I happen to know, Yamur," Roygan continued, "that this cabinet meeting is not sanctioned by my father. Today is a holiday. I will not meet in any unsanctioned meetings, and I will not meet on a holiday. I will see you the day after tomorrow in my father's court."

Yamur did not try to hide his annoyance at the prince. "You would rather waste your day here with mere—"

"You have been dismissed!" Roygan said through clenched teeth.

Yamur stood in shocked silence for a moment. Then he regained his composure, turned on his heel and left.

"I cannot stand that man," Roygan said.

"You certainly put him in his place, sire," Arriah said, still grinning.

"You did nothing to help," Roygan said laughing at his friend. "I do not understand why my father keeps him around."

"Yes you do," Arriah said.

Roygan turned to Katyan, "Forgive me, Miss Amman. That man is just short of pure evil, I'd say. He is the son of my grandfather's top advisor. My father kept him on his advisory cabinet out of respect for both fathers. When I am king, he and his family will have no part in my rule." Then he turned to Arriah. "You know what he was going to say, don't you?"

"Yes, Sire, I do."

"He has no tolerance for servants," Roygan explained to Katyan. "He despises these holidays. He thinks he's better than everyone. He tries to ruin every fine day I have." Then the prince smiled. "He has no idea that he has not succeeded yet."

"Very good, sire," Arriah said.

"Oh look," Ania said. "The races are about to begin."

Roygan then took the time to tell Katyan the names of each rider and a little about their background. Katyan was pleased to see that the prince knew so much about the servants at the palace.

The day was extremely exciting for Katyan. There were six horse races in all. The first five were two racers each. The last one was a race of the ten best riders among the stable staff. Katyan cheered along with everyone else.

After the races were finished, a new group of horses and riders emerged. Roygan explained that these were the entertaining horses. They performed tricks such as jumping fences, one rider standing riding two horses, riders jumping from running horse to running horse, even horses jumping through fiery hoops. Katyan was in awe of the performance.

"Next is the spectacular finale," Roygan said, after the entertaining horses were finished.

"What is the finale?" Katyan asked.

"Fireworks," Roygan answered excitedly.

"Fireworks!"

"Yes, have you ever seen fireworks?"

"No, sire, never."

"You are in for a real treat." Roygan said. "Our blacksmiths are masters at the trade and they put on fantastic shows."

Roygan was right. The show was fabulous. Katyan couldn't tear her eyes from the night sky. The explosions of color left her in awe throughout the show. The whole audience "oohed" and "aahed" over the demonstration. They erupted in thunderous applause after the grand finale.

"That was beautiful," Katyan exclaimed still amazed at the day.

"I'm so glad you enjoyed it," Roygan said.

They began to pack their things. It seemed everyone on the lawn stopped by to wish the prince a good night. Roygan chatted with nearly everyone on their way out. Katyan's respect for the prince grew as she watched him with his people.

The prince and his friends were the last ones to leave the lawn. They chatted about the day as they walked back.

"Miss Amman," Roygan asked, somewhat shyly. "Do you play Match?"

"Yes, Sire, I love to play card games."

"Wonderful! Do you play Double Match?"

"I play with my aunt, uncle, and cousin all the time."

"Perfect. Would you care to play tomorrow? I have a treasury meeting in the afternoon, but would love you and Ania to join Arriah and me for dinner and a game of Double Match."

"I would love to," Katyan smiled. "Ania?"

"I would enjoy that," Ania answered.

"Great. Arriah and I are always playing Single Match with Ania playing the winner. We've wanted to play Double Match but have never had a fourth player."

"I'm glad I could oblige," Katyan said.

"Well, then, until tomorrow evening, Miss Amman," Roygan bowed.

"Tomorrow, Your Highness," Katyan curtsied.

The four separated and went their separate ways to turn in for the night.

———

"I believe you've met your match, sire," Arriah said happily as Katyan won the second game in a row for her team with Ania.

Roygan simply stared at Katyan with a mix of awe and disbelief. Katyan smiled confidently in return.

"I believe she's considerably more than my match," Roygan chuckled, not missing the irony in the fact that Katyan had chosen to play the Queen of Hearts to win both games. "It is a rare person, indeed, Miss Katyan, who would be victorious over their prince in anything, even a simple card game. And, not only be victorious, but seek out that victory twice in a row."

"It is a rare, low servant, Highness, who would be privileged to play her high prince in a card game," Katyan responded sweetly. "I'm simply taking advantage of the situation."

Roygan chuckled again.

Arriah and Ania were enjoying the playful exchange between friends. They were happy their prince and friend had finally found the one he wanted.

Katyan stifled a yawn, for it was getting late in the night. "Forgive me, sire," she smiled. "All this winning is making me tired. I must beg your leave to turn in for the night."

"Not another game? You won't give me a chance to redeem myself? Oh, so that is your strategy," Roygan said in mock offense. "You continue to win and then leave while you're ahead."

Katyan smiled coyly at him. "Always leave them wanting more, Your Highness."

A broad smile spread across Roygan's lips. Little did she know how much he wanted more with this woman. He would have to tell her soon. "In that case, Miss Amman, you have succeeded in your strategy. However, in lieu of the lateness of the hour, I will bid you good night." He grasped her hand, kissed it, and bowed.

Katyan blushed at the attention, curtsied, and bade him goodnight.

"Miss Amman," Roygan called as she was leaving the room. "I wonder if you might join me tomorrow for a ride around the grounds. Perhaps a picnic as well?"

"I would love to, sire," Katyan smiled.

"Wonderful. I will have the horses saddled and send Arriah for you after my cabinet meeting. Tomorrow, then."

"Tomorrow, sire," Katyan curtsied again and left the room with Ania.

Chapter 6

"I believe it is time to revisit the issue of the failed alliance with Janier," began Sotu, the king's cabinet leader.

"I believe the prince's offenses have had time to blow over," murmured Yamur not quietly.

Roygan's head shot up, and he glared at Yamur. "Are you suggesting that I am responsible for the alliance failure?"

"Well, sire," began one of the other cabinet members, "your behavior—"

"Could have been better, I know," snapped Roygan. "However, I have since apologized for my actions. The princess has genuinely forgiven me, and she is now quite happily engaged to the Duke of Sem. My behavior, gentlemen, is not the reason the alliance failed!"

"And I suppose you know why the alliance failed, then," Yamur sneered.

"Yes, I do," seethed Roygan. "The alliance failed because we continue to have closed borders between our country and theirs. They are willing to open their borders to us, yet you continue to close ours. They know you do not trust them. Why should they trust you with an alliance?"

"Are you suggesting we open the borders?" another member asked.

"Absolutely!" Roygan exclaimed.

"Why would we do that?"

Roygan feigned pensiveness. "Um," he began sarcastically, "perhaps to let them know we trust them enough to have an alliance with them; that we're not just using them because we're afraid of the Carturans on the other side."

This discussion was getting on Roygan's nerves. Why did his father surround himself with these narrow minded people? Where was his father, anyway? This was his cabinet meeting. Roygan had been left to oversee it while his father tended to some other matter.

"I think opening the borders would be ill-advised," Yamur said. "Do we really want the slow-minded, dim-witted, Janiriens infiltrating our land? They will completely bring our class of person down. They are only one step above the manipulating, barbaric Doriians, in my opinion."

"That is enough!" Roygan bellowed as he jumped out of his chair slamming his fists on the table. He was furious. "How dare you speak of others in that manner. My father may allow such talk in his presence, but as long as I am here, you will speak respectfully of others. You have no basis for your prejudice. I will not listen to one more word of this." He stopped to catch his breath and glare at his father's cabinet members who all sat staring at him in stunned silence. "You will open the borders, or I will do it myself. You are dismissed."

"But, your highness," Sotu interjected, "we have not finished-"

"I said you are dismissed!" Roygan yelled. He remained standing, fists on the table, glaring at each member as they quickly gathered their belongings and left the room.

He sat down shaking with anger. Were these the men he would need to deal with when he was king? Surely not. He would replace them, no question about that.

The door opened and his father entered the room. He looked around at the empty table and chuckled as he closed the door. "Is the meeting over already? Have you solved the world's problems?"

"You may laugh, Father," Roygan said argumentatively, "but these men you have surrounded yourself with are fools! They blame me for the failed alliance with Janier, when the obvious reason is the border closing. They don't want to take responsibility for their own actions.

All they want is power. They would take it from you in an instant if you gave them the opportunity."

The king considered his son for a moment before speaking. "Sometimes, you need to keep your enemies close, son. And never give them an outright reason to get rid of you. When you are in charge, you must attempt to keep peace while still getting your own way. Otherwise, they will try to find a chance to take the power from you."

———

Roygan was still upset when he went to ride with Katyan. She sensed his frustration the moment she saw him, but chose to wait to inquire until they were on their way.

Roygan chose a beautiful chestnut mare for Katyan to ride saying the horse was gentle enough to take a new rider, yet feisty enough to make the ride fun. He was right. Katyan thoroughly enjoyed the ride. Roygan took her all over the palace grounds. He showed her several ponds and the big lake. They rode along the river that fed each one. They rode through paths in the woods, along cliffs, and down in the valley. The day was beautiful. Arriah and Ania joined them as they stopped for a picnic.

Sensing the prince was still uneasy, Katyan decided to ask him about his mood. "Forgive me, sire, but you do not seem yourself today."

"Am I that transparent?" he asked wryly.

"I am afraid so," Katyan smiled.

"The cabinet meeting this morning did not go well," he told her. "They blamed my offensive behavior with the princess during the banquet for the alliance failure with Janier—"

"That's ridiculous!" Katyan exclaimed coming to the defense of her prince. "Anyone with a brain can see the failure is due to the closed borders..." she caught herself knowing public criticism of the government could land her in prison. "Forgive me, sire, I did not mean to criticize the government."

"No forgiveness necessary," he said chuckling. "I said the exact same thing to them." He then went on to recount the morning's events.

"I am sorry you must deal with these men, sire," Katyan said. "I am very proud of you, though, for defending those who were not there to defend themselves."

"I believe in equality of people," he said simply. "I do not care one whit where a person is from, or who their parents are. I want to know the person inside. That is what matters to me."

Katyan smiled. She felt relieved at this statement. She knew she did not need to divulge her secret to this man. If he would love her, it would be for who she is, not where her mother came from.

Roygan seemed to relax after their short conversation. The respect he saw in her eyes warmed his heart. The rest of the day was spent in laughter and enjoyment.

Chapter 7

Katyan leaned back in the overstuffed chair and relaxed as Roygan stoked the fire. They had just spent a riotous evening of games with Ania and Arriah who were now out taking a walk together. Roygan finished with the fire and relaxed in a chair next to Katyan.

"Tomorrow, I would like it if you would join me for dinner in the formal dining room," he invited.

"That would be lovely, sire," she accepted.

"I would like for your first meal there to be pleasant," he joked, knowing that foreign dignitaries were invited to dine in the formal dining room and meals were not always agreeable.

Katyan flinched at his words. In the week they had been seeing each other, Roygan continued to make comments about the future. He was never specific about what future they would have together. At times she thought perhaps he would choose her for his wife. Then, she would see him interact with Ania and Arriah and realize he was treating her the same way he treated them. She wondered if he meant for her to be another servant-friend; after all, she was only a low servant. She was beginning to care for him deeply and did not think she could handle serving him as he chose someone else for his bride. She was determined to ask him about his comments soon.

There was that look on her face, again. It was just a flash, but Roygan caught it, nonetheless. He didn't understand it. He'd seen it several times during the week they'd been together. He decided that now was the time to ask about it.

"Miss Katyan," he began slowly, "I don't understand the look that just flashed across your face."

"Sire?" she questioned.

"I have seen a look flash across your face several times that I cannot figure out. What are you thinking at this moment?"

Katyan took a deep breath. It was now or never. "Well, Your Highness makes comments about the future quite flippantly. I don't understand what kind of future you are desiring. I know I am here as one of one hundred women vying for the position of your wife. I have thoroughly enjoyed every moment I have spent with you. I can't help but notice, though, that the relationship you seem to have with me is the same as that of the relationship you have with Arriah and Ania. Does Your Highness see me as a servant-friend or something more?" There she'd said it. There was no turning back now. She looked down at her shaking hands, fearful of the answer.

Roygan smiled tenderly and moved from his chair to sit at her feet. He grasped her trembling hands in his right hand while tipping her chin up with his left. He waited until her gaze met his.

"My dear, Katyan," he said for the first time, "from the first evening I met you, I knew I would never be the same. You were perfect in every way for me. You are strong-willed, funny, charming, easy to talk with, and so much more. I told Arriah that night to begin sending the other women home. The last one left this morning. I wanted to give you as much time as possible to know me and decide if you liked me before I said anything. I wish I could give you a proper courtship; you deserve it.

"I was going to wait until tomorrow night, but..." he paused and rose to one knee, still holding her hands in his. He looked directly into her eyes and said, "Katyan Amman, will you be my wife?"

Tears sprang to her eyes as a smile spread across her face. "Yes, Roygan," she said using his given name for the first time.

He squeezed her hands, took a deep breath, and asked another question. "Will you be my queen?" He knew from previous conversations that she was unsure of high royalty and was not confident in her ability to be a leader.

Katyan mirrored his deep breath, but hesitated no more. Looking steadily in her fiancé's eyes, she said, "It would be an honor."

They both relaxed as he pulled her out of the chair into a long embrace.

——

The next evening, they had a formal dinner in the formal dining room to celebrate their engagement. Katyan was intimidated by her surroundings, but Roygan toured her through the finery in the room that would soon be theirs to entertain. He was gentle with her as she asked questions about what would be expected of her as princess and then queen. She was nervous, but knew she would be able to handle it with this man at her side.

The following day, Katyan would meet the king and queen for the first time. Roygan knew she was uneasy at the prospect, but helped to coach her through the impending process.

Chapter 8

Dinner with the king and queen had been quite pleasant. Katyan found their company agreeable. They were not as easy-going as their son, but were not as high and mighty as many others of royal position. They engaged her in amiable conversation, genuinely trying to get to know their future daughter-in-law. If they had any reservations about their son marrying a low servant, they did not show it. Katyan was comfortable around them.

The only discomfort Katyan had felt during the meal was when Queen Glorvana had innocently asked about her family. Katyan hoped she gave a satisfying reply.

"My mother and father died when I was twelve," she had answered. "My aunt and uncle took me in and have raised me since."

"They are good people?" the queen had inquired.

"Oh yes, very," Katyan replied enthusiastically. "They are honest and hard-working. They continued in my parents footsteps to teach me on all subjects of etiquette and morality."

This had sparked a short conversation about Katyan's fine etiquette and no more was asked about her family, saving Katyan from divulging or hiding her true heritage. They had talked well into the night and all seemed very comfortable with each other.

After Katyan left to her chambers, the king and queen gave their approval to their son, only questioning his decision once.

"She seems a lovely young woman, son," King Cortierre had said. "You are fine with her current position?"

"Position has never mattered to me, father," Roygan replied. "It is the woman I wanted to find, and she is the woman I want. I have chosen Katyan. She will do an admirable job in her future position."

The king smiled, patted his son on the shoulder, and said, "I do believe you are right, son."

———

The next day, the two young couples took a ride on the grounds to have a picnic lunch together. Naturally, the subject of weddings arose.

"Have you set a date, sire?" Arriah asked.

"Actually, we have talked about it," Roygan answered.

"What have you decided?" Arriah wondered.

Roygan looked at Katyan who nodded her consent for him to continue. "The date we have picked," he said, "is two weeks after the date you pick for your wedding."

Arriah and Ania looked at them quizzically.

Roygan smiled at his friends. "I know you have been waiting to set a date until I have found someone. Please forgive me for being so selfish as to allow you to wait. Now that I have found Katyan, I want to marry her immediately. I can only imagine that is the feeling you have shared since announcing your engagement. We have agreed that we desire for you to marry first, have at least a week long honeymoon, which will be our gift to you, and then we will wed."

"But sire …" Arriah began.

"I will not entertain any thoughts to the contrary," Roygan said good-naturedly. "This is our decision, and it is final."

"Well, then, I guess we have no argument to make," Ania said cheerily.

"None at all," Katyan agreed.

"Thank you, sire," Arriah said humbly.

"We also have another, rather unconventional, question to ask of you," Roygan said.

Arriah and Ania looked at their prince with amusement. He was anything but conventional.

"We would like for you two to stand with us at our wedding," Roygan announced.

They were shocked. It was unheard of for servants to do anything but serve their masters at their weddings.

"We know it is unconventional," Katyan said. "But you are our friends. There are no others that we call friends as we do with you. There is no one else we would rather have stand with us. Please say yes!"

They smiled and laughed at Katyan's enthusiasm. Then Ania answered, "We will stand with you, if you stand with us."

"Really?" Katyan and Roygan asked together.

"We feel the same about you. Please say yes," Arriah mimicked Katyan's plea.

"Of course, we would be honored," Roygan answered emotionally.

It was settled. Each couple would stand with the other at their wedding. Arriah and Ania set the date for their wedding for one month away; Katyan's and Roygan's wedding was set for two weeks after.

————

The next weeks were filled with wedding planning. Katyan and Ania had dress fittings for each wedding. They picked out flowers and food and decorations.

Each wanted a simple wedding. Katyan had to compromise a little on hers since the queen insisted on a large guest list. Katyan gave Queen Glorvana the task of setting up music, much to the queen's delight. They worked together to plan the wedding feast.

In the end, Ania had planned a small, simple wedding in accordance with the custom of the high servants. The wedding would include only family and the reception following would be a large party put together by the palace servants.

Ania was beautiful in her simple, white, silk dress and veil. She carried a bouquet of white roses down the candle-lit aisle of the servant's chapel. It was an intimate, moving ceremony. Katyan shed a few tears as her new friends exchanged vows.

The reception was indeed a party. The palace servants prepared a large feast. Several brought out instruments, and lively dances followed. When the party was over, the couple was sent off to their honeymoon on the coast where Roygan had, years ago, purchased a house. Both couples would use this house for their honeymoon.

———

Two weeks later arrived faster than Katyan could have imagined. During the week Arriah and Ania were gone, she finished what wedding preparations she could. When they arrived home, she helped them set up house in their new quarters near Katyan's and Roygan's future quarters.

All of a sudden, her wedding day arrived. Katyan was glowing with excitement. The only ache came when she remembered her aunt and uncle would not be here to share her special day. She had gone home to see them after her engagement was announced. They had agreed it would be best for them to remain home. Her uncle's Doriian features would be too obvious. They had heartily given her their congratulations and love.

Katyan shook the melancholy feeling away and focused on her day. Ania helped her into her dress. It was a simple, elegant, silk dress with beading around the bodice and down the skirt. Her veil had similar beading on the trim. She carried a single calla lily down the aisle.

The aisle was adorned with tall candelabras decorated with roses. The ceremony took place in the palace cathedral which was already ornately decorated with wood carvings and stained glass windows.

Both Katyan and Roygan let tears fall as they exchanged vows and rings, knowing their lives would now be changed forever, for better.

The reception following was a formal dinner in the formal din-ing room. Katyan was thankful that Roygan had dined with her here alone before she was required to entertain. The dining room was daunting in its richness and formality. Roygan never left Katyan's side as he guided her through her first task as Princess of Groy.

The music the queen arranged was formal, yet lively and fit the tastes of the young prince and princess as well as the king and queen. The dinner was an exquisite five course meal set with the palace fin-ery. The palace cook had certainly outdone himself with each course.

When the reception was over, the young couple set out on the same road as their friends two weeks previous to enjoy their honey-moon at the coast.

Arriah and Ania remained at the palace to help arrange the new quarters for the young married prince and princess.

Katyan and Roygan left for their honeymoon with no servants. A few guards accompanied them for security, but as far as daily serv-ants, Katyan and Roygan were on their own. Katyan was in her ele-ment enjoying doing for herself what Ania had been required to do for the past five months. She enjoyed watching Roygan attempt life without Arriah.

Roygan had always prided himself on not being overbearing with his servants. Yet, now, without Arriah or other servants to attend him, he realized how much he depended on them. He did enjoy the independence and freedom that came with providing for himself and was determined to do more when they returned to the palace.

Chapter 9

"Are you ready?" came a gruff voice.

"Of course I'm ready," replied a whiny voice. "I've been ready for three months."

"Well, it seems if that were true, the job would be finished by now," replied the gruff voice.

"He didn't leave the palace for two months before the wedding. What was I supposed to do?" retorted the whiny voice.

"Well, he left today with the king," answered the gruff voice. "They're going to Janier to talk about the alliance. Now we need that alliance, so don't do anything until they return. But I want the job completed before they arrive home. Do you understand me? Get it done!"

"What about the women?" whined the voice.

"We'll worry about them later," came the gruff answer. "Finish the men off first. The women will be easier to deal with when the men are out of the way."

"Are you ready?" the whiny voice asked.

"Of course I'm ready," mocked the gruff voice. "You just worry about your job. My men and I are in place to take over once the king and prince are gone."

———

At the sound of retreating footsteps, Dadaan emerged from the corner he was hiding behind. He was on his way to the palace to deliver a message. He had recently received the middle servant job as a messenger to the palace. He ran through the streets in the rain. He needed to tell Katyan. He reached into his pocket for the locket that would serve as his entry key to see the princess. Since receiving the messenger job, he carried her aunt's locket in his pocket for just such a time as this. He just did not expect to need it this soon.

The rain came down harder as Dadaan ran faster down the cobble stone streets to the palace. Finally he reached the messenger door and pulled the rope ringing the bell as fiercely as he could.

Mrs. Fasi answered the door with a scowl on her face. "You needn't be so insistent, sir. One pull on the rope is sufficient to alert my staff."

"I do apologize, ma'am," Dadaan bowed. "I have two messages. One to be delivered by hand." He handed her the message which originally sent him on this mission. "And the other to be delivered in person only to her Highness the Princess."

Mrs. Fasi openly laughed. "I will take the hand delivered message, but I cannot simply let anyone in to see the princess."

"I completely understand," Dadaan answered. "Perhaps you would be so kind as to show this to Her Highness. I feel certain she will agree to see me." Dadaan handed Mrs. Fasi the locket.

Mrs. Fasi stared down her nose at Dadaan. Then, something like realization crossed her face. She remembered that the current princess was once a low servant. Surely she still had friends among this population. She agreed to take the locket to the princess. If Katyan did not recognize the necklace, she would simply send the man on his way.

Leaving Dadaan just inside the doorway, she retreated down the hall toward the princess's chambers.

Katyan lounged on the sofa near the window watching the rain fall as she attempted to read a book Roygan had purchased for her during their honeymoon. They had returned from their trip a month ago. Life had fallen into a routine since then. Roygan continued with his cabinet meetings. Katyan learned everything she could about the palace and the servants. She would be given the first year of their marriage to learn how things were run at the palace before she was given more particular tasks to oversee.

Thus far, she had spent much of her time getting to know the kitchen and stable servants. These were her two favorite places in the palace. Gazing out at the rain, she smiled as she recalled her new friends.

A knock sounded at her door. Having given Ania the night off, she went to answer it herself. Mrs. Fasi stood on the other side trying to hide her disapproval at the princess answering her own door.

"Mrs. Fasi," Katyan smiled. "How good to see you. Won't you come in?"

"No, my lady," Mrs. Fasi curtsied. "There is a messenger here desiring to see you. When I told him not simply anyone was allowed to see the princess, he handed me this locket to show you in hopes you would agree to see him."

Katyan took the locket Mrs. Fasi handed her and smiled. "Yes, of course, Mrs. Fasi. Thank you for being so diligent in your work." Katyan had long since discovered that Mrs. Fasi's ego needed to be filled. "I do recognize this locket. Please send the messenger in. I will agree to see him."

"The man is Doriian, my lady," Mrs. Fasi informed.

"Please send him in," Katyan said steadily.

"Yes, my lady," Mrs. Fasi sounded disappointed, but turned to leave and fetch the messenger.

A few minutes later, Mrs. Fasi knocked on the door again. Again, Katyan opened it and was delighted to see Dadaan. She did not show more than just a simple smile, so as not to give anything away. She turned and allowed him into her front room as she dismissed the head house servant.

When she was sure the door was securely closed she turned to hug her uncle. "Uncle!" she cried. "How wonderful to see you! What brings you here, and on such a stormy night?"

Dadaan's smile did not match that of his niece. "I rejoice in seeing you, my dear, but I fear it is not good news that brings me here tonight."

"Oh dear," Katyan said as she stumbled back to the nearest chair. "Is it Aunt Barria? Is she ill?"

"No, my dear, it is not your aunt," Dadaan rushed on. "It is your husband and father-in-law. I have reason to believe their lives are in danger." He went on to repeat the conversation he heard on the street.

"Oh, no," Katyan cried. Then she jumped up, grabbed Dadaan by the arm and rushed him out the door. "Come with me," she commanded.

They ran down the hallway to Arriah and Ania's rooms, their feet echoing on the stone floor. Hearing them come, Arriah had flung open the door to see what the commotion was about. Katyan pulled Dadaan crashing into the front room. Slamming the door behind them she said, "Sir," giving thanks for having the presence of mind not to call him uncle, she continued, "Tell this man what you just told me. He is the prince's head assistant and is trustworthy."

"Your Highness," Arriah said, "what is going on?"

"Go on, tell him," Katyan ordered.

Dadaan went on to repeat the story.

"Sir, are you sure of this?" Arriah questioned.

"Absolutely, sir," Dadaan answered.

"And you have reason to believe this man's word?" Arriah asked Katyan.

"Absolutely," Katyan assured.

"We must act now," Arriah sprung into full action as the prince's head guard. "Thank you, sir, for this information. I will handle it now."

Dadaan stepped aside at this dismissal. Katyan nodded her thanks to him as he slipped out the door.

Arriah pulled a rope ringing for help. Quickly, two men arrived at the door. "The lives of the prince and the king are in danger. Saddle up the horses. We ride tonight. I want twelve men with me." He named the twelve men most trustworthy for this mission.

"I can ride, I want to go as well," Katyan insisted.

"No!" Arriah nearly shouted. "You must stay here with Ania. If the prince's life is in danger, yours will be, too. This country still recognizes the authority of the queen. Queen Glorvana has already said she will decline the throne once the king passes. That means you are next in line after Roygan to run the country. You must stay here!" Then he turned to Ania. "Keep her here!" he demanded.

Katyan looked to Ania for confirmation of this danger. Ania nodded her agreement with her husband.

"Arriah?" Katyan said in a meek voice. "You will keep him safe?"

He took Katyan's hand in his and looked her directly in the eyes. "We have taken an oath with our lives to protect you. We will fulfill that oath to the most extreme point necessary." He squeezed her hand, turned to embrace Ania, grabbed his coat and flew out the door, leaving the two women he cared about most staring mute and unmoving at the planks of the closed door.

Ania came to her senses first and rushed to the door to bolt it. The two women stared at each other in equal fear for their husbands.

———

Arriah pushed the horse as fast as he dared through the torrential rains. It was half a day's ride to Janier. He prayed he and his band of men would reach the prince and king before they left, knowing especially the prince's desire to depart early, if possible.

———

"Here they come," alerted the leader of the renegade posse. "Two security in front, the king and prince in the middle and one security in the back. The prince is on the left, the king on the right. We outnumber them eight to five. Wait until the first two security pass, then everyone for his man."

The first two men rode by the hiding place. The second two horses approached.

"Ready!" the leader hissed. "On your guard. Char-"

The command was cut off by a gurgling gasping sound as the man was grabbed from behind and his throat slit. Four of the posse members had anticipated his command and ran to fight the oncoming group. The other three turned at the strange sound to see their leader fallen in a pool of his own blood. Turning again, just as quickly, they faced their attackers.

The three left behind had not time enough to fully draw their swords. The attackers quickly gained the advantage.

The four rushing ahead unaware of the fight behind them had swords drawn. To their surprise, the men on horses were ready for them. They jumped down from their mounts, swords brandished. The prince and king threw off their cloaks.

"That's not the prince!" "That's not the king!" two of the attackers shouted at once.

The two replacements took this opportunity to gain the upper hand in the fight. Swords clashed. Horses skittered and whinnied at the commotion. The men struggled. Sword met flesh in painful agony for the victims.

The three posse members left behind were no match for their attackers whose orders were to leave none alive.

The four renegades who rushed ahead were bigger and stronger than the other posse members and gave a strong fight, but in the end were overtaken by the security detail and stand-in prince and king.

Arriah, posing as the prince, stood over his quarry, sword pointed in his neck. This was the only one of the posse still alive. The other members of the group joined Arriah, swords drawn.

"Tell us who you're working for," he said breathing heavily from the exertion of the fight.

The man glared defiantly at Arriah, but kept his mouth clamped shut.

Arriah pushed the sword tip closer until it was poking the man's neck. "Tell us, or I will kill you."

"I have sworn not to tell," the man sneered.

"Sir," one of Arriah's men came to him with a piece of paper. "This was found in the coat pocket of the leader."

"What does it say?" Arriah asked never turning from his prey.

"It says they are to meet with Magdorn at the Oak Inn once they have completed the assassination of the prince and the king."

Arriah's sword bearing arm had been sliced during the attack and began to quaver under the pressure of holding his sword. The last surviving member of the posse tried to lift his sword against his attacker as Arriah put an end to his life.

Arriah dropped his sword and stared at the ground. This was the part of his job he hated. He would do anything to protect the prince, but he would never get used to killing.

"You have done good work tonight, men," he said as one of the men wrapped his arm in a bandage. The other wounded men were being tended to as well. "Our job is, unfortunately, not complete. We must go to the Oak Inn and confront the prince's cousin. I pray Their Majesties made it home safely on the alternate route."

He then assigned some of the men to carry the fallen bodies to the waiting cart to be carried back to the palace. Other men he assigned to accompany him as he challenged the man behind the assassination attempts. His danger was not yet over.

Chapter 10

Katyan and Ania had fallen asleep in their chairs, exhausted from fear. They were suddenly awakened by pounding on the front door of the rooms. They jumped up, silent, and stared at each other wide-eyed.

"Katyan, Ania, open up!" came the frantic yell.

Katyan shook with relief as she ran to the door. "Roygan!" she called as she slid back the bolts.

Roygan fell into the room into his wife's arms.

"Thank goodness you're safe," they cried in unison.

Then Roygan turned to Ania and embraced his friend.

"Where's Arriah?" the three asked together.

"He's not back yet?" Roygan inquired.

"No," Ania answered. "He's not with you?"

"No," Roygan replied. "He found us and sent us on an alternate route. Then he and his men dressed up like Father and me and took the route we originally were supposed to be on."

"Oh, no," Ania sighed as she sank back into her chair.

"I will go to the stables and inquire," Roygan said. He hugged Katyan again and left the room.

Down at the stables, Roygan met the two servants just returning with the cart carrying the victims from the attack.

"Zandi, Cama," he addressed the two on his security detail, "Where is Arriah?"

Zandi answered, "He is at the Oak Inn, sire, confronting Magdorn."

"It was he who was behind the attacks, sire," Cama added.

"What can you tell me of the attacks?" Roygan asked.

The two men recalled everything to their prince.

Roygan sighed at the loss of life. "Thank you, gentlemen. Your loyalty and valor is appreciated beyond expression and shall be rewarded." He bowed to the servants who bowed back. He then left them and returned to Katyan and Ania.

Roygan relayed everything Zandi and Cama had told him. Ania sat silent in her chair while Katyan brought her tea.

"We will wait with you here until he arrives," Katyan said.

Ania did not answer.

They waited in silence for almost two hours. Then Roygan jumped up. "I can stand it no longer. I must go out and look for him."

"No, sire!" Ania almost shouted. These were the first words she had uttered since Roygan returned. "You must stay here or you will succumb to the same fate I fear Arriah has met."

They sat in silence for a few more minutes.

"What is that?" Katyan jumped to the window at the sound of horse's hooves galloping up to the palace.

They all ran to the window. The security detail was back, though they could not see who all was with them.

They waited tense, to hear any news from anyone. Soon, an urgent knock came to the door. Roygan went to answer it.

Arriah stood dripping wet and muddy in the hallway. Ania jumped up and ran to him, embracing her wet husband, freely letting the tears fall.

"Welcome home, my friend," Roygan said, obviously emotional.

"It is good to be home," Arriah answered tearfully.

"Come, tell us what happened," Roygan urged. "Zandi and Cama told me about the attack and that you went to Oak Inn to confront Magdorn. What happened there?"

Arriah came in as Ania retrieved a dry robe to wrap around him. "When we arrived at the Inn, I placed the men outside in case Magdorn decided to run. I went in, wearing the clothes of one of his men. As soon as I sat down, however, he recognized me. I confronted him with what we knew and he ran. In the rain, it was easy for him to slip by the security guards, but not so easy to keep going.

"One of the guards had the foresight to station himself at Magdorn's horse. Seeing this, Magdorn took off running through the woods. We chased him for nearly an hour and finally caught up to him. We seized him and brought him back here. He is in prison under the palace guard awaiting trial. Though, I doubt there will be much of a trial. In anger, he confessed to the whole thing on the way back."

"Thank you, my friend," Roygan said emotionally. "There are no words to express my gratitude."

"None are needed," Arriah said.

Roygan considered his friend carefully. Arriah sat back in his wife's arms, clearly spent from the night's events. His eyes were downcast seeming defeated. There was pain behind his eyes.

Roygan leaned forward in his chair toward his friend. "You have proved your loyalty again and again, Arriah. I know this costs you. We can change the head of security, if you'd like."

"No, sire," Arriah said forcefully. "We have had this conversation before. I owe my life to you. I will pay it, if necessary."

Roygan nodded silently and stood. "Thank you, my brother. Let us pray it does not come to that. Get some sleep. We will clear the day tomorrow. Relax. I will see you the next day." He clasped Arriah's hand in farewell. Then, helping Katyan up, they left their friends' living quarters to walk to their own.

Once in their rooms, Katyan inquired after the conversation. "What did Arriah mean when he said he owed his life to you, dear?"

Roygan took a deep breath and sank down on the sofa, pulling Katyan next to him. "When I was about thirteen years old, my father gave me a new puppy. We decided to take him for a walk one day. The puppy pulled out of his leash and ran down an alley way. Father and I chased after him. We were horrified at what the puppy found. He was sniffing and nudging the limp, bloody, beaten body of another thirteen-year-old boy. It was Arriah.

"Arriah's father was a drunk. He owned a tavern in town. When he drank, which was often, he would beat Arriah to within an inch of his life. He not only beat Arriah, but occasionally he would pull a sword or a knife on him. Arriah has several scars from his father, but one rather large one on his back. The day we found him, his father had pulled a sword on him and when Arriah tried to run, his father slashed him in the back with the sword. Arriah was unconscious from the wound and the beating. His father had simply thrown him out into the alley."

Katyan gasped as tears sprang to her eyes at the cruelty.

Roygan pulled her close in a protective hug. "My father was incensed. He threw open the back door and stormed into the tavern with the security guards who were with us, leaving my puppy and me in the alley with Arriah. A few minutes later, my father stormed back out the door leading the security guards carrying a man passed out from liquor. It was Arriah's father.

"Arriah came back to the palace with us where we nursed him back to health. He has stayed with me ever since. We became friends, and he asked to be head of my security."

"What happened to his father?" Katyan asked.

"He was thrown into prison for the cruelty he inflicted upon Arriah. Soon after, he died from tuberculosis. He'd had the disease before my father found him. The palace doctors tried to help him, but nothing could be done."

"Poor Arriah," Katyan sighed. "I'm so glad you found him."

"So am I," Roygan answered emphatically. "He has been the best friend and brother anyone could ask for."

"You also told him that he has proved his loyalty again and again," Katyan said. "Has something like this happened before?"

"Yes," Roygan answered. "A few years ago, a man confronted me in the streets. He was drunk and pulled out a sword. Arriah jumped on him before I could even pull my sword out of its sheath. Arriah simply wanted to capture him and take him to prison, but the man gave such a fight and pulled his sword on Arriah, that Arriah killed him."

"Oh, my," Katyan gasped.

"Arriah is the best swordsman I know, but he gets no joy out of using them," Roygan said. "It brings back too many painful memories of his father. But he refuses to let anyone else be the head of my security."

Katyan didn't know what else to say. Hearing this explained why the two never touched a drop of alcohol. She determined to do the same.

The two sat in each other's arms until they fell asleep, content to be together.

Chapter 11

One year later

The ear-piercing scream split the night air sending chills up Katyan's spine.

"It's a boy!" announced the mid-wife excitedly.

Katyan fell back against the pillows on the birthing bed. It was over. She'd done it. They now had a boy to carry on the family name as well as the crown. "Is he healthy?" she asked weakly.

"Yes, my lady," the mid-wife answered.

"May I see him?"

"Let me clean him up a bit, and I'll bring him right back."

"May my husband come in now?" Katyan asked eager to show Roygan their new son.

"I will bring him in as soon as I give the boy to you, my lady."

"Thank you, Rema," Katyan said.

"You're welcome, my lady," the mid-wife answered, as she handed the clean bundle to the new mother.

Moments later, Roygan entered the room with excitement on his face. "Is everything alright?" he asked.

"Yes, my dear," Katyan answered. "Everything is wonderful. It's a boy. A beautiful, healthy, baby boy."

"A boy!" Roygan exclaimed. "How wonderful."

"His name, my lord?" Rema asked.

"His name is Zedan," Roygan answered proudly, "named after the princess's father."

Katyan beamed up at her husband as she cradled their son.

"Zedan," Rema repeated. "I will go and make the announcement." Then she left the room.

"How wonderful it is!" Katyan exclaimed. "What an exciting way to end a wonderful year."

The child had been born five minutes before the first day of the new year.

"It has been a wonderful year, hasn't it, my dear?" Roygan asked lovingly.

"It has been extraordinary!" Katyan said excitedly. "Who would have guessed I would be a princess, for one thing? Then the excitement and fear over the assassination attempt as well as the trial convicting and sentencing your cousin afterward. Not to mention my extreme happiness in helping in the stables and kitchen. I have even thoroughly enjoyed the few parties I've thrown for the dignitaries. I have loved getting to know your parents. They are truly wonderful people. They have helped and coached me through everything I have needed to know. And finally, giving birth to a healthy baby not one month after my best friend gave birth to hers! It's been an extraordinary year!"

"Speaking of Ania," Roygan said smiling at his wife's enthusiasm, "she's outside waiting to see you. Shall I bring her in?"

"Oh yes, please."

"I'll wait out with Arriah. I love you," Roygan said.

"I love you, too, dearest."

Moments later, Ania entered the room, beaming at her friend. "How wonderful for you, sister."

"Thank you, dear," Katyan answered the woman who had been closer than any sister.

"He's beautiful," Ania proclaimed.

"How is Emaria?" Katyan asked of Ania's newborn daughter.

"Wonderful," Ania answered proudly. "She's sleeping in her father's arms just outside the room."

"How amazing is it that we have children not one month apart?" Katyan exclaimed again.

"Very amazing," Ania replied. "We can endure every experience together!"

"With each other's help, I know we can do this!" Katyan said with a giggle. The two were nervous first time mothers. They determined to lean on each other and learn together.

"Happily!" Ania said.

———

One month later, as Katyan was caring for her son in the middle of the night, an urgent knock sounded on the door. Roygan rose to answer it.

"Your Highness," Arriah said somberly. "Your presence is requested in the king's chambers. He is ill."

———

"What is the diagnosis, Doctor?" Roygan asked. He and his mother were sitting outside the king's sick room waiting for the doctor's examination.

"He is very ill," the doctor replied. "He needs constant care. He must not be left alone for more than a few minutes. His breathing is extremely shallow, and he is still coughing blood. Only family must see him. He needs nothing to upset him now. I fear he may slip into unconsciousness shortly."

"Thank you, Doctor," Roygan answered. His mother was unable to speak through her grief.

"I will return tomorrow, unless summoned sooner." The doctor bowed and left the room.

"That is utterly ridiculous, Your Highness," one of the cabinet members said.

"How dare you speak so rudely to me, Fa," Roygan said heatedly. "Lest you forget, in my father's absence, I am in charge of this council."

"Well," Fa said as he stood from the table, "in your father's absence, I shall be absent as well." He turned to leave.

"Wait just a moment," Roygan said.

Fa turned around expecting an apology and invitation to return to the table.

Roygan pulled something out of his pocket and flipped it to the councilman. "Here's a silver coin. On your way off the palace grounds, buy a comb from one of the vendors. Your head looks as if a rat is sleeping on it."

Fa's face turned red. He was speechless as he stormed out of the meeting room.

The other members sat silently as Roygan finished his speech and dismissed them.

———

"You said what?" Katyan exclaimed, laughing. "Dearest, you really should hold your tongue."

"It was true!" he said. "His hair was bunched up on top and had a long tail down the back. It truly looked like a rat! Anyway, I don't know how my father stands meeting with those men," Roygan adjusted the warm cloth over his eyes in an attempt to relieve a headache. "All they want is power. I'm sure they would take power from him in a heartbeat, if he offered it to them."

Katyan giggled as she picked the baby up to nurse him. "Dearest?"

"Yes, my love?" Roygan answered sweetly.

"Do you know what I was thinking?"

"I haven't the slightest idea," Roygan said, chuckling.

"I was thinking that you have never told me what you said to the princess of Janier."

Roygan groaned sheepishly as he removed the cloth from his eyes to look at his wife. "Do you really want to know?"

"Of course!"

"Well," he began, knowing he would not get out of telling her. "As we danced," he began slowly, "I stepped on her feet a few times, some on purpose, and I commented that they were the size of a small elephant's feet."

"Oh no!" Katyan cried, trying not to laugh.

"Then, when we sat down to dinner," Roygan continued, this time not looking his wife in the eye, "I pushed her chair in too closely to the table and…" he took a deep breath, obviously embarrassed by his behavior. "I said she was large enough that carrying a child should be easy."

"Oh!" Katyan didn't even try not to laugh at this. "You're terrible! And she forgave you for this?"

"Actually, she did," Roygan said, laughing with his wife. "Her father was so embarrassed at having set her up with me that he allowed her to choose whoever she wanted. She already had her eye set upon her current husband. She actually sent a letter to thank me. Without my rudeness, she might not be married to the man she loves now. Oh, and by the way, she just gave birth to twins!"

Katyan laughed heartily at this statement.

Roygan rose from his chair to kiss his son and wife on the forehead. "I'm glad I can amuse you so!" he said smiling. Then his smile faded and he added, "The strange thing about the whole situation at the council meeting is that Yamur remained silent throughout the whole interchange."

"Really?" Katyan asked interested.

"Really. He even looked at me with an expression akin to approval."

Katyan raised her eyebrows in curiosity.

"I don't know. I'm inclined to be suspicious. Though, it would be nice to have an ally in the council. They don't look very highly on me or my ideas, being so different from Father's. And it would be great not to fight with Yamur anymore." Roygan sighed and sank back into his chair. "I don't know," he repeated as he placed the cloth over his eyes again.

Katyan furrowed her brow now that her husband couldn't see her. She was inclined to be suspicious of Yamur as well. She didn't want to cast concern over these already trying times, so she decided to remain quiet.

The weeks passed tensely. The king's health was deteriorating. The weight of the kingdom pressed on Roygan. He wanted to be king when the time came. He had many plans for the kingdom. At the age of twenty-six, he would be the youngest king ever to rule over Groy, should his father not pull through. He knew his mother did not want to be queen without his father, so she would relinquish the crown upon his father's death.

Yamur continued to change his attitude and became an ally for Roygan in the council. Roygan was still somewhat suspicious, but needed the ally in the council. King Cortierre's council members were power hungry. Roygan was learning more and more how they tried to manipulate his father. Roygan was a stronger leader than his father and did not allow himself to be manipulated, thus he found himself butting heads with each member at times.

Chapter 12

One month after his father became ill, Roygan went to visit the king during the early morning, as he did daily. However, this time he stopped just outside the sick room for a moment to cover his mother with a blanket. Usually she slept in the sick room near his father, but his father's labored breathing had become so noisy that his mother was unable to sleep. She now took to resting just outside the sick room.

As Roygan finished covering his mother, the door to the sick room opened. Expecting the doctor, as no one besides family was permitted to see the king, Roygan was taken aback to see Yamur exiting the room.

"Yamur!" Roygan exclaimed.

"Good morning, Roygan," Yamur replied and continued out the door of the king's chambers.

Roygan was uneasy. None of the recent niceness was present on Yamur's face. In fact, his look was quite sinister. A chill coursed up Roygan's spine. "Mother," Roygan decided to wake the queen.

"What is it?" Queen Glorvana woke with a start.

Roygan placed a hand on her shoulder to calm her. "Did you know Yamur was in visiting Father?"

She became concerned. "No, dear, I had no idea. I had fallen asleep out here and did not hear anything."

"Puzzling," Roygan said. "He did not look pleasant as he left and all but ignored me on his way out. I don't like it."

She put a hand on his arm, now trying to calm him. "Dear, your father is unconscious most of the time. I am sure Yamur could do no harm."

"I hope you are right, Mother," Roygan said. He went into the room to visit his father. After checking the room, he was satisfied that nothing seemed out of place, and his father was asleep. As he left, he promised his mother he would return in the afternoon.

When he returned to Katyan, he told her of the disturbing encounter.

———

The next morning, Roygan and Katyan were awakened by a knock on their door. Roygan answered it.

"I'm sorry, Roygan," Arriah said.

"Father's gone?" Roygan asked.

"Yes," his friend answered sadly.

They embraced, both feeling the sadness of losing a father.

"Go to Ania," Roygan said. "Be with her today."

"Go be with Katyan," Arriah said.

The two shook hands and left to the comfort of their wives.

———

The funeral procession three days later was an impressive tribute to a great man. The king lay in state in the great hall of the palace as his subjects and foreign dignitaries passed by to pay their respects. The priest gave a beautiful service, and the king was laid to rest.

The day after the funeral, Queen Glorvana arrived at Roygan's and Katyan's chambers.

As they sat in the sitting room, Katyan noticed the calm peace which had come over her mother-in-law. Not wanting to force the queen into talking, Roygan and Katyan simply sat with her and waited.

"You two have done beautifully these few days," Queen Glorvana praised her son and daughter-in-law. "Cortierre would have been proud. You spoke with the foreign dignitaries with grace and dignity. I am proud of both of you."

"Thank you," the two answered.

"I am not sure how much you know of our past, Katyan," Queen Glorvana continued. "If you will indulge me, I would like to tell you."

"Please," Katyan said, not having heard their story.

"Cortierre and I were married when we were twenty-four," the queen began. "Cortierre was the second son of the king. Did you know that?"

"No, my lady," Katyan responded interested.

"He had no kingdom responsibilities. He had been schooled along with his brother, but, being the second son, was not educated in the ways of kingdom leadership. During those lessons, he was allowed to learn whatever he wanted. His passion was with the out-of-doors. He enjoyed animals and farming.

"My father was a wealthy land owner just on the other side of town. I learned how to raise animals and farm the land as well. When we married, our one desire was to own a piece of land and work it. The king gave us some land near the palace. A house was built and we began to work the land. Roygan was born in that house.

"Six years later, Cortierre's father and brother were on a trip attending some kingdom business or another. An accident occurred, and both were thrown from the carriage. His brother died instantly. His father died en route to the palace. Cortierre was now to be king.

"He had no training at all in leading the country. He kept many of his father's advisors and replaced them with their sons as the time came. He never wanted to be king. He thought by surrounding himself with people who had advised his father before him, they would help lead the country, and he might not need to do much.

"Unfortunately, the council members quickly realized this. They became power hungry and manipulative. Cortierre allowed himself to be manipulated by these men, therefore rendering him a weak leader. He knew this, however he could not devise a way to get out of it."

Roygan and Katyan remained silent, intently listening.

"I never wanted to be queen, either. I supported him in every way I could. We were not good at the roles into which we were thrown. Without Cortierre, I have no desire to continue with the title, and the leadership role. I know you have known this. Therefore, I am relinquishing the crown to both of you. A ceremony will be held tomorrow to make it official."

She turned to her son and grasped his hands. "Roygan, you are strong. You are brave. You love the people. You have wonderful ideas for this kingdom. You will be a wonderful king. I have every confidence in you to lead this country."

"Thank you, Mother," Roygan said.

Then she turned to Katyan and grasped her hands. "Katyan, you are beautiful. You are loving. You are caring. You know the people. You treat them fairly. You will be a wonderful queen. I have every confidence in you to support Roygan in his leadership and- should you be called, and should you desire it- to lead the country yourself one day." Then she smiled looking at Roygan, "Though I sincerely hope nothing ever happens to either of you."

"Thank you, Mother," Katyan said. "Will you stay in the palace?"

Glorvana smiled at the hopefulness in her daughter-in-law's voice. "No, dear. I will return to our house in the country to live the life we desired."

"It is not too far away, I hope," Katyan said.

Glorvana stood and went to the window, beckoning Katyan to follow. "Do you see that second hill?"

"Yes," Katyan answered.

"Our house is just beyond that hill, in the valley," Glorvana said proudly. "It has been kept by two wonderful people who will remain there to help. I will take a few servants with me. I will be close enough to visit every day," then she smiled. "Though, I will not."

Just then, Zedan began to wake from his nap. "Please allow me to get my grandson," Glorvana asked.

"Of course," Katyan said.

———

The next day Roygan and Katyan were crowned King and Queen of Groy.

Chapter 13

Two weeks later

"Please, Mrs. Fasi, I know you are simply doing your job, and you are doing it quite well, but I must see the queen. It is a message only for her. I cannot pass it to anyone else. It is of extreme importance."

"I cannot simply let anyone off the street in to see the queen! I let you in once when she was princess. This is another matter entirely!"

"Mrs. Fasi," Arriah said as he approached, "what is all the commotion? We can hear your raised voices down the hall."

"Forgive me, sir," Mrs. Fasi said without a hint of apology, "this messenger is insisting on seeing the queen. I cannot simply let anyone off the street in to see the queen."

"Sir, the message is of the utmost importance," the messenger pled. "It is for the queen's ears only. Please, if you would just tell her Dadaan must speak with her, I am sure she will allow me in."

Arriah looked intently at the man at the door. He recognized the man as the one who brought the news of the assassination attempt a year ago. His gut feeling told him it would be alright. He decided to take the chance. "Come with me."

"Thank you, sir," Dadaan said as he brushed past Mrs. Fasi.

"Wait here," Arriah pointed to a chair and continued down the hallway.

Dadaan was too nervous to sit. He paced the hallway as he waited. The last time he came, he brought news of an assassination attempt. Now the news he brought was much more dire. "Please let her see me," he hoped.

Arriah returned, "Queen Katyan will see you now." He led the way toward the sitting room.

"Thank you, thank you," Dadaan repeated.

"Queen Katyan," Arriah said when they entered the room, "the messenger to see you."

"Thank you, Arriah," Katyan said.

Arriah left and closed the door, standing watch just outside.

"Uncle!" Katyan exclaimed as she jumped up to hug him. "How wonderful to see you! I hope your news is not as bad as the last time you came to see me."

Dadaan hated to ruin his niece's mood. "I'm sorry, my dear. I'm afraid it is worse."

Katyan's face fell. "What is it?" she asked as she sank back onto the settee.

He decided to come right out and give her the entire news. "An executive order has been written and signed by the king for war to be waged on all people of Doriian decent."

"What?" Katyan exclaimed in horror. "How could this be? How could Roygan do this?"

"Forgive me, dear," Dadaan said contritely. "It was not Roygan. It was Cortierre."

"Cortierre?" Katyan asked confused. "How is that possible? When was it signed?"

"It was signed three weeks ago, just before he died. I overheard some councilmen talking in the pub. The king was tricked on his deathbed."

"Yamur," Katyan whispered.

"Yes," Dadaan confirmed.

"Roygan saw him coming out of the sick room the day before Cortierre died. Why would he do this?"

"Yamur has always hated the Doriian people. His father was once cheated by a man from Dorii. He lost most of the family fortune to that man. And," he paused, "I am afraid I might have added to his hatred."

"You?" Katyan asked. "How could that be?"

"Yamur is intense about courtesies to royalty. He believes everyone of servant position must bow or curtsy to anyone of royal position. As I was bringing a message to him one day, I failed to bow. When he ordered it, I refused. He tossed me out, and the next day went to see the dying king. I am so sorry, Katyan."

"You have nothing to be sorry about, Uncle. You could not have known his pettiness would go this far. What will you do?"

"I have come to you to ask for help. You must talk to the king. It is time to tell him the truth about your heritage."

"I cannot do that!" Katyan said fearfully. "He will never trust me again. The penalty for lying to the king is death. If he knows I lied to him, I could face execution!"

Dadaan looked sternly at his niece. "Do not think you will escape this edict, Katyan. There are many people who know you and know your heritage. Some of them are quite jealous of your new position. They are simply waiting for an opportune time to reveal your secret for you. Do not think you will be spared."

Katyan buried her face in her hands.

Dadaan placed his hand on her shoulder and waited until she looked up at him. "Who knows, my dear whether you have come to the kingdom for such a time as this. Perhaps you have been called to this position to save your people."

Katyan sighed. "Perhaps, however I have no idea how to do it. When is the edict to be carried out?"

"One week from today."

"One week!" Katyan practically shouted. "I must tell Arriah and Ania. I need their support."

"Whatever you think is best."

"Ania!" Katyan called.

Ania entered the room.

"Please get Arriah. We need to talk."

———

Katyan left the room and walked purposefully to her husband's study. Arriah and Ania were left to pray for her safety with Dadaan. She knocked on the door.

"Come in," Roygan called.

She opened the door and found Roygan meeting with Yamur.

Catching her breath, she strode purposefully into the room.

"Hello, my dear," Roygan rose to kiss his wife.

"Hello," Katyan answered sweetly.

"What can I do for you?"

"I came to invite you to a special dinner tonight," Katyan said. "I would also like Yamur to come."

"Yamur?" Roygan asked.

"Yes, sire," Katyan answered firmly. "I would like to know your council members. Yamur is a great one to begin with."

Yamur was flattered to dine with the king and queen. "I accept, Your Highness."

"Wonderful," Katyan said. "We will dine in the formal dining room tonight at seven."

Katyan kissed Roygan on her way out.

Trembling, she went to order the dinner.

———

The food was wonderful. She encouraged Yamur to eat and drink plentifully. When he was in high spirits, Katyan decided to reveal her true intent.

"My lord," Katyan said to Roygan, "I fear I have some bad news."

"What is it," Roygan asked, concern etched on his face.

Katyan took a deep breath. She knew the king had every right to sentence her to death as well for keeping her identity hidden. She hoped Roygan was true to his word and did not care the bloodline of a person, only their personality. "I fear, my lord, that someone has conspired to kill the queen and her family one week from today."

"What?" Roygan practically exploded from his chair. "Who would do such a thing?"

"It is Yamur, Your Highness," Katyan said calmly.

Yamur's head snapped up. He was wide-eyed in shock.

"Why you!" Roygan towered over Yamur menacingly.

"I have done no such thing, Your Highness," Yamur whimpered.

"Now you call the queen a liar!" Roygan shouted.

"No, sire, I, I," Yamur stammered.

"Sire," Katyan said, "Yamur tricked your father into signing an edict declaring war."

"Is that what you were doing in my father's sick room while he was on his death bed? Conspiring to kill the queen and her family?"

"No, sire," Yamur was cowering in his chair. "He did sign an edict waging war on the Doriian people. I have no intention of harm on the queen!"

"Katyan?" Roygan asked.

"It is true, Your Highness," Katyan said. "My ancestors are Doriian."

Roygan briefly looked hurt by Katyan's confession. Then he turned to Yamur, furious. "That you would conspire to kill anyone for no reason, is treason enough. I have had it with you. I thought perhaps you could be an ally, but all you were doing was getting close so you could commit treason. You're finished, Yamur. Guards!"

Three security guards and Arriah burst through the dining room door.

"Take this man and execute him. He has conspired to kill the queen and wage war against her people."

"How would you like him executed, sire?" Arriah asked.

"Whatever way you see best, just get it done," Roygan snapped.

"If I may, Your Highness," Arriah said as the other guards tied Yamur's hands, "a gallows has been built just outside the palace walls."

Roygan was taken aback. "Gallows? I gave no orders for gallows to be built."

"Yamur had them built, sire," Katyan answered. "They were for a messenger named Dadaan. This messenger is my uncle. Yamur had them built because Dadaan would not bow to him."

"Dadaan?" Roygan asked. "Is this the same man who saved my life and the life of my father from the assassination attempt?"

"Yes, sire," Katyan answered. "He has risked his life twice to save your life and attempt to save mine."

"Arriah," Roygan said. "Take everything that belonged to Yamur and give it to the messenger Dadaan. He will now hold the position and wealth once coveted by Yamur."

"Yes, Your Highness," Arriah said smugly. Then he ordered the guards to take Yamur to the gallows.

When Katyan and Roygan were alone, Roygan turned to his wife with sad eyes. "Katyan…"

"I am sorry, sire," she said. "I did not mean to lie to you. My uncle feared for my life should my heritage be known. Now, I know I face the same fate since I have lied …"

Roygan covered the distance between them and kissed his wife.

"My dear," he said, tears brimming his eyes, "I do not care what your heritage is. I only care for you. I am so sorry you had to keep it from me. I completely understand why you did it, though. It was safer for you. I love you."

Katyan smiled and hugged her husband, safe in his arms. "I love you too."

Roygan pulled gently away and looked at his wife with concern in his eyes. "I fear your safety may still be in question, though."

Katyan looked questioningly at him.

"If my father really did sign this edict, I cannot undo it. If it was signed before his death, it cannot be undone."

"Something must be done, sire!" Katyan cried. "If my life must be taken, so be it, but spare the life of our son!"

"I will do all I can in my power to spare the lives of you both! Let us talk with your uncle. Perhaps he can advise us."

They ran down the hallway to speak with Dadaan.

"Write another edict, sire," Dadaan said. "In this edict, pronounce that all people of Doriian descent may assemble and fight back, annihilating anyone who attacks them. Then give them permission to plunder the property of their enemies. Proclaim all of this to occur on the same day as the previous edict."

"It shall be done," Roygan said rising to write the edict. Once several copies were written, he stamped his royal seal on them. "Take these," he said as he handed the copies to Dadaan, "hand them to my messengers. Tell them to ride to all the neighboring peoples and announce the edict." Then he handed another piece of paper to Dadaan. "You take this one to the king of Dorii. Deliver this yourself."

"It shall be done," Dadaan said. Then he rose and kissed his niece and left to do the king's bidding.

Chapter 14

Word came of Yamur's death. Katyan and Roygan grieved for the man. "How sad his life has been," Katyan said.

"What a miserable life to lead," Roygan said. "I pray his mischievous and hurtful acts end here."

The next day, Dadaan returned with news that he had delivered the message to the king of Dorii.

"Thank you," Roygan said. "Now, I want you to go to your home, gather all of your family and belongings. You must move in to Yamur's house now and be with us on the day of the edict. I do not want you or your family away from here on that day. I will send men with you to help you move."

"Yes, sire," Dadaan bowed and left with Arriah to gather men to move his home.

"Thank you, dear," Katyan said, "for caring for my family."

"They are my family too," Roygan said, as he hugged her. "I am so glad to know them now. Your uncle is a wise and noble man."

Dadaan returned two days later and moved into Yamur's house. Katyan was overjoyed to see her aunt and cousins.

Over the next three days, reports came in of the edict being delivered to all the Doriian people. With it came reports of the Doriian people gathering together to defend themselves.

Roygan set up a double guard on the palace and quadruple guard surrounding the queen and her family for the day of the edict. "I will take no chances," he declared.

The day of the edict came. Katyan, Roygan, and their son gathered in their chambers along with Arriah, Ania, and their daughter. Katyan's family stayed with them as well. The mood was tense. No one knew what to say. Arriah and Roygan paced the rooms, constantly checking on the guards. Katyan and Ania cared for their children with the help of Barria.

Soon, messengers began pouring in with reports of the battles.

"Your Majesties, there has been an attack at Markel. The Doriians are fighting strong."

"Your Majesties, an attack has been waged at Shender. The Doriians were taken by surprise. They fell back, gathered more support and pushed forward. They are on the offensive and winning now."

"My lord, my lady, there was a quick attack at Corma. The Doriians won easily."

"My king, my queen," this messenger was downcast, "there was a bloody attack at Henai. One Doriian family has been lost." This was Katyan's hometown. Katyan and her family mourned the loss of this family they knew well.

"Your Majesties," another messenger said, "the biggest attack so far has been at the Doriian border. The Doriians have overpowered their enemies and are pushing them back."

The reports continued to come from all over the country. It was wearing to hear the reports of bloodshed. By nightfall, Katyan and Ania had retired. They could not stand to hear any more. The killing was senseless. They had no heart for it.

———

The next day dawned bright and clear. Birds were singing outside the window. Katyan arose, refreshed. After getting ready, she went to the sitting room and found Ania serving her family tea and breakfast. The final messenger had just arrived to give report.

In all, the Doriians had lost three families and two farms. However, their enemies had been annihilated and possessions plundered for the victors. Yamur's plan had failed. It was victory for the Doriians.

The rest of the day was spent in mourning for the three families lost during the horrible day long war. Katyan and her family especially mourned the loss of their friends in Henai.

After the day of mourning, the next two days were set aside for celebration of the victories which far outnumbered the losses. Banquets and parties were set up all across the country as well as throughout the country of Dorii. Katyan and Roygan invited the king of Dorii to come for a special banquet. The king graciously accepted, having found strange allies in the new king and queen.

"Welcome, Your Highness," Roygan said to their neighboring king. "We are so pleased you decided to accept our invitation."

"Anyone who would pass an edict to save the people of a neighboring country at the expense of their own subjects is worth a strong alliance," the Doriian king said.

"I have always believed in the equality of people," Roygan explained. "I hate war. I hope it never comes to that again. The people had a choice to follow through with the senseless edict or not. Those who decided to follow through made their own decision and must suffer their consequences. Thankfully, I found that most of my subjects did not participate in the horrors. Those that did were of the seedy underground or from other countries."

"I had heard that as well," said the Doriian king. "You have a strong class of people as your subjects. I guess we all have those few who belong to the seedy underground."

The people of Groy also showed great respect for their new king and queen as well as for the Doriian people. They showered their new king and queen with gifts and an outpouring of devotion.

Over the next few weeks, Roygan replaced his father's council members with people of his own choosing. Roygan, Arriah, and Dadaan interviewed people for the positions for three weeks until Roygan was satisfied they had the right men. Arriah stepped down from his position as head of security and became second in command to the king. Dadaan was third.

The former members of the king's council lost their position and status. Many left the capital city to live in humiliation. Their dreams of power were never realized.

Roygan and Katyan ruled the country for many years together, always enjoying the devotion of their people.

One night, as Katyan and Roygan were retiring, Katyan turned to her husband and said, "Do you remember how nervous I was about becoming queen?"

"I remember it like it was yesterday instead of many years ago," Roygan said lovingly.

"It is still hard for me to believe that I arrived here from my humble background."

"You, my dear," Roygan said, as he wrapped his arms around his wife, "have been the most favored of all queens in this country. You have ruled with a fair and generous hand. You have been the helpmeet I searched for all those years before. Thank you, my love."

"Thank you for choosing me, my dear," Katyan said.

"Thank you for accepting." Then he kissed her.

The Unlikely Helper

"Our lives for your lives!" the men assured her. "If you don't tell what we are doing, we will treat you kindly and faithfully when the Lord gives us the land."

Joshua 2:14 (NIV)

To: Alex, Bethany, Brooke, Melissa, Anne, and Julie; amazing helpers in trying times.

Chapter 1

February, 1945 Remagen, Germany

"He's coming!" Tilly burst through the door.

Alia jumped, knocking over the dressing table, spilling its contents. "What?" she cried. "He's fifteen minutes early."

"I know," Tilly said urgently, "but I saw him turn the corner as I came in the house. You must hurry! Which one?" she asked, as she ran to the armoire and threw the doors open.

"The pink one," Alia answered in a panic as she began undressing.

"Herr Wolf is coming," Nixie came sauntering in dreamily unaware of the urgency in the room. "You're so lucky, Alia. He's so handsome." She walked over to the window and peeked through the curtains to watch the man stride down the sidewalk.

"I know," Alia snapped, as Tilly slipped the negligee over her head.

Nixie looked hurt at her new friend and suddenly noticed the flurry of activity in the room. "Why are you moving so fast?" she asked innocently.

"I must be ready on time for the man," Alia snapped again.

"Robe?" Tilly asked.

"Yes," Alia answered.

"Tied?"

"Yes."

"Hair?"

"Pulled back with the matching ribbon."

"Where is the ribbon?" Tilly asked, trying to remain calm.

"It was on the dressing table," Alia answered, panic beginning to rise again. "I don't know where it is now." She dropped to the floor to find the ribbon. "He gave it to me and likes me to wear it when he comes. Where is it?" she cried.

"This one?" Nixie asked as she held up a pink lace ribbon.

"Yes!" Tilly cried snatching the ribbon out of the girl's hand. She deftly tied Alia's long brown curls back in a loose tail leaving some curls to frame her face.

"Why are you so panicked?" Nixie asked again.

"You tell her," Alia told Tilly as she applied lipstick and blush.

"The last time Alia was not ready when the colonel came, he showed his displeasure with a backhand to her face," Tilly explained fearfully. "He left a bruise so dark on her cheek that makeup wouldn't cover it. She couldn't work for a week and a half."

"Oh, my," Nixie said. "What about having someone else take him?"

"Tried that, too," Alia answered looking apologetically at Tilly. "Same thing, plus he used some choice words to lash out at Tilly."

"And Madame Giselle still allows him to come?" Nixie asked in unbelief that the proprietress of the brothel would allow this dangerous man in her house.

"He's such a high ranking Nazi official, she's afraid of arrest, or at the very least the shutdown of the house," Tilly explained.

"He's coming up the walkway," Nixie announced, this time with a little more fear in her voice.

"Ready?" Tilly asked.

"Ready as ever," Alia answered. Taking a deep breath and shutting her emotions off, she walked out the bedroom door and stood seductively on the landing at the top of the stairs.

The front door opened, and Colonel Leon Wolf entered the house.

"Heil Hitler, Colonel," Madame Giselle greeted in a business manner.

"Heil Hitler, Madame Giselle," Wolf answered gruffly, "is Alia ready?"

"I believe so," Giselle answered shakily.

"Good evening Herr Colonel," Alia spoke quietly and coyly from her perch at the top of the stairs. "Heil Hitler."

Wolf's eyes roved over her, taking in every inch hungrily. He moved past Madame Giselle without another word to her and strode purposefully up the stairs. Firmly grabbing Alia's arm, he turned her around leading her to his favorite room. "Is the room ready?" he asked gruffly.

"Yes, sir," she answered quietly.

He opened the room and breathed in the aroma of incense he enjoyed. Leading her into the room, he closed the door behind him.

Alia walked over to the chest of drawers where two glasses and a decanter of brandy sat. Turning to him, she batted her eyelashes and asked, "Would you care for a drink?"

"Not tonight," he answered, unbuttoning his cuffs. "I have a meeting soon."

Alia affected a pout. "Oh, how soon?" She asked.

"In an hour, across town," he said, unbuttoning his shirt.

"Well," she said sauntering closer to him and putting her hand on his arm, "that still gives us plenty of time."

He stopped unbuttoning and looked hungrily at her again. Then, snatching her to him, he forcefully kissed her neck.

Knowing he could not see her face, she grimaced at his touch. Cursing him in her head, she reluctantly allowed his advances.

Just as soon as he started, he stopped and let her go. She cleared her face just as fast.

He licked his lips as a twisted smile spread across his face. "Well, no sense in letting anything go to waste," he said. "I might as well have that drink, and enjoy the show." He sat down on the edge of the bed as she poured his drink.

Alia hated this part of the interaction. Actually she hated everything about what she was getting ready to do. Not wanting Wolf to know her feelings, she didn't allow herself the luxury of anger and disgust at the time. The man paid handsomely, and she needed the money to get out of the situation she was in. Again, she turned off her emotions and began undressing. When she was finished, Wolf came to her, and she let him have his way with her.

When the interaction was over, it was always harder to turn off her emotions. Alia let a single tear slip down her face before she turned back to her client. He was already out of the bed and dressing.

"The money's on the table," he said without feeling.

She didn't answer.

He finished dressing and gathered his things. "Next week," he said, referencing their standing weekly appointment and walked out the door.

Alia lie in the bed a few moments more and allowed the tears to flow. She cursed the God she no longer believed in. She cursed her mother for leaving her in Madame Giselle's care when she and her older sister were but twelve and ten years of age. She cursed Madame Giselle for not attempting a better life for the girls. She cursed every man who had ever used her and her sister. She cursed herself for being the victim and allowing herself to be used in such a way.

After her lament, she put the robe on and walked to the bathroom.

Chapter 2

Back in the dressing room shared by the girls, Alia sat alone at her table brushing her hair.

Another image appeared in the mirror behind her own. Alia groaned. "Yes, Odette?" she said wearily. The older woman didn't share the dressing room with the younger girls. At thirty-five, Odette Hahn thought herself too good for the girls in their early twenties.

"Well, well, Miss Schmitt, how was he?" Odette sneered.

"What do you care?" Alia snapped. The two did not get along. Before Alia began working, Odette was the most sought after lady of the house. Alia's beauty, charm, and class far surpassed Odette's, therefore making her more appealing to the more prominent gentlemen callers. Odette would not forgive Alia her good fortune.

"No reason," Odette said with a smirk on her face.

"I don't believe you," Alia challenged. "You always have a reason. What do you want?"

The smirk quickly left Odette's face. "I want him!" she practically shouted.

"What?" Alia asked warily.

"He is the most prominent, high paying customer in the house. I have worked too hard and too long in this business to let a mere child take him away from me."

"I didn't take anyone away from you, Odette," Alia countered. "You weren't even here the first night he came."

"That doesn't matter," Odette whined. "I have seniority here, he should be my client."

"What do you want me to do about it, Odette?" Alia asked, tired of the woman's antics.

"Give him to me!" Odette ordered.

By this time, Tilly and Nixie had finished for the night. Coming in to the dressing room, they listened to the confrontation with interest.

"I'd gladly give him to you, but you know what happened the last time we attempted to give him to someone else."

"That's just an excuse," Odette shot back. "She just wasn't good enough for him. If he had the chance with me, he'd see what a real woman is like and what he's been missing."

"What is going on here?" Madame Giselle came into the room.

Nixie answered for them all, "Odette has challenged Alia for Colonel Wolf."

"Stay out of it, girl," Odette spat.

"Is this true?" Madame Giselle asked.

Alia remained silent.

"I have seniority, Giselle," Odette pled her case. "I deserve to have the high paying clientele."

"Alia?" Madam Giselle questioned.

"You know my history with the colonel," Alia explained. "I would gladly give him up to someone else. However, I fear the repercussions for both of us."

Odette huffed her disbelief.

Madame Giselle thought for a moment then answered. "I give you my permission, Odette to attempt to lure the man. However, I do have a reputation to uphold with myself and any woman working for me. I will not allow you to badmouth each other. Agreed?"

"Agreed," Alia answered.

Odette rolled her eyes, "Agreed," she said reluctantly.

"And," Madame Giselle continued, "Alia must be ready and available should he want her. Agreed?"

Alia sighed, "Agreed."

"But…" Odette protested.

"Agreed?" Madame Giselle pressed.

"Fine," Odette agreed.

"Very well," Madame Giselle said with finality and left the room.

"Come next week," Odette said threateningly, "he's mine." Then she turned and stormed out of the room, slamming the door behind her.

Alia shuddered at the thought of what she knew would inevitably transpire. As she finished brushing her hair, Nixie began chattering.

"You sure do get the high class clientele, Alia," she commented. "How do you do that?"

Alia smiled. Nixie had only been at the Trosten House for a few weeks. She came when Alia's sister Adele left. She enjoyed talking with the two younger girls.

"She knows how to act high class," Tilly answered for her.

"How do you know?" Nixie questioned.

Alia put the brush down and turned around to chat. Tilly didn't know the whole story, so she decided to start from the beginning.

"When I was about ten years old, my mother died. She had worked for Madame Giselle and gotten sick. She left my sister, Adele, and me for Madame Giselle to raise. Since we were too young to do what we do now, we did a lot of odd jobs around the house. When we were finished with our work around the house, I would go sit in the parks and watch the people go by. I loved watching the high society people in their fancy clothes and their fancy way of walking and talking. I started mimicking them. Adele and I would practice with each other. Eventually, it became second nature for the both of us. We hoped to do something else with our lives.

"Unfortunately, Madame Giselle never sent us to school, so we never learned anything beyond some English and what she had to offer, so we ended up where we are now. The high society men like the company of women who at least seem more high society. It pays well, though it does attract some rough men. The higher rank they are in the Nazi regime, the more aggressive and sometimes violent they can be."

"I never had a chance to be around high society people," Nixie said. "Could you teach me some things?"

"Sure," Alia agreed. "Tell me your story."

"Well," Nixie started, eager to talk about herself, "I lived with my parents until they died and then ended up on the streets. I was there, begging and stealing for about five years until Madame Giselle found me and offered me the job. So, I have definitely not lived with the high society. What can you teach me?"

Alia smiled and tried to think of where to start. "Well, first," she said, "don't wear so much makeup."

Chapter 3

Two days later, Alia woke early for her day off. Quietly, so as not to disturb the sleeping girls in the same room, she quickly changed into one of her favorite dresses, which she designed and tailored. Then she picked up her portfolio of designs and slipped out of the house. Pausing under a tree, she breathed in the crisp cool air. Spring was on the way.

Alia reveled in the thought that she didn't have to go back to the Trosten House for more than twenty-four hours. A broad smile crossed her face, and she took another deep breath of the fresh air.

Clutching her portfolio, she walked purposefully toward the main street. She enjoyed the anonymity her outfit provided. Here in the open, she blended in with the other pedestrians. No one gave her a second glance, because no one knew what she did behind the closed doors of the Trosten House.

Hailing a cab, Alia gave the driver her destination. As they drove down the streets, she enjoyed watching the people as they drove by. She tried to watch their mannerisms so she could imitate them later on. This trick helped in her profession, though she hoped it would help in her life post-prostitution, whenever that time came.

At last, the cab driver pulled to a stop in front of Alia's desired destination. Paying the man, she thanked him and stepped out. She stood in front of the building and gathered her nerves before entering. Squaring her shoulders and lifting her head high, she pushed the doors open and strode up to the receptionist.

"Heil Hitler," the receptionist snapped.

Alia hated the Nazi regime. Most of the entire regime didn't affect her personally except the officers who required her services. She hated the Nazis for what they did to her and how they used her. However, she wanted to impress the designers she was here to see, so grudgingly, she raised her hand and repeated, "Heil Hitler," to the receptionist.

"May I help you?" the receptionist asked through piercing eyes.

"Yes, please," Alia said as strongly as she could muster. "I would like to see Herr Dehn."

"Herr Dehn is a very busy man," the receptionist said haughtily. "Appointments are needed. Why do you need to see him?"

"I have a few designs I would like him to take a look at, if he has time," Alia said, gathering strength from the frustration she was feeling at the woman's haughty nature.

"Have a seat over there," the receptionist pointed to a cluster of three leather chairs in a waiting area.

Alia chose the middle chair and waited. Glancing at the clock, she noted the time as 9:00 a.m. She waited and waited and waited. The receptionist never rose from her desk and never looked again at Alia.

At 11:15 a.m., a door opened to the reception area and a well-dressed man came out. "Helen, I will be at lunch with…" He stopped mid-sentence as he noticed Alia sitting in the waiting room. He walked over to her and held his hand out. "Good morning," he said as he shook her hand.

"Good morning," Alia replied politely, noticing he did not use the required Nazi greeting.

"Have you been helped?" He asked.

"Yes, sir," Alia answered. "I requested to see Herr Dehn when he might be available."

The man's eyes narrowed. "When did you place this request?" he asked.

"I arrived shortly before nine, sir," Alia answered.

The man's face reddened, and he turned to the receptionist. "Helen, why was I not told of this visitor?"

Helen looked slightly flustered, but composed herself in a hard glare at Alia. "I told the fraulein that you are a busy man, and she needed an appointment."

He noted Alia's portfolio and said, "Please forgive my receptionist. She is new. I am never too busy for potential designers. Come, step into my office."

"But your lunch—" Helen broke in.

"My lunch can wait, thanks to your rudeness," Herr Dehn snapped as he ushered Alia into his office and shut the door. "I apologize, fraulein. She is new and has some competency issues." He smiled.

Alia returned the smile. She liked the man already. "It is no problem, sir. Thank you for agreeing to see me."

"Of course," he said genuinely. "I always enjoy seeing fresh designs, as I assume you have brought me." He pointed to her portfolio.

"Yes, sir," she handed the portfolio to him.

"First things first," he said and extended his hand to hers again. "I am Charles Dehn, owner of Dehn's Fashions. Who's hand do I have the pleasure of shaking?"

"My name is Alia Schmitt. I am afraid I have nothing so glamorous on my resume as you," she smiled. "These are my first designs."

"Excellent," he said. "Am I correct in assuming the outfit you are wearing is of your own creation?"

"Yes, sir," Alia smiled in pleasure that he noticed.

"Very nice," Charles remarked. "Might you be comfortable turning, so I may look at it?"

Somewhat taken aback at the man asking permission to observe her, Alia hesitated.

Picking up on her hesitation, Charles quickly spoke, "I apologize if I made you uncomfortable. I simply assumed that by wearing your creation, you might be willing to model it."

"Of course," Alia said comfortably. "I have just never modeled before."

Charles smiled, "Just turn, and stop when I request. I assure you, I am only looking at the design."

"Of course," Alia complied. She turned and stopped as the man requested, enjoying his approving remarks of her creation. Never had she stood before a man who frankly appraised her handiwork and not her body. Inwardly, she basked in the experience.

"Excellent," Charles declared after she had turned completely around twice. "I love the fabric you chose for the skirt and jacket. The red, wool plaid compliments the black blouse. The red hat is an excellent accent as well. Is this design in the portfolio?"

"Yes, sir, third design in."

"Wonderful," Charles said as he began to leaf through the pages. "Please have a seat while I take a look at your other designs."

Alia sat in the chair offered. She was surprised when he sat in the adjacent chair, not behind his desk.

Charles turned each page carefully as he examined the designs. Periodically he made approving comments or asked questions about her ideas. Alia was thoroughly enjoying her encounter with the head of the design company.

"Well," Charles said as he finished examining the final design, "I can certainly tell you that I am impressed. You have very creative ideas. Your lines are nice and precise. The color schemes you have chosen are very flattering. I think you have a great future ahead of you in design."

Alia beamed. Was she hearing him correctly? Was he actually praising her work?

"Unfortunately," he continued.

Her heart sank.

"I am not able to make the decisions for the firm on my own. I have a board who helps make the decisions on what designs to accept. Fortunately, though, they have much the same taste as I do." He smiled.

Alia let herself breathe easier. Hope began to rise.

"Would you be willing to allow me to keep your portfolio and show it to my board? We meet twice a week and would have a chance to look at these together to make a decision."

"Yes, sir, you may keep them this week," Alia began to feel some excitement as she thought about the possibilities ahead of her.

"When would you be available to return next week to discuss the results of my board's perusal?"

"I am available on Tuesdays," Alia answered, hoping he would not ask her what she did other days.

"Great, Tuesday it is. Will 9:00 a.m. work?" He asked, showing no interest in asking her about her other weekly duties.

"Nine would be perfect," Alia said excitedly.

"Wonderful," then he smiled, "Let's make sure Helen gets it on the appointment calendar, shall we?"

Alia smiled, but refrained from commenting.

After personally adding the appointment to the log, Charles informed Helen that he would be taking his full lunch break and would return in an hour. He shook Alia's hand and they parted ways.

Alia walked down the street toward the banks of the Rhine River. She walked toward the Ludendorff Bridge that led into her town of Remagen. She breathed in the smell of water and fish, actually enjoying the smell. It seemed so fresh after the stale air of the Trosten House which smelled of old incense, cigarette smoke, and alcohol. Reaching the street she was looking for, she turned right and walked up the stairs to an apartment complex.

Finding the apartment of her destination, she inserted her key quietly and entered. Opening a window, she went to the kitchen to brew some tea. After setting the kettle on to boil, she went to the curtain that separated the living area from the sleeping area in the studio apartment. Pulling the curtain back, she looked in on the sleeping form of her sister. After convincing herself Adele was sleeping peacefully, Alia returned to the kitchen to fix the tea.

A half hour later, sipping her tea, Alia was still enjoying her day. The curtain parted, and the disheveled form of her sister appeared. Alia smiled. "Good afternoon," she greeted.

"Afternoon?" Adele sleepily asked. "If its afternoon, then you are late, dear sister."

"I have been here for a half hour, sleepyhead," Alia bantered.

"Still a half hour means you are late, and you should have awakened me when you arrived," Adele admonished sweetly. "We don't have that much time together."

Alia smiled. "You're right. I apologize. You are supposed to sleep, and I didn't want to disturb you. I will next time."

"Thank you," Adele said. "Why are you late?"

"I had the most incredible morning, Adele," Alia said excitedly. "I took my portfolio to Dehn's Fashions. I met with Herr Charles Dehn in person!"

"That's wonderful! What did he say?"

"He liked my designs, Adele. He liked them! He kept the portfolio, and I have an appointment with him next Tuesday at nine in the morning. Can you believe it?"

"I'm so proud of you, Alia. I knew he would like it. Did he like the outfit you're wearing?"

"Yes, he did. He had me model it for him. And, Adele, it was the first time a man saw me for me and my brain, and not for my body. I can't tell you what an incredible feeling that was."

"I can't imagine. I'm so glad for you." A shadow fell across Adele's face.

"I'm sorry you haven't had that experience, yet," Alia apologized.

"No time for sorries here," Adele brushed off the shadow.

"How are you feeling?" Alia asked with concern.

"I'm alright," Adele answered. "A little lethargic today, but alright." Five months before, Adele had become pregnant by a client. When she began to show, she became unable to work. She was unable to see a doctor due to the precariousness of her situation with the client – he was a married Nazi officer.

After a pause, Adele quietly offered, "I saw Conrade."

Alia nearly spit her tea out. "What?"

"He was walking outside by the river. I could see him from the window."

"That means he's close to finding you again," Alia said in a near panic. "We have to find another place."

Conrade Lange was the father of Adele's unborn child. When she was unable to continue working and told him she refused to abort the child, he flew at her in a blind rage, beating her and raping her. She was no longer able to remain at the Trosten House, for her safety and the safety of the other girls. Alia had found another apartment for her to stay in, hoping the man would not find her.

Conrade was a major in the Nazi army and every bit as vicious as Colonel Leon Wolf. He also had many connections in the S.S. and had been able to use those connections to find Adele's last hideout.

Both girls shuddered, thinking of the last altercation three weeks earlier. It had been Alia's day off, and she was spending it, as usual, with Adele. Conrade had come barging in the door with no notice. Adele had no chance to hide. Alia tried to stop him, only to meet his fist. He beat her and knocked her to the ground unconscious for a few minutes while he'd had his way with Adele one more time. They moved Adele two days later.

The next week, when Alia arrived at the new apartment, Adele told her the sad news. The last altercation with Conrade had resulted in a miscarriage of the baby. Now, Adele was left emotionally and physically broken.

Unbeknownst to Adele, Alia had bought a pistol off the black market. She kept it with her when she was with Adele, vowing to shoot the major if she saw him again.

"I'll look for another apartment," Alia said. "Until then, make sure you have quick access to the closet."

The house this apartment was in had been an old mansion. The flat Adele occupied had a closet that covered the old servants' stairs. The back of the closet was shoddily made and Alia discovered that it came off leading to a hidden passage way. The two decided to hide Adele in the passage way, if need be, should they get the chance.

"Of course," Adele said. "Meanwhile, let's enjoy your day off."

"Gladly," Alia said.

Chapter 4

That evening at the Trosten House, an unexpected guest arrived.

Bursting the door open, Colonel Leon Wolf stepped drunkenly into the foyer. "Where's Alia?" he bellowed.

"Good evening, Colonel," Giselle said, trying to steady her nerves.

"Quit with the pleasantries, Giselle," Wolf slurred. "I'm here for Alia, where is she?"

"This is her night off, Colonel," Giselle said shakily. "She is not here."

"What?" he screamed. "She'd better be here, or there will be consequences."

Odette saw this as her opportunity. She stepped in. "Why, Colonel," she crooned, "you're looking tastily handsome tonight."

"What do you want?" he snapped.

"I simply thought you might want a taste of something new," Odette stepped closer to him and ran her fingers along his arm.

He slapped her hand away. "Why would I want that? I get the best one in the house. Why would I want some old hag?"

The words stung Odette, but she was not to be deterred. She was determined to show him she was every bit as good or better than Alia. "Just give me a chance, Colonel," she said coyly. "I'm sure I could change your mind."

"Giselle," he shouted drunkenly, "if Alia is not here in the next ten seconds, someone is going to feel my wrath!"

Giselle's strong façade cracked. She knew what the man was capable of and knew that she could not produce Alia. She didn't know where Alia went on her days off. They agreed to hide Adele without telling anyone, to keep everyone safe. Unfortunately, it looked like that would backfire on her now. She simply stood there, mute.

"Giselle!" Wolf screamed again.

Odette tried again, "Oh, come, Colonel. I'm sure I could satisfy you in ways you never dreamed."

Realizing Alia would not appear and Odette would not go away, he turned his full wrath on her. "Woman," he growled as he clutched her arm in a vice-like grip, "you're going to see what you get when you step in my way."

He dragged her upstairs to his favorite room. Seeing it was occupied, he yanked her harder to the next available room, the whole time ranting and raving. He shoved her into the room and slammed the door shut.

Tilly's client finished in the room Wolf wanted and quickly exited. Tilly changed as fast as she could and met Nixie and Giselle downstairs. The girls stood frozen stiff as they listened to the horrific sounds coming from the room. They heard furniture crashing, Wolf beating Odette, and Odette screaming.

When it was over, Wolf came out of the room still buttoning his shirt. He slammed the bedroom door, stomped down the stairs and stood inches away from Giselle. She could smell the alcohol on his breath and see blood on his fingers.

"Alia had better be here next time I come back, or you're next," he said to Giselle and stormed out the front door.

Tilly and Nixie stared at Giselle and back at each other in horrified shock. Then they ran upstairs to see if they could help Odette. What they saw made them want to wretch. The armoire had been turned on its side. The mattress was flung off the bed. The bedside table had been flung across the room. Odette lay in the middle of the mess, naked and bleeding. She began to moan.

The girls picked her up carefully and took her to the bath to wash up. As they took care of her, she remained quiet except for a few moans when they washed areas that had been especially beaten. They were tremendously haunted by the vacant stare in her eyes.

When they finished, they wrapped her in her robe and laid her in her bed. Thankfully, Odette fell asleep, and they closed the door behind them.

They quietly went downstairs to find Giselle. She was in the sitting room on the sofa with her head in her hands, crying.

Tilly and Nixie sat next to her and cried with her.

Chapter 5

"What would you like for breakfast?" Alia asked as Adele came in to the kitchen.

"What do we have?" Adele asked sleepily.

Alia showed her the spread of breads, cheeses, and fruits she had picked up from the market that morning. Adele's eyes widened in pleasure as she pointed out her choice.

The two sat in companionable silence as they ate their breakfast and drank their tea.

"Soon, this will be a normal morning for us not just a rare occasion," Alia said with dreamy confidence.

Adele was silent as she sipped her tea.

"Won't that be nice?" Alia asked, noting her sister's silence.

Adele hesitated a moment. "That would be wonderful," she said. "But how is it going to happen? You know how hard it is to get out of the profession. You know I can't even go out the door. I fear Conrad's wrath daily. I fear I will not make it long enough to live the dream."

"Sister, don't talk like that," Alia said, concern etched in her voice. "Of course you will make it. I'll make enough money soon with my designs and perhaps get a job as a seamstress. We'll get out of here to a new place without fear of Conrade Lange or Leon Wolf. We'll go to England or perhaps America. We will," she added with more conviction than she actually felt.

"I hope so," Adele said sadly.

"Meanwhile," Alia continued, "we just need to wait out this week and see what happens with my designs and Dehn Fashions. Besides, perhaps the Allies are coming closer and will liberate us from the Nazis and this whole nightmare will be over."

"That would be wonderful," Adele said. "I wish we knew what was really happening in the war. I know we're not getting the full story. I listen to the radio and all is wonderful with the Nazis, but I have a feeling it is all propaganda."

"You're probably right," Alia agreed. "Since when have we ever gotten the full true story from the Nazis?"

"Oh, that there would be some way we could help thwart the Nazi regime," Adele dreamed.

"I would love to be able to do something to get back at every Nazi officer who ever used you and me. Every man who ever treated us with anything but respect, which would be just about every man we have come in contact with," Alia said.

"That would be nice, but don't think just about yourself, dear sister," Adele gently admonished. "What about the thousands of Jews around who have been mistreated and killed by the Nazis as well?"

"I know all about that," Alia said with slight irritation. "But that hasn't affected me personally. I want revenge on Leon Wolf and Conrade Lange and all the other Nazi men who have beaten, abused, and humiliated us and the other girls. That's my motivation. And, believe me, Adele, if I ever get the chance, I will take it."

Adele shuddered slightly at the intensity in her sister's voice. She knew the passion Alia was capable of and was afraid it might get her into trouble.

Deciding to change the subject to the beautiful weather outside, the sisters enjoyed the rest of their meal together. All too soon, it was time for Alia to return to the Trosten House.

"Be safe," they told each other simultaneously, then giggled at their coinciding thoughts. Hugging each other tightly, they bid good bye until Alia's next day off.

Upon entering the Trosten House, Alia could tell something was wrong. Usually, the girls were up and cleaning the table from the mid-day meal with laughter and joking. This morning, no one was downstairs and the shades were drawn. Alia walked quietly up the stairs to the room she shared with Tilly and Nixie. She found them sitting quietly on Nixie's bed looking out the window.

"Is everything alright?" Alia asked as she hung her jacket in the closet and removed her hat.

The two younger girls looked at each other, neither wanting to be the first to answer.

"What's going on?" Alia asked fearfully. "Please tell me." She crossed to the bed to join the other two.

"Wolf was here last night," Tilly said somberly.

Alia's heart skipped a beat, and she could feel herself beginning to panic. "Wolf?" she whispered. "He's not supposed to be here until Sunday."

"He stopped in unexpectedly," Nixie stated the obvious. "He was drunk," she added.

"Oh, no," Alia had seen the man drunk several times and knew how aggressive he could be, especially in that state. "What happened?" she pressed.

"Since you were gone, Odette thought she had the perfect chance to lure him," Tilly supplied.

"Oh, no!" Alia exclaimed, guessing where the story was leading. "Is she all right?"

Both girls silently shook their heads. "She's in her room," Tilly offered.

Alia jumped up and hurried down the hallway to Odette's room. The door was closed. Alia leaned her ear to the door and heard soft moaning. Quietly, she opened the door. Odette lay on her bed, wrapped in her robe. The blinds were closed, but Alia could see bruises on her face and arms. She hurried over to the bedside.

"Odette," she whispered lightly holding her hand. "I'm so sorry."

"What do you want?" Odette rasped angrily.

Taken aback that the woman would be angry with her, even when she was trying to be comforting, Alia stammered, "I-I just want to say I'm sorry. I feel badly that this happened to you."

Odette slapped Alia's hand away. "What do you care?" she growled.

"I'm just sorry you're hurt, that's all," Alia said.

"I'm sure that's all," Odette snapped. "You just want to come here and gloat that the man wanted you."

"No!" Alia argued.

"Well, I'm not finished yet," Odette vowed. "This won't deter me. I've been in this business a long time, girl. I am not about to let some snippy, uppity little thing take the big business away from me. I'll be back on my feet soon and giving you competition again. Just you wait. Now get out!"

Alia knew better than to press Odette. She quickly left the room. Once in the hallway, she let the tears flow. She and Odette had never gotten along, but it wasn't for lack of effort on her part. Odette had simply always viewed Alia as competition and couldn't stand the success the younger woman had. Alia had enough challenges in her life. She didn't want to continue adding hostility with housemates to the list.

Chapter 6

The next few days at the Trosten House passed by quietly. Odette remained in her room allowing only Giselle to attend to her. Alia, Tilly, and Nixie remained away and continued with their daily activities. Wolf did not return unannounced again.

Sunday arrived, and Alia's nerves were tense. She readied herself an hour before she knew Wolf was scheduled to come, to make sure there were no complications.

Right on schedule, Colonel Leon Wolf arrived at the Trosten House. Alia was taken aback when he arrived with a small bouquet of flowers. He cordially greeted Giselle as he passed her to meet Alia at the top of the stairs. No mention was made of his last visit.

"Heil Hitler, and good evening, Alia," he said almost sweetly.

"Heil Hitler, and good evening, Colonel," Alia returned.

Wolf gently took her hand in his and led her to his favorite room. He sat her on the edge of the bed. Pouring brandy into two glasses, he handed her one.

"My, my," Alia said coyly, actually enjoying the attention, "you're in an exceptional mood this evening."

"I certainly am," he replied, though did not expand.

The evening passed, and he was more gentle and attentive than he had ever been. She actually found herself enjoying his company for the first time since she had met him two years prior.

After their interaction was complete, Wolf took his time dressing. Curious, Alia allowed herself to ask, "What has you in such an exceptional mood, Herr Colonel?"

"We had an extremely successful raid tonight, my dear," he answered proudly.

"Raid?" Alia asked almost afraid to hear the answer.

"We found a pocket of resisters – Jew hiders," he answered. "We routed them out, arrested the resisters and killed the Jews. It was a triumphant evening."

Alia was sorry she asked. She did not ask for more details.

He came back to her, lifted her hand to his lips and kissed her fingers one by one. As he did, she noticed blood on his hands. When he finished, he placed the money on the table and left. Alia promptly wrapped the sheet around her, ran to the bathroom, and wretched.

She bathed extra long to try to rid herself of the filthy feeling of having been with such a terrible man. She contemplated her lot in life, especially focusing on her position of being somewhat highly sought after by the higher ranking Nazi officials. The money was good, but she wondered how much longer she would be willing to compromise herself.

Tonight was the first night she truly thought upon the plight of the others whose mere existence drew the Nazi hatred. They, like she, did not deserve the treatment they received. Her determination grew to do whatever she might be able to do to thwart the Nazi regime. She had no idea how it would come about, but she resolved to keep an open eye and ear for possibilities.

The next morning was quiet. Odette came down for breakfast. Not wanting an altercation, and still pensive about the previous evening's musings, Alia remained in her room.

The day passed quietly and Alia began to ready herself for the evening's callers. She didn't have a regular for Monday night, but usually was able to fill her evenings. All of a sudden, she heard a crash downstairs. Then an all too familiar voice yelled out, "Alia! Where are you?"

Tilly looked at her in fear. It was Wolf.

There was nothing for her to do, but go meet him. She trembled as she turned the doorknob to walk out on the landing. When she reached the top of the stairs, she saw Wolf swaying drunkenly as he grabbed hold of Odette's wrist. She was wincing in pain but would not allow herself to scream.

Knowing Odette would be mad, but fearing what Wolf would do if she did not let her presence known, Alia said, "I am here, Herr Colonel."

"Go away!" Odette swore at Alia.

Wolf threw her on the ground and strode purposefully up the stairs to Alia. Grabbing her arm, he twisted her roughly around and took her to his favorite room. The door was locked indicating it was occupied. He swore and kicked at the door.

Turning down the hallway, he dragged Alia to the next available room. Alia's arm was twisted painfully, his vice-like grip never loosening. She stifled a scream. He threw her into the room and slammed the door shut. Moving swiftly to her, he made quick progress of his desires. Her evening meal threatened to come up as she smelled the alcohol on his breath and remembered his sickening triumph of the night before.

When he finished, he left her lying on the bed as he made quick progress of the decanter of brandy on the table. Leaving his money next to the glasses, he left without a word.

Alia cursed herself for allowing the man's advances and not fighting for herself. She threw the pillow across the room knocking over the decanter and glasses, sending them shattering against the wall.

A soft knock sounded on the door breaking her inner lament. "Who is it?" she asked shakily.

"It's Tilly. There's another customer downstairs asking for you."

Alia groaned and got up. Opening the door, she said, "Who's down there?"

"Brock Peters," Tilly answered.

Alia rolled her eyes. She would describe the young officer as silly, immature, and annoying. He was far too patriotic and eager for her tastes, but he paid well, so she kept him as a client.

"Alright," she sighed, realizing she would not have the luxury of lamenting any longer. "Let me get washed up and changed, and I'll be right down."

Alia had one other customer for the evening after Brock. After bathing, she sat at her dressing table brushing her hair, looking forward to her day off the next day.

Madame Giselle knocked on the door and opened it. "Alia," she said in a business-like manner.

Alia knew this voice. She also knew she would not like what followed. "Yes, Madame?"

"I need you to remain at the House tomorrow," she answered firmly.

Alia's heart sank. "But tomorrow is my day off," she said. The next day was the day she had her appointment with Herr Dehn about her designs. She would also miss seeing Adele.

Giselle's voice softened a bit. "I know. But since we've had these troubles with Colonel Wolf, I fear for all of us if you're not here."

"But you don't fear for me, if I am?" Alia countered. She had never been so forthright with the Trosten House proprietress before and was shocked at her own directness. Though, it did feel good to speak her mind.

Madame Giselle was equally as shocked at Alia's candid statement, though she did not take kindly to being countered. "I have a reputation to uphold and a business to run. You will be here tomorrow in case the colonel returns." With that, she turned and walked out the room.

Alia walked over to her bed and sank down. Oh how she wished for a different life! She needed to get word to Adele that she would not be there. She felt exhausted. Wearily, she rose from the bed and got dressed.

"Where are you going?" Nixie asked sleepily.

"I have some things I need to take care of since I can't take my day off tomorrow," Alia said and headed out the door.

Aware she was out past curfew, Alia kept to the shadows to avoid detection. A few times, she saw a Nazi watchman on the street, but was able to escape his eye.

She reached the apartment and quietly slipped inside. "Adele?" she whispered, hoping not to startle her sister.

"Alia?" Adele whispered back fearfully. "Is something wrong?"

"I'm sorry to scare you," Alia crossed to the bed and tried to comfort her sister. "I just needed to let you know that Giselle won't allow me to take my day off tomorrow."

"Why?" Adele asked sympathetically.

"Wolf," Alia explained. "He came unexpectedly on my last day off and hurt Odette pretty bad. He came yesterday as scheduled and was fine." She decided not to worry Adele with the details he shared with her about the raid. "Then he came back unexpectedly today, yelling for me, and would have hurt Odette again had I not been there."

"Did he hurt you?" Adele asked with a mix of fear and protectiveness in her voice.

"Just my arm as he dragged me to the room," Alia confessed.

"I fear for you, Alia," Adele said.

"I know," Alia said thinking of her sister's own plight. "I'm afraid, too."

"I wish it were easy to get out," Adele said, knowing how difficult it would be.

"The worst part of it, besides not getting to see you," Alia said, "is that I'll have to miss my appointment with Charles Dehn."

"No!" Adele exclaimed. "You can't miss that. Couldn't you slip away in the morning?"

"You know I can't. You know Giselle. She won't let me leave the house. She'd kill me if she knew I was gone now."

"You're right," Adele agreed. "But you need that appointment."

"Oh well," Alia tried to sound nonchalant. "I'll figure it out."

Adele knew her sister and did not believe she was resigned to the fact she would have to miss her appointment.

"Well," Alia said, "I'm not ready to leave you, but I need to. Have you seen Conrade again?"

"No," Adele said.

Alia stood to leave. "Be safe, sister."

"You too."

They hugged and parted.

Chapter 7

The next day, Adele woke early and got dressed, trying to disguise her features as much as possible. Keeping a close watch out for Conrade, she stayed along the side streets. Reaching Dehn's Fashions at 9:00 a.m. sharp, she squared her shoulders and went inside.

As she approached the receptionist desk, she said, "Heil Hitler. I am here to see Herr Dehn."

The receptionist looked suspiciously up at her. "Heil Hitler," she repeated. "Do you have an appointment?"

"Yes," Adele answered. "I am here for Alia Schmitt."

Helen narrowed her eyes at Adele. "You're not Fraulein Schmitt."

"Yes, I am," Adele answered. "I am her sister."

"Why is she not here?"

"I don't believe it is any of your business," Adele answered haughtily. "I am here for the appointment with Herr Dehn."

At that moment, the door to the office opened and Charles Dehn walked out. "Good morning," he said. "May I help you?"

"I am Alia Schmitt's sister," Adele said. "I am here for her appointment."

"Of course," Charles said, not asking questions. "Please, step into my office." He led her to his office and shut the door behind them. "I can tell you are sisters. You look very much alike. Please, have a seat." He pointed to a chair and chose the adjacent chair.

Adele decided to jump in with as little explanation as possible before the man started asking questions. "I apologize for my sister's absence. Something came up. I am here to see if I can relay any message to her."

"I understand," Charles Dehn said with empathy. "These are precarious times." He did not elaborate on that comment. Adele wondered just what the man had gone through. Only then did she realize that he had not greeted her with the required Nazi greeting. He continued, "I can tell you, fraulein, that my board was very impressed with your sister's designs."

Adele smiled and let out a breath she didn't realize she had been holding.

"We are willing to pay handsomely for the designs," Charles continued. "However, we do not have a seamstress position open, so we are unable to hire your sister otherwise."

"Oh," Adele said.

"Believe me, I tried. I thought your sister's abilities quite impressive and would love to have her employed here. However, as I said, we are willing to pay handsomely for the designs."

"Wonderful," Adele exclaimed, thrilled for her sister.

"I cannot give the money to you, though," Charles said. "I need to give it to your sister."

"I understand," Adele said. "I will tell her and have her come as soon as she is available."

"Great," Charles said. "Is there anything else I can help you with?"

"I don't think so," Adele said smiling. She rose and shook Charles' hand. "Thank you very much. I appreciate your seeing me. My sister will appreciate this as well."

"Thank you for coming, fraulein," Charles opened the door and guided Adele out before Helen could ask questions.

———

"I'm thrilled at the news, of course," Alia told Adele that night after she snuck out of the Trosten House again.

"You don't seem thrilled," Adele said, seeming hurt.

"I'm just nervous that you left the house and might have been seen by Conrade," Alia explained.

"I know," Adele answered. "But it was a risk I was willing to take for you. You deserve this chance, Alia. You're good with the designs. I hated for you to miss the appointment, so I took the chance and went for you."

Alia considered her sister for a moment. "Thank you so much, Adele," she said sincerely. "I really appreciate it."

Adele relaxed, knowing her sister was not mad at her.

"Perhaps I'll sneak out tomorrow morning and meet with Herr Dehn," Alia said.

"Good, but be careful."

"I will," Alia agreed.

———

Alia was able to sneak out the next morning and return before anyone was awake. She was thrilled with her meeting with Charles. He had again been so kind to her. She was not used to being treated thus by any man. She began to wonder if there really was a life for her beyond her current status. She had always dreamed of it, but now it began to seem more of a reality. Tucking the generous amount of money away, she began to get ready for her daily chores.

Wolf returned every night that week. Each night he proved to be progressively more aggressive than the night before. He didn't talk while he was with her. She became increasingly more fearful each time she saw him.

"I found out what's been driving him," she said to Adele one night she'd been able to sneak out.

"What did you find out?" Adele asked as she applied a cold washcloth to Alia's cheek where Wolf had beaten her that night. "Hold still, I need to wipe the blood. This may hurt."

Alia winced, but did not cry out. She began to tell what she knew. "Well, Brock came by the other night in a foul mood as well.

I asked him about his mood. He's easy to get to talk. He said that they had been out attempting several raids on resisters this week that hadn't gone well. Two of their officers were shot, and some of the resisters escaped."

"Oh, my," Adele gasped.

"I figure Wolf was coming to me to relieve tension from his failures," Alia went on. "And the fact that things weren't going well, explains his foul mood."

"Yes, it does," Adele agreed. "I fear for you going back there, Alia."

"I do, too," Alia confessed. "I just don't know what else to do."

"I understand," Adele said.

They both fell silent. Alia gazed out the window. "What's that," Alia said sitting up in her chair and leaning toward the window.

Chapter 8

"I saw something on the river," Alia said as she strained to see more.

"A fisherman?" Adele asked.

"Too late to be a fisherman," Alia said. "Besides, it didn't look like a fishing boat, more like a raft or something." She jumped up and grabbed her jacket. "I'm going to go see," she said.

"No, Alia!" Adele said fearfully. "It's way past curfew! What if you get caught? What if it's the Nazis?"

"I don't think it is the Nazis," Alia said. "I'm not sure what it is. I'll be right back. You stay here. Don't turn the lights on." She left before Adele could protest further.

Alia quietly slipped out the apartment building, thankful her sister's apartment was on the first floor. Keeping to the shadows, she quickly maneuvered to the river. As she approached the water, her suspicions were confirmed. It was a raft with three military men. They had reached the shore nearest her by the time she arrived and were climbing up the bank. This was an obvious sign that they were not Nazis. For one thing, this was Nazi territory, and they would not sneak around.

As the men climbed the banks, she studied them. They were wearing Nazi uniforms, but something was wrong. Two of the men wore army uniforms with SS helmets, a slight difference to foreigners, but a blaring difference to a Nazi officer. The other was even worse. He wore an SS officer jacket with the cap of a Panzer enlisted man.

Spies! Alia thought. This could be her chance.

Just then, she heard the unmistakable sound of hobnailed boots down the quiet street coming closer. The night watchman!

Alia ran closer to the men. "Psst!" she whispered urgently.

They halted.

"Hurry," she said. "An officer is on his way."

They didn't answer.

"I know you're spies," she said. "I'm here to help you."

No answer.

"I can see you," she said irritably as the sound of boots steadily got closer. "I'm right above you. Come here, and I'll take you to safety. If you stay there, the night watchman will find you and notice your uniforms are wrong. You'll be caught."

"How do we know you aren't waiting to capture us?" One of the men finally whispered back.

"Please, hurry," she said, now fearing for herself. "If I am here to capture you, either way, you'll be captured. Who's more likely to capture you, a small woman or a Nazi officer? Hurry!"

After a short hesitation, she heard the men quicken their paces as they climbed the banks. Then she was met face-to-face with the three spies. Without a word, she motioned them to follow her into the shadows. She could tell they had doubts, but she ignored them and moved quickly. She could hear their shuffling right behind her. Taking a chance, she took them straight to Adele's apartment.

As she reached the door to the building, she turned and motioned for them to remain quiet. They nodded and followed her in.

Once inside, they all simply stared at each other. Adele broke the silence, "What's going on?" she whispered.

No one answered.

Adele repeated with irritation, "I said, what's going on?"

"They're spies," Alia answered as she took her jacket off and hung it on the peg.

"Obviously," Adele said as she motioned toward their mismatched uniforms.

"I know," Alia replied with annoyance at the carelessness of the spies.

"What are they doing here?" Adele asked with a hint of fear in her voice.

"They were out in the river, and I heard the night watchman coming around, so I brought them here to avoid detection, hopefully."

"Why?"

"Something needs to be done, Adele. The Nazis cannot stay in power forever. We need to get out. Perhaps this is our way out."

"So, you really are not Nazi sympathizers?" one of the spies asked in an obviously American accent.

"Not at all," Adele answered for the two of them.

The men seemed to relax a little.

Then a soft knock came on the door. Adele and Alia looked at each other. No one was supposed to know they lived here. Everyone froze.

The knock came again, a little louder this time and followed by a voice.

"Adele?" came the familiar voice, though it was uncharacteristically kind sounding.

Now, both women showed obvious fear. The spies moved to take action, only to be halted by Alia.

"No!" she hissed and began to move them toward the closet. "Get in there," she ordered. "Adele, show them." Then turning to the spies she said, "Whatever you do, do not let her out. No matter what you hear, do not open that door until I tell you. Do you understand?"

The men seemed to realize the urgency of the situation and agreed as they quickly hid in the secret room.

Alia shut the outer door, making sure everything seemed normal.

The knock sounded again, harsher this time. "Adele, I know you're there. Open the door before I break it open." The kindness seemed to have left the major's voice.

Alia opened the door and met Major Conrade Lange.

"Where's Adele?" Conrade said as he pushed past Alia and into the apartment.

Alia did not answer.

"Woman, I know she's here. She doesn't leave the apartment. Where is she?" Conrade snapped.

Again, Alia did not answer.

Conrade laughed at her. "No matter, I'll find her." He began turning furniture over and making a mess of the apartment.

"You cannot have her," Alia finally said.

Conrade laughed again. "Who are you to say who I can and cannot have? I'll have whomever I want."

"Not her, Conrade," Alia said bravely.

He turned on her. Striding to within arm's length of her, he said menacingly, "Do not address me as such. I am a major in the Nazi Army. You will address me with respect."

Alia met his gaze with a steely one of her own. "I am addressing you with more respect than you deserve."

He slapped her hard across the face.

Her eyes stung with the blow. She tasted blood, but she did not move. She stood staring unwaveringly at him.

A twisted smile came across his face, and he reached out to touch her arm seductively. "I will find her," he said. "And I will take what I want from her. Perhaps, though, it will be after I get what I want from you." He jerked her close to him.

At that same moment, he slumped forward clutching his stomach.

Alia had pulled the trigger on her pistol, which she had kept in her pocket.

As he fell forward, Alia pulled the trigger once again and shot him through the head. He fell on the rug with a thud.

Alia dropped the gun next to him, thankful she'd had the foresight to buy the silencer. She hoped no one in the apartment building heard anything, including those hiding in the closet.

Taking a few breaths to steady herself, she went to the closet and opened the door.

"You can come out now," she said.

The four in hiding stumbled out the opening and gasped at what they saw.

"Alia," Adele exclaimed, "what did you do?"

"Something that needed to be done a long time ago," she answered with conviction. "He won't be bothering you again."

Adele was speechless.

Alia turned to the spies, "Now will you tell us what you're doing?"

No one answered.

"I've just killed a Nazi officer," Alia explained. "If that doesn't prove I'm not a Nazi sympathizer, I don't know what will."

The three men looked at each other. Two seemed to defer to one. The one took a deep breath and began to explain.

"We are part of the United States First Army," the man said in perfect German. "I am Lieutenant Mark Hoyle."

He paused. Silence.

"Nice to meet you, Lieutenant Hoyle," Alia said testily, "but that does not explain why you are here."

He cleared his throat and continued. "Our army is poised to attack and invade your country. We were sent to find the best place for invasion."

The other men remained silent and stared expectantly at Alia and Adele as if to see if they might turn them in.

"How close is your army?" Adele asked.

"They will attack within the next day," Lt. Hoyle replied.

"Did you find what you were looking for?" Alia asked.

"Yes," he answered. "It looks as if your Ludendorff Bridge is intact and virtually unguarded, though set with some explosives."

"Yes, it is," Alia said.

"That seems strange," Hoyle ventured. "Why would they leave such an obvious entrance point unmanned? Surely they know we are close."

"That I cannot answer," Alia said. "Although, I would venture to guess that their interests lie in other more sinister activities."

"What do you mean?" one of the other men asked curiously.

Alia looked at them quizzically, unsure of whether or not to answer.

"Tell them what you know, Lia," Adele urged gently.

Alia took a deep breath and explained. "I mean that they are too busy rounding up what is left of the Jews."

"What for?" the man asked.

Adele and Alia looked at the men not believing that they truly did not know what she meant.

"Do you know why you are fighting the Germans?" Adele asked.

"All we know is Hitler is bad and is trying to take over Europe, if not the world," the third man said.

The girls stared at the men, unbelieving.

"What else is there to know?" Lt. Hoyle asked gently, seeing that there was more to the story than their army knew.

"Yes, Hitler is a bad man," Alia agreed. "Yes, he is trying to take over Europe, and I believe he would take over the world, if the world would let him. Hitler is bad for many reasons. One large reason is that he hates the Jews. He has vowed to rid the world of the Jews in any way possible. He has his armies round them up and take them away, if they don't kill them on the spot."

"Take them away?" Hoyle asked.

"I don't know for sure, but I have heard rumors."

"Rumors of what?" Hoyle asked gently.

Adele answered. "Rumors of camps. Work camps, experimental camps, death camps."

"It's not just the Jews," Alia continued. "Anyone who disagrees vocally with Hitler is taken. Anyone who is different in any way – physical or mental challenges, different nationalities, homosexuals, gypsies – but mainly Jews."

"That's terrible!" the second man said.

"Yes it is," Alia said. "It's what we have been living with since Hitler came in to power."

"And now, the reason the bridge is unmanned?" Hoyle asked.

"I believe," Alia said haltingly, "the army is searching out anyone left of Jewish descent, though I cannot imagine there being many left. My guess is that they know you're coming and are afraid."

There was silence around the room as the men digested the information.

Finally, Lt. Hoyle spoke quietly. "How do you know this information?"

The girls knew the men feared they were part of the Nazi regime. They looked at each other, knowing that in order to convince the men they were not, they would have to tell them what their profession was. Neither was proud of their profession. In fact, they went to great lengths out of the house to hide what they did. Adele nodded solemnly for Alia to tell.

Alia looked at the men with a mixture of sadness and defiance in her eyes. "We are prostitutes. Some of our customers are high ranking Nazi officers. During drunken moments, they would share information privy to the army."

Lt. Hoyle looked at them for a long time. His eyes searched theirs, never once dropping lower. The other men tried to hide grins at their fortune for meeting up with two beautiful prostitutes. Hoyle was the ranking officer, so the others waited to see what he would do.

Finally, after what seemed a long scrutiny, Hoyle spoke. "This profession is not what you want, nor what you sought, is it?"

"No," both women said strongly.

"And this man?" Hoyle nudged Conrade's body with his toe.

"He was my client," Adele explained. "He was very aggressive and beat me. I could not go to a doctor for fear of his wife finding out. I have not been able to work since."

The expressions of the other two men softened, though they still eyed Alia with pleasure. She glared at them.

Hoyle spoke up. "I give you my word, ladies, that no one will touch you." He glared at his men who shrunk back in shame.

"We have plans for other professions after the war is over, and we can get away from these officers," Alia opened up.

"Well, I will do my best to help that to happen," Hoyle said in a gentlemanly manner.

"What can we do to help?" Adele asked.

"We need to get a better look at the structure of the bridge," Hoyle said. "Also, whatever information you can give us on military positioning would be most helpful."

"We will help you," Alia said, "but we need your guarantee that we will be safe in the coming invasion."

"You have my word," Hoyle said. "You and your family will be safe as long as you do not tell anyone what we are doing."

"We promise," Alia and Adele said.

"If you keep your promise, we will keep ours," Hoyle said. "As for anyone who is in the house with you, his blood will be on our head if a hand is laid on him. If anyone goes outside your house into the street, his blood will be on his own head; we will not be responsible." Then he looked around the room. He walked over to the coat rack and picked up Adele's red scarf. "Tie this out your window. This will be the sign that no one shall lay a hand on anyone in this apartment."

"What about him?" one of the other men asked, pointing to Conrade.

"Take him with you," Alia said. "Roll him up in the carpet and dump him in the river. The current is swift tonight. He'll be several miles down-river by the time anyone knows he's missing."

The next hour was spent discussing military positions and anything else Alia and Adele could tell the men. Soon, the expressions of lust on the two men's faces, whom they came to know as Private Sam Jenson and Private Adam Compton, changed to expressions of admiration for all of the information the two women were able to share and help they were able to give.

When Alia and Adele had given all the information they knew, the men rolled Conrade's body in the rug and prepared to leave.

Lt. Hoyle turned to Alia. "Don't forget the scarf in the window. Look for us to come soon. I will return. Thank you for your help."

"Wait," Adele said. "Go out the back window. It opens up right to the riverbank. There will be less chance of detection."

Adele and Alia helped the men out the window and shoved Conrade's rug-wrapped body out after them. They watched in silence with the light off as the three men carried the body to the river and threw it in. The river was indeed swift and, the rug bobbed in and out of the water as it was quickly swept out of sight.

Both women heaved a sigh of relief as they closed the window and began making preparations for the coming invasion.

Chapter 9

The next morning, Alia left early as planned to go to the House. She snuck in knowing everyone would be asleep. Quickly, she went upstairs to the room she shared with Tilly and Nixie. She woke them, motioning for them to remain silent.

Tilly sat up quickly, thinking something was wrong.

Nixie sleepily rubbed her eyes and stretched on the bed.

"Quick," Alia whispered. "Don't ask questions. I want you to pack a few regular clothes and follow me."

"Why?" Nixie asked lazily.

Already on her feet, Tilly shot her a glare. "She said don't ask questions," she whispered back. "You know Alia wouldn't make a strange request without a reason."

"Please just trust me, Nixie," Alia said. "Your life depends on it."

At that, Nixie's eyes shot open, and she almost jumped out of bed.

Alia quickly silenced her. "You must be quiet. We can't wake Odette or Giselle."

"They aren't even here," Tilly said as she finished her bag.

"What?" Alia exclaimed. "Where are they?"

"Don't know," Nixie joined in as she grabbed a few things.

"Wolf came again last night." Tilly said.

"I know, I was here, remember?" Alia said pointing to her cheek.

"No, he came back."

"What?"

"He was completely drunk," Tilly said. "Didn't even remember being here earlier that night. Since you weren't here, he took it out on Odette. Afterward, Giselle and Odette both left. We thought they were out looking for you."

"Well, they never found me," Alia said as she grabbed a few things as well, "and that's a good thing. Now, hurry. That's all the more reason for us to get out now."

"Where are we going?" Nixie asked.

"I'll tell you when we get there. Have everything?"

Both girls nodded.

Alia grabbed her things and peeked out the bedroom door. Everything was quiet. The three tiptoed silently out the hallway. Peeking out the front door, they saw no one. Slipping quickly out, they ran down the sidewalk.

"Wait," Nixie said. "Look down there." She pointed down the next block. Giselle and Odette had just turned the corner toward them.

Quickly, they back tracked to the alley a block away from the house and waited until the other two passed by. As the other two came closer, Alia could hear part of their conversation.

"We've got to find her," Giselle was saying, "she knows too much. She'll ruin my business if we lose the officers."

"But where will we find her?" Odette asked in a whining voice.

"She's with her sister, I'm sure," Giselle answered. "We just need to find out where she's hidden and silence them both."

"Silence?"

"They'll never know what hit them," Giselle answered menacingly.

The voices died away. Alia shivered. She knew what "silence" meant. Giselle had a gun and had used it before on a customer. The urgency intensified now.

They waited a few more minutes to be sure they were alone, then Alia motioned silently for the others to follow her. Keeping to the shadows as best they could in the morning sunlight, they crept along the way to Adele's apartment.

Once at the apartment, Tilly and Nixie settled in while Alia told Adele what she'd heard. "What do you think it means?" Adele asked shakily.

"You know what it means," Alia said. "She wants to kill us. She's afraid we're going to go tell someone about Conrade and Wolf, and the way they've treated us or something. She doesn't realize that nothing would happen to them, if we did tell. So far, she doesn't know where your apartment is. I'm sure she'll try to find it. Hopefully the invasion will come before that."

"So the best thing we can do is to lay low, right?" Adele asked.

"For now."

"What do you mean?"

"I want to go get Herr Dehn."

"What?" Adele asked incredulously. "You can't be serious. You can't go back out there. What if you run into Wolf or Giselle and Odette?"

"I have to take that chance," Alia said defensively.

"Why?"

"Because, he took a chance on me. He gave me my life back, and I need to try to do the same for him."

"But…" Adele began.

"I won't argue about it, Adele," Alia cut her off. "I'll help get these two settled and then I'm going." She turned around and effectively ended the conversation.

After everything was settled, Alia grabbed her coat, whispered some words of instruction in case she failed to return, hugged her sister, and left.

Despite her show of confidence within the apartment, Alia was actually quite scared. She knew many of the officers on the street. They knew her "relationship" with Wolf. If he wanted to know where she was, they would tell him where they saw her. They also would tell Giselle, if she asked them. She needed to stay in the shadows, which wasn't easy as the sun rose higher in the sky.

Dehn's fashion store was a ways away from Adele's apartment. It took Alia an hour to get there as she crept quietly from shadow to shadow. She had to jump into alleyways several times as she came near an officer who looked familiar. One caught sight of her and called to her in a friendly manner. She pretended not to hear and turned down the nearest street. Afraid he would follow her, she quickly zigzagged her way through a few allies, nearly getting herself lost.

Finally, she arrived at the store and walked purposefully through the front doors. She gave a sigh of relief as she noticed the reception-ist was not at her desk. Then her nerves quickened as she wondered how she would get Herr Dehn's attention from his office without rousing suspicion. She didn't have to wait long. He must have heard the front door open and came to see who entered.

"Fraulein Schmidt," he said pleasantly, "how nice to see you. I trust you are feeling better?"

"Yes, sir," Alia answered, noting with pleasure how he again did not use the required Nazi greeting. "It is nice to see you as well."

"How can I help you?"

"Is there a place we may talk privately, sir?" Alia asked, glancing at the reception desk.

His demeanor immediately changed to one of concern. "Of course," he said as he held out his arm to direct Alia to his office. "Helen is out for lunch and won't be back for an hour, but we can meet in my office."

"Thank you."

Once in the office, he closed the door but made no move to sit down or offer her a seat. "How can I help you?" he asked seriously.

Alia glanced around nervously, wondering if his office were tapped, but not voicing her concern. "I noticed you have never offered me the required greeting, sir," she began hopefully.

He eyed her with a little suspicion. "I have been in the practice of offering it when it is offered to me," he answered.

She took a deep breath and lowered her voice, "Can I assume, then, that you are not one of them, either?" she asked.

He put a finger to his lips and walked around the room running his hands under furniture and by the windows. After several minutes he returned. His voice matched hers in a hushed whisper. "I am not."

"No bugs?" Alia asked.

He smiled. "No," he answered still whispering, "but it doesn't hurt to still be careful."

"I agree."

His face became serious again. "What is this all about, Fraulein?"

"Well, sir," Alia began nervously. She took a deep breath and continued with as much confidence as she could muster. "I have come to warn you."

"Am I in danger?" he asked fearfully.

"We all are," Alia answered.

Dehn remained quiet allowing Alia to continue.

"I have it on good authority that the allies are poised to invade within less than twenty-four hours. I have come to offer you and your family safety."

He looked at her intently.

She continued. "If you are agreeable, I will tell you where to bring your family. I pray you will come soon. I cannot guarantee your safety if you don't accept my help."

He narrowed his eyes. "Why would you do this?"

"Sir, I give you my word I am not part of the Nazis. I truly am trying to help you."

"I think I believe you," he said. "Why, though, would you come to save me and my family? You don't even know us."

Alia took a deep breath. "You saved my life, sir," she said. "I am trying to repay the kindness."

"How did I save your life?" he asked confused.

"Sir, my former profession was as a prostitute. You gave me the hope that I could do more with my life. This hope has given me the strength to leave the only terrible life I have ever known, to embark on an aspiration of a new and better life. I consider it saving my life. Now, I want to do the same for you and your family."

He took a deep breath and let it out slowly. They stood there for a while staring at each other, judging if the other was telling the truth in their disloyalty to the Nazis.

Finally, Dehn spoke. "I believe you. I am terribly sorry for your former life. I'm sure I could not imagine what you've been through. I accept your offer of help with deep gratitude. I fear I might have some trouble explaining to my wife how I know of this, but that is my problem." He smiled.

Alia's nerves eased, and she smiled as well.

Over the next few minutes, she helped him memorize the address and directions to Adele's apartment. He told her he had a wife and two small children. She helped him decide what to bring and how they could make the space for his family in their apartment. He decided to finish the work day, so as to not arouse suspicion from his receptionist and agreed to meet Alia at the apartment as soon as he could get his family ready.

"Don't take too much time," she cautioned. "I have no idea as to the time of the invasion and, as I said, I cannot guarantee your safety outside of the apartment."

"I will hurry," he promised. "And thank you very much."

They shook hands and Alia left. The trip back to the apartment was less eventful than the previous trip. Alia was thankful for that. She wasn't sure how much more her nerves could take.

Once back at the apartment, Adele fixed a pot of tea, and the four women tried to rest knowing they would be up all night waiting for the invasion.

"Do you really think this will be a victory for the allies?" Adele asked nervously.

"I do," Alia answered strongly.

"How can you be so sure?" Nixie asked. "All the soldiers say we're winning the war and the allies will never reach us."

"The allies are across the river," Alia asked. "I think the soldiers repeat what the officers tell them, and I think the officers make the Nazis out to seem better than they are. You know the radio never says anything but that the Nazis are winning."

"How do we know they're not?" Tilly asked.

"I think our friends from last night are proof that they're not," Alia answered.

"How do we know they're telling the truth?" Nixie asked.

Alia paused for a moment and considered the question. "I guess we don't," she finally said. "I think we just have to believe." She paused another moment. "I truly believe that their God has handed our country over to them."

The others looked skeptically at her. "What do you mean?" Adele asked.

"We have lived our lives under the tyranny of the Nazis," Alia began. "They have performed horrific acts all in the name of Hitler and against God. They have taken God out of everything, even the churches. I know our lives aren't exactly what God would want. I know I have said that I don't believe in a God or anything, but so much has been done to us in the name against God. I can't help but believe that perhaps he is real and is going to deliver us from this hell we're living in now without him."

The others sat silently considering her words. No one knew what to say. One-by-one they leaned back in their chairs and fell asleep.

Chapter 10

A soft, cautious knock came on the door. In the silence of the room, the knock sounded deafening. Alia jumped up and ran to the door. Again, the knock came. It was the prearranged knock she had asked Charles Dehn to use. She opened the door and ushered the family quickly inside. The other women in the room were slowly arousing from sleep.

"Why did you wait so long to come?" Alia asked, noting the darkening sky out the window.

"Helen wouldn't leave the office," Charles said. "I think she might have been suspicious as to my anxiousness to get out. Usually I stay later."

"Do you think you were followed?" Alia asked.

"We took several precautions," he answered. "I don't think so."

Alia relaxed, and the two made introductions. Tilly and Nixie began playing with the children as Adele made a pot of tea.

Alia was nervous around Frau Dehn until the woman took her aside.

"Fraulein Schmidt," the woman began, "I want to thank you for risking your life to save ours. My husband told me everything. Please know that I am fine and very appreciative of your and your sister's kindness."

"Thank you, Frau Dehn," Alia replied relieved. "Please come in and sit. May I offer you some tea?"

The woman smiled. "Yes, I would love some, thank you."

Alia showed her to the table as Adele poured the tea.

As they waited, Frau Dehn proved invaluable at putting everyone at ease making small talk. She did this without ever bringing up anyone's past or profession.

"Charles showed me some of your designs," she told Alia. "They are beautiful."

"Thank you," Alia replied modestly.

"If I remember correctly, you're wearing one of them now."

Alia blushed. "Yes, ma'am."

"It's beautiful. I hope to wear one of your creations someday."

Alia smiled her thanks and looked shyly away.

"Adele," Else Dehn turned to Alia's sister, "your apartment is lovely. I'm very impressed with the décor."

"Thank you, ma'am," Adele beamed. Having been in hiding, she had never been able to entertain guests in her apartment. Alia knew her tastes and had brought home what decorations she could without being obvious. Adele spent her time sewing drapes, pillows and other amenities as well as other decorations for the apartment. "Decorating is something I truly enjoy."

"You do it well. And, please, both of you call me Else."

"Yes, ma'am," both girls replied, then smiled at their formality.

Next, Else moved to Tilly and Nixie and praised them for their ability with children. Everyone in the room felt immediately comfortable and relaxed in spite of their circumstances. Charles Dehn simply watched his wife proudly, knowing she was helping take everyone's mind off their uncomfortable past and uncertain future. He loved his wife for her ability to do this.

Alia and Adele went to work fixing a meager dinner for eight mouths. This was a challenging task given the usual one or two mouths present in the apartment. No one complained at the small portions and soon the children were asleep on the one bed in the apartment. None of the adults felt they would sleep much that night.

When they were confident the children were asleep, conversation turned to the upcoming invasion.

"I know you couldn't tell me much back at the office, and we came here on blind faith," Charles began. "Could you tell me more about what is happening and how you came to know this?"

Alia and Adele recounted the events of the night before in as much detail as they could. Nixie asked questions, many of which were unanswerable, throughout the account.

"And as I told your husband," Alia turned to Else, "he saved my life, and I want to repay the kindness. We are guaranteed safety for a while here until the allied soldiers come for us." Then she turned to Adele, "Is the red scarf hanging out the window?"

"Yes," Adele answered. "I put it on the clothes line so as not to arouse suspicion."

"Perfect," Alia replied.

They talked more and tried to answer questions, though neither Adele nor Alia could answer more than they had already told. Soon, everyone became quiet and by mutual, unspoken consent, began to close their eyes and rest.

They were awakened by a loud explosion. The building shook. The children screamed and jumped out of the bed to the comfort of their mother and father. Alia went to the window, cautiously peeking out.

"Looks like the Nazis were more prepared than we thought," she said grimly.

"What do you mean?" Adele asked.

"Take a look," Alia said making room on the window seat. "The invasion looks to be on the way, but the explosions came from the bridge. I know the allies wanted to keep the bridge intact."

"I don't think the allies will let the bridge go very easily," Charles added. "They're right on the other side defending it."

Explosions continued to shatter the air. Planes flew overhead dropping bombs at their targets.

"Something tells me this is not how the allies planned it," Alia said. "I'll be honest, I don't know how Lt. Hoyle is going to be able to keep us safe in this bombardment."

No one replied. Alia had voiced the fears of everyone in the room.

All of a sudden, a thunder of thumps came to the door of the apartment. Everyone jumped at the sound that was so close.

No one moved to answer the door.

"Alia, open the door!"

Alia ran to the door and flew it open. Lt. Hoyle along with Privates Jenson and Compton rushed inside and closed the door behind them. They were panting.

"Get your things, we need to leave now!" Lt. Hoyle ordered.

No one asked any questions. They gathered their previously packed bags and followed the allied soldiers.

"I cannot guarantee your safety in that apartment any longer," Lt. Hoyle explained as they followed him. "The Germans were more prepared than we thought. They began an attempt to destroy the bridge before our army arrived this morning. Thankfully, it hasn't worked yet. We've put up a pretty good perimeter and are in good position to capture the bridge. However, they are putting up a good fight. I got permission to come get you all out of there and take you back to my company's headquarters."

"What will our status be?" Charles asked cautiously.

"Don't worry, sir," Hoyle explained. "You will be as refugees, not as prisoners of war. I have explained to my commanders how the Frauleins Schmidt helped us. My commanders are very grateful."

The refugees followed their American liberators along the river's edge a ways past the city. They found two small boats and crossed the river undetected by the enemy.

"They're pretty engaged at the bridge," Private Jenson explained to the worried passengers. "We should be alright here. We'll take you to headquarters and then go back to the front-line units."

They traveled the rest of the way in silence, the refugees trying hard to keep up with the well-conditioned soldiers.

Soon they reached the unit headquarters.

"Colonel," Lt. Hoyle saluted. "These are the people I was telling you about. Fraulein Alia Schmidt, and her sister Fraulein Adele Schmidt, are the ones who hid us the other night."

"Welcome," the colonel said. "Please come in the tent. I have some weak tea to offer you. As you can see, we're a little busy, but we can offer you a place to rest while we continue with the attack."

The refugees thanked the colonel and took the tea he offered.

The colonel turned to his men and gave them their assignments to return to their unit.

Lt. Hoyle turned quickly and looked at Alia, "I'll see you soon." Then he led his men to the battlefield.

Chapter 11

For the next several days, the eight German refugees remained in the care of the American colonel and listened to the officers command their men. They learned that the allies had crossed the bridge and were now into Germany.

It was intense and relieving listening to all that was happening. They were sad to leave their homeland, but all knew the country was no longer even a shadow of what their real homeland had been. Evil had taken over. Finally, light was penetrating the darkness and hope was real.

The refugees said little as they experienced a new life. All knew their former lives were over in some capacity or another. Some could return to a semblance of their past, while others were headed in new directions. Each had different feelings toward the matter.

Alia and Adele, having faced their horrors head on, were relieved beyond measure at the prospects of a new life. Neither knew what the future held, but both believed it would be better than the past.

Tilly felt excitement at the unknown. Experiencing how the men treated her, knowing they had been without female companionship for months, left her feeling confused in a pleasant way. She realized that a woman could be treated with respect. A hope she had never known began to take root inside as she looked toward a new life.

Nixie felt the same confusion as Tilly did, though it was not as pleasant for her. The confusion took root but did not allow room for hope. It would take time for her to see the possibilities laid before her.

Charles and Else Dehn wanted to return to their former life and knew it was possible. They remembered life before the Nazis and were excited at the prospect of some semblance of that as a future for their children.

After a few days of waiting around the allied headquarters camp, a military doctor came to the colonel's tent to report.

Casualties were pouring in. They were being treated as best they could, but the medical staff was shorthanded. The colonel came to the eight refugees.

"So that's the situation," he said after repeating what he could that the doctor had reported. "Would any of you be willing to help in the field hospital? It would be small jobs so the trained staff could be more able to do their jobs."

Adele, Alia, Tilly, and Nixie readily agreed to help. Charles and Else decided to remain with their children and wait to be transferred to a refugee camp at the first chance.

As the group of eight separated, goodbyes were said all around. As Charles and Else came to Alia, tears were visible.

"You saved our lives, more than anything I did for you," Charles said. "Thank you."

"Thank you," Alia replied.

"I will be returning to my shop at the first chance I get, whenever that is," Charles said. "Wherever you are, please contact me. I still plan on getting your designs out."

Alia smiled, thanked him, and hugged his wife.

"Thank you, dear one," Else said hugging Alia tightly.

The four girls then left to gather their few belongings and follow the doctor. Catching a ride on a military jeep, they raced to the field hospital.

The jeep pulled up to a group of large tents. The doctor led them to the first one. Calling a nurse over, he explained who the newcomers were.

"This is Nurse Carson," the doctor said introducing them to the young nurse with a bright smile. "She'll tell you what to do. Thank you for coming." Then he left them.

"You are most welcome," Nurse Carson said. "We've had a large influx of patients with the invasion, as I'm sure you can imagine. We're pretty busy around here. Until you're more comfortable, we could really use some help just feeding the patients and giving them water. Do you think you can help with that?"

The girls nodded and followed her.

Having no experience with wounded men, they were shocked at what they were greeted with. Some were missing arms, some missing legs. Some had bandages over their faces and were barely recognizable as people. Fortunately, they were not given much time to think about what they saw. They were put to work right away.

For the next several months, they stayed with the US Army medical staff helping with any odd jobs they were given. They got to know the nurses well and learned much from them. Nixie especially found her niche. She enjoyed helping the patients and working to heal. She found that the gratefulness and acceptance of these men far exceeded anything she ever felt with her former profession. The confusion she felt earlier in her experience with the allied army gave way to hope in a future. She followed Nurse Carson loyally and learned all she could, gaining herself much respect from the medical staff.

The others enjoyed helping as well, though the horrors were too much for them to want to continue past what was necessary.

A few weeks after they began their work in the field hospital, one of the nurses found Alia as she was writing a letter for a wounded soldier.

"Alia," the nurse said, "you have a visitor."

Thinking it was one of the doctors asking for help, she told the soldier she would return shortly, put down the paper and pen, and walked in the direction the nurse indicated.

What greeted her outside the tent made her heart flutter. It was Lt. Mark Hoyle. He was dirty and had a bandage around his left arm.

"Hello, Fraulein Schmidt," he said almost shyly.

"Hello, Lieutenant," she answered, matching his shyness. "Were you wounded badly?" she asked noting his bandage.

"No," he answered. "The bullet ricocheted off a nearby tree and grazed my arm. It bled a lot, so they sent me to the aid station. I'll be fine. This was the first chance, since I'd heard you were here, that I'd had to get away and come find you."

"I'm glad you did," she said.

"Would you care to walk with me?" he asked.

"I'd love to," she answered. "Let me make sure they can do without me for a few minutes." She ducked back into the tent and returned a few minutes later.

They began walking around the compound. She asked him about the invasion. He told her of the battles. He commented on her work with the military medical staff. She recounted her experience.

"I've been relegated to light duty for a few days and will be around here for the duration of that time," he explained. "May I come back and see you again?"

Not used to a man asking permission to see her, Alia was taken aback and unsure of what to say. These new events were giving her a fresh look on life. She enjoyed the respectful attention. "I would enjoy that. Thank you for asking."

He smiled. "Thank you for accepting."

Their walk brought them back to the tent she had been working in. "I'd better return to Sgt. Collins," she said hesitantly. "I'm writing a letter home for him."

"I'll see you later, then," Lt. Hoyle said.

She smiled and went inside.

The next few days, Alia and Lt. Mark Hoyle spent much time together. They also discovered that Adele and Private Adam Compton had become reacquainted and were spending equal amounts of time together. The sisters were extremely happy for each other. It seemed the two had overcome incredible odds and were now facing better lives than the two dreamed possible.

Tilly had also found a young soldier who treated her with more respect than she had ever experienced before. He had been wounded in the battle. They were introduced when she was assigned to help him eat. She spent as much time with him as she could.

Nixie was in her element in nursing. For the first time in her life, she was more interested in helping others than in the attention she could receive from men. She wore no make-up and drab, army-issued uniforms. The men appreciated her help more than what they thought they could get out of her.

As the days and weeks went by, each girl grew emotionally into the woman she was intended to be. The farther removed they were from their former lives of self and other-inflicted oppression, the stronger their character grew. Everyone around them saw the changes, though few knew their past. They became the most sought after helpers in the compound.

Chapter 12

On May 8, 1945, word came of the unconditional surrender of Nazi Germany. Relief was felt throughout the medical compound as well as the entire Allied Armed Forces. Individual celebrations were held throughout the units.

When they heard of the surrender, Alia and Adele fell in each other's arms weeping. The oppression they had lived under for most of their lives was demolished.

"Do you still think God had something to do with this?" Adele asked Alia.

"I am more convinced now than ever," Alia answered. "After spending time with these people, listening to them read their Bibles, hearing their prayers, I am more convinced that God exists and that he had a hand in this victory. What do you think?"

Adele thought for a moment. "I think you're right," she finally said. "Especially after talking so much with Adam and hearing his beliefs, I think God is good. I wonder at his ways and why he would allow such evil to happen, but I still think he is good."

"I agree with your questions," Alia said. "Perhaps we can talk with Adam and Mark about it later. But for now, let's celebrate!"

The two sisters laughed and continued with their rounds celebrating with the men who had fought so hard for their freedom.

Later that night, Adele, Alia, Mark, and Adam found themselves celebrating together. As the celebration wound down, the two soldiers noticed the sister's pensiveness and questioned them.

"We were talking earlier," Alia said, "and wondering about God's hand in all of this. We have come to believe more in your God and believe that he has had a hand in this victory over evil. However, we wondered at the goodness of God, that he would allow the evil in the first place."

"That's one of life's great questions," Mark answered. "It is confusing, and I don't know that I fully know the answer. I do know, though, that God is good and there is evil in the world. God doesn't like the evil, but he allows it because he has given man free will. He wants us to choose him, but knows some will not, and he is saddened by it. He will step in when his timing is right and then all will be well again."

"I guess that's about all we can know and accept, and we have to go on faith for the rest," Adele said.

"That's right," Adam answered and put his arm around her.

The next day, each of the two couples were able to find time alone together. Alia and Mark took a stroll outside of the camp.

"Alia," Mark said as they were walking, "I have truly been enjoying every minute we've been able to spend together. I find you fascinating and lovely and simply a wonderful person. I'll be going home soon, and I hate the thought of going home without you. Would you consider giving up your country to marry me and come with me to America?"

Alia stopped and looked him in the eye. "Mark," she began softly, "you have shown me that there is life beyond what I have ever known. You have given me the life I have dreamed of, and now you offer more. There is nothing for me in Germany. I have left that life behind. My life is with you now. I would be honored to be your wife."

Mark threw caution to the wind, picked her up in a giant hug, and swung her around in a circle. "You have made me the happiest man alive! Though," he said, "I think Adam is a close second."

"What do you mean?" Alia asked.

Mark pointed behind her where Adam was mirroring Mark's previous actions with Adele.

"What? Did he…?" Alia couldn't finish her questions. She knew the answer. Adam had just proposed to her sister who accepted as well. Alia's eyes filled with tears of happiness and joy for her sister.

Unsure of how to proceed with wedding ceremonies, the two couples awaited Army orders. When it was sure they would be heading back to the United States, they went to the army chaplain who was more than happy to perform the double ceremony.

Epilogue

Alia stood on the deck of the ship and let the salt water spray in her face. She had never felt more alive, more at peace. She and her sister were on their way to America! They were free from the oppression of the Nazis in more ways than one. The evil that had clung to their country for over a decade had come to a glorious end. The men who had used them and abused them were far behind. They would meet their new husbands in their new country in just a few minutes.

They were sad not to have been able to travel together, but Mark and Adam were required to travel with the army, and Adele and Alia were not allowed to go with them. Mark and Adam had arrived with the army a few days before.

As Alia leaned over the rail, she could just make out people on the dock past the famous Statue of Liberty. Her husband was among the crowd.

Her husband! She never thought she would be able to say those words. The dream of every young girl had been planted in her heart long before she entertained her first customer at Madam Giselle's establishment. Living the life she did, she never thought it possible that a kind, loving man would see beyond her past and treat her like a lady.

She had found just that man climbing up the bank of a river. She had hid him from danger. He had led her to a life she could feel proud of with a God who was proud of her.

The Confident
Leader

"… has not the Lord gone ahead of you?"

Judges 4:14 (NIV)

To: Grammy (Anna Ruth) whose love of stories encouraged mine.

Prologue

"Joanna, Joanna, quick, take these and run to your grandfather's house!" Joanna's mother thrust a bundle into her hands and began shoving her out the back door.

"But, mother, I don't want to leave you!" Joanna cried.

"You must go!" her mother urged. "Your grandfather is too sick to come here alone. Corbin's army is on the move. They are at the edge of the village. You know he preys on the elderly first. I would go, but I must stay with the little ones. You are the fastest and strongest in the family."

"Where's Papa?" Joanna asked.

"You know where he is," her mother answered impatiently. "He's joined the army to help fight. Now no more. Go!" With one final push, Joanna's mother sent her into the dark street on the mission to bring her grandfather to the family house.

Her grandfather lived five houses and five long fields away. Tonight, those five houses seemed an eternity away. Looking over the houses, Joanna could see the familiar red glow of fire. Since King Maxim had come into power in the nearby land of Gabon, his military commander, Corbin, had done everything he could to torture the people of Thadon. Each time he came to their village, he burned something. This time, however, the fire seemed closer than before.

Thirteen-year-old Joanna stood staring at the fire, shaking. The sound of horse's hooves galloping near didn't penetrate her brain until it was too late. She turned and saw the stampede bearing down on her. Frozen in fear, she couldn't will her feet to move. All of a sudden, someone crashed into her and knocked her out of the way. She began screaming, not knowing if it was friend or foe she was wrestling with. Quickly, though, she was pinned.

Opening her eyes, she saw a boy near her own age holding her down. The boy's hand clamped over her mouth, leaving her right arm free. She swung at him and caught his jaw in a solid punch. This seemed to rattle the boy, but not enough for him to let go.

"Will you be quiet?" he snapped. "I'm on your side. Don't you recognize me? It's Ethan. Our fathers farm together."

Joanna stopped struggling and looked harder. She barely recognized the boy in the dark. She'd only seen him a few times before.

Seeing some recognition on her face, Ethan took his hand off her mouth. "Do you recognize me?"

"Barely," Joanna said angrily. "It's pitch black out here. You've got dark paint on your face. I've only met you a few times. How do you expect me to know who you are?"

"Well, at least you know now," he said and let go of her. He helped her up from the ground. "What are you doing out here? Don't you know Corbin's army has come?"

"Of course I know," she spat, still angry. "I've come out to get my grandfather."

"Why you?" Ethan asked.

"Because, my mother has to stay home with the babies to keep them quiet. Now, if you'll excuse me, I'm in a bit of a hurry. I'd like to go get my grandfather before Corbin's army does." She turned and ran down the street.

"I'll help you," Ethan said running next to her.

Too scared, Joanna didn't reply, but let him come along.

Joanna suddenly realized why the fire looked so much brighter and closer. It was closer. It was just on the other side of her grandfather's house! She ran faster cursing the fields between each house.

When they reached her grandfather's house, they realized they were too late. The fire had beaten them there. Joanna's heart filled with dread. Unthinking, she ran toward the house only to be wrestled again by Ethan.

"Let me go!" she screamed.

"You can't go in there," he said. "The fire's already claimed the house and everything in it. We don't know how close Corbin's men are. You know what they will do to you, if they find you."

This last statement stopped Joanna. She did know. It had happened to many of her friends. She was still haunted by the hollowness of their eyes after being treated in such a manner. Joanna had so far been able to avoid such treatment by hiding.

Suddenly, a dark figure came around the house. He looked demonic with the flames rising behind him. The closer he got to the two children, the more they could make out his features. His eyes were dark and cold and menacing. His mouth was grim and determined. He looked only at Joanna hiding behind Ethan.

The man raised his sword to get rid of Ethan, when Ethan surprised him with his sword skills. The two fought for what seemed like an eternity. The man was a better swordsman, but his size was a disadvantage. He was very heavy and this slowed his movements. Ethan was quick as a cat.

After several moments of fighting, the man took a glance at Joanna to make sure his prey was still there. She was frozen to the spot. Ethan took advantage of this distraction. Rolling under his assailant, he rushed behind him and thrust the sword into the man's back. The big man fell to the ground.

Ethan didn't take time to catch his breath. Taking his sword out of the man's back, he grabbed Joanna and rushed her home.

They stopped short of her house. Flames shot out of the windows. Joanna tried again to rush to a burning house. Ethan again held her back.

"You can't do anything for them," he said apologetically, but strongly. "If you go in there, you will reach the same fate."

They hid behind a tree watching the horror unfold before their eyes. They could see dark, clad figures inside the house taking what they could before the flames did.

"My family," Joanna whispered.

Ethan didn't say anything. He just held her close and covered her up with one of the blankets she had brought to her grandfather's.

The two stayed in the shelter of the tree through the night. Joanna fell asleep from exhaustion and attempt to block out the trauma. Ethan stayed up and kept watch.

Soon the attackers left the house and moved on to other houses. As the night wore on, the army took what they wanted and burned the rest. The first fires set died down toward morning, but the rest of the outskirts of town still burned throughout the next day. Part of the army was called back from battle to rescue duty.

The enemy army focused most of their destruction away from the center of town. The leaders of Joanna's tribe thought they would be back for the rest of the town that night.

Ethan stayed with Joanna. Both were too scared to move from their hiding place. Midday of the second day, Joanna saw her father coming to the remains of their house. She jumped out of Ethan's protection and ran to her father.

Her father's face was streaming with tears of joy at finding Joanna alive and sorrow at the loss of the rest of his family.

Chapter 1

Sixteen years later

"Your honor, I think the little ones are wearing out. They might need a rest soon."

"Thank you, Joel. I think you're right." Joanna looked ahead. "Send word to Jonas in the back and find out what the status is on Corbin's army."

A few minutes later, Joel reported, "No sign of them, your honor."

"That's three days, without sign of them, correct?" Joanna asked.

"Yes, your honor," Joel replied.

"I think that's plenty of breathing room. We can rest at the top of the ridge," she announced. "Send word back through the people."

"Yes, your honor." Joel turned and did as the judge requested.

As they reached the top of the ridge, Joanna guided her people to places where they could lay their belongings as the scouts checked for the best passage into the valley. The group of six hundred enjoyed the time of rest. They had been on the march for nearly three weeks fleeing the enemy army of over two thousand. Hopelessly outnumbered, they were traveling fast. Hearing the news that their enemies had not been spotted for three days gave everyone cause to breathe and relax.

"Your honor, we must begin looking for a permanent camp. We cannot remain on the run forever," said Liam, the captain of the Thadon army over which Joanna ruled.

"You're right, Liam," Joanna agreed. "We must find water and there we will set-up camp. As for now, let the people rest. Perhaps we can send the scouts out farther in a few hours and see what they find."

Liam agreed and left.

"You know it will take many of the people quite a long time to ever be able to fully rest," said Ethan, Joanna's husband. "They have seen and experienced too much at the hand of the king of Gabon and his followers. They have lived in terror most of their lives. One doesn't easily forget that."

"True," Joanna replied shuddering at her own memories of cruelty against her family. "They must have hope, though. We must hope that they can find rest somewhere. Finding a permanent camp is as good a place as any to start."

"You are good for the people, my dear. Just look at them and how they respond to you. They've always been more comfortable with you than with your uncle."

"There wasn't much I needed to do to help that," Joanna replied bitterly. Her uncle had conspired with the enemy. He had sold some of his people into slavery merely for the money. The people had been in such an uproar about his dealings. A group was formed and in the middle of the night, Joanna's uncle was dragged from his bed and hanged from the nearest tree.

The man's sons were not considered for leadership after their father's death. Prejudice ran strong against his family. Joanna's father had been a well-respected man of the council. Since his death, she had taken his place. Wanting something far different than Joanna's uncle, the council had elected Joanna to replace her uncle as judge and ruler over the Thadon people. In her three years of rule, peace had reigned within the tribe. The people trusted her now to keep them safe from the enemy army.

Maxim, the ruler of the nearby tribe of Gabon, was a ruthless man. His desire was to rule over any people he came in contact with.

He had his sights set on the Thadon people. They had been at war with each other off and on for over sixteen years. Finally, he'd had enough. He had sent his army commander, Corbin, to the Thadon village once and for all to annihilate them or take them as slaves.

Liam and Jonas had learned of the latest plan shortly before the invasion. Joanna managed to get her people on the run, fleeing night and day from the enemy army. For three weeks they had wandered in the wilderness trying to lose Corbin's army. It seemed now that they had succeeded.

"Do you really think three days is enough?" Ethan asked, not wanting to undermine his wife's authority.

"I don't know," Joanna answered wearily. "Corbin's army has either given up on us or gone back for reinforcements. I pray it's the former. I don't want to show signs of fear to the people, though. They've been through enough."

"I agree," Ethan said.

Joanna smiled at her husband. She loved this man. She had loved him from the first time she'd really set eyes on him when he saved her from Corbin's army at age thirteen. Not once had he shown any signs of jealousy of his wife's power. He supported her fully. He questioned her only in private. He advised her lovingly. She leaned over and kissed him.

"What was that for?" Ethan asked laughing.

"I just love you. That's all," Joanna said smiling.

The next few hours were quiet and peaceful. Joanna sent scouts out to see if there were any signs of water nearby. The children began playing together. Some of the adults could be heard laughing.

"This rest has been good for the people," Joanna said enjoying basking in the sun.

"And for their leader," Ethan replied kissing his wife on the forehead.

Just before nightfall, the scouts came riding back.

"What did you find?" Joanna asked.

Martha spoke up first, "There's a valley with high mountains on this side and low hills on the other. A river runs through the valley. Lush vegetation spreads through the entire area. It's big enough to hold three times as many people as we have here."

The others caught her excitement quickly. No one else found anything.

"How far away is it?" Joanna asked.

"It will take the tribe about a day and a half to walk it. I rode my horse pretty hard to get there and back," Martha answered.

"Wonderful," Joanna exclaimed. "We'll sleep here tonight and head there tomorrow. Martha, tell the other scouts where the valley is. I want some to remain behind and keep a lookout for Corbin's army. Well done, everyone. Thank you. Sleep well. We'll head out after first light in the morning. Spread the word."

The scouts did as she requested and the camp settled for the night.

The next morning was met with eager anticipation by the entire tribe. Everyone got ready quickly, eating what meager rations they had left and packing up their few belongings. Then Joanna followed Martha leading the tribe in the direction of the valley.

The pace was quicker than Joanna anticipated since everyone was so excited about the possibility of their new home. They reached the valley early in the morning on the second day. It was everything Martha had said and more.

The children ran down the slopes of the mountain and splashed in the water. Some of the adults followed suite. Joanna basked in the happiness of her people.

Everyone relaxed in their new home. Before setting up camp, they all rested or played and explored the new environment. There was more than enough room for the tribe. The adults searched the area finding the right places for their homes. After a few minor disputes, every family had their own space in the valley. Joanna and her husband claimed land in the middle on a small hill overlooking the entire valley. She wanted to be available to her people and have the vantage point the hill gave of the valley and beyond.

"This is beautiful," Joanna said to Ethan as they began setting up their tent.

"It is perfect," Ethan replied.

Joanna sighed contentedly and hugged her husband.

Chapter 2

The next day Joanna sent scouts out for a day's ride in every direction to make sure they were safe from enemies. While the scouts were out, the rest of the tribe began to settle in. Joanna encouraged the people to take advantage of the resources the valley had to offer.

The people quickly formed groups to search for food, wood, farm land, and land for the livestock. As the search parties found what they were looking for, some rearranging was made of living space according to who would farm the land and who had the animals to graze.

By the third day, everyone seemed to have settled on their preferred land for their homes and then began to size up the trees to make cabins. They were used to living in wooden houses and few wanted to remain in their tents, though they knew it would be months before everyone had cabins to live in. Still, everyone seemed peaceful as they began their new life in their new settlement.

The evening of the third day, the scouts returned from their trek. The first ones to report said they were clear of enemies. Jonas and Martha were the last to report. They informed their leader of a Gabonite military camp a day's ride to the west.

"We couldn't tell if it was specifically Corbin's army or not, but they were definitely flying the flags of Gabon," Martha said.

"You're sure it was military?" Joanna asked.

"Yes, ma'am," Jonas answered. "Though I think it is a training camp. They seemed to be settled in and not on the move."

Joanna thought for a while. "Liam, what do you think?"

"If they are a training camp, they probably have no idea we are anywhere near. I think we're safe," he said.

"I agree," Joanna replied. "We'll set up a regular guard at intervals a few miles out around the perimeter. Liam, tell the commanders and get the guard set up tonight."

"Yes, your honor," Liam replied.

"Thank you all for your hard work," Joanna said to her scout team. "Now, go find your families and enjoy your new home. We'll have a tribe meeting in a few nights."

They all thanked her, bowed, and left her tent happily in search of their families.

"Liam," Joanna said to her military commander, "I'd like a regular guard set up to keep an eye on the Gabon camp. I don't want any surprises, alright?"

"Yes, ma'am," Liam replied. "Anything else?"

"No. Thank you."

"You're welcome," Liam bowed and left the tent to talk with his military commanders.

"Do you really think we're safe?" Ethan asked when everyone was gone.

"I don't know," Joanna replied. "I have to hope, though. These people have been on the run and in fear for too long. They need peace. The children need to grow up without the fear their parents have faced throughout their lives. All we can do is pray."

"Without ceasing," Ethan said, smiling.

The tribal meeting a few days later raised some concern with the people. Joanna had the tribal meeting tent set up in the center of the valley, near her tent, so it was easy for everyone to reach. Each member of the council arrived and milled around talking excitedly about their new homes.

When Joanna began the meeting, everyone sat down in respect for her. She began by thanking everyone for their attendance and hard work with getting the camp setup. She praised the people for the good work in beginning to make the settlement home. She had talked with Ethan and Liam before the meeting, and all came to the agreement that the council should know about the Gabon military camp. She took a breath and began, not knowing what their reaction would be.

"It is my duty to inform you all," she said, "that the scouts have found a Gabon military camp a day's ride from here. We have kept a watch on the camp. I believe it to be simply a training camp, and not one searching for us. I have placed scouts constantly to watch the camp and report any movement. I have also placed guards at regular intervals around the perimeter of the camp. I fear no attack from this camp, but wanted you all to be aware of it."

Joanna paused as the council began to murmur frustrations and fears. She raised her hands for quiet. When the group had quieted some, she said, "I am open to hear your concerns in an orderly manner."

One councilman stood up. "Your honor, are you sure this is wise? Haven't the people been through enough? Do we need to be so close to our enemies? Why not continue a few more days?"

A murmur of agreement rippled through the council.

"I understand the concern, Herman," Joanna said when the group had again quieted down. "I know what our people have endured. I know the pain and the fear. I believe our people need some good news now. This land is the best land we have seen in our journey. I don't believe we will find land like this a few days away."

"So you're trading our safety for land?" one of the council members spoke up.

"Not at all," Joanna said, trying not to sound defensive. "What I'm saying is that our people are downtrodden. They are weak and weary. If we continue moving, they will have little to no hope. I want our people to have hope. This land, the prospect of settlement, has given them hope."

"The prospect of an attack looming just a day's journey away will snatch that hope away, your honor," came another voice in the group.

"Only if the council shares the fear," Joanna replied. "If the council joins me and shows strength and courage, the people will join in that courage."

"It doesn't seem as though the council shares your courage, your honor," Herman spoke again.

"What can I do to remedy that?"

"Send the scouts out to see what other land there is. See if we can reach new land farther away."

"I have done that," Joanna replied. "I am awaiting their return."

At that moment, the scout's brigade entered the council tent. "Forgive us, your honor," Martha said. "We were waiting for all scouts to return."

"Of course," Joanna said. "What have you found?"

"Well, we know what is to the south of us," Martha began. "We just came from that direction. We did not find much during our three week journey. Jonas and I rode to the west and found the Gabon camp. Report is still no movement."

"To the north, your honor, is nothing but desert. We found no water, no trees for shelter, only harsh desert land," one scout reported.

"To the east is more forest land as we have seen here, however no water until we reach the sea," another scout reported.

"So, this land we are on supplies wood, water, and fertile land for farming, correct?" Joanna asked.

"Yes, your honor," the scouts replied.

"The land surrounding us does not supply all of that collectively, correct?"

"Yes, your honor."

Joanna turned to her second in command, "Liam, is our army fitted?"

"Yes, your honor," Liam said. Then he went on to describe the weapons the army had, a few of the tactical maneuvers they were trained in, and how they could use the land and cover the forest gave for protection against enemies.

"We would not have that in the desert, correct?" Joanna asked.

"Correct," Liam answered. He suppressed a smile understanding his commander's tactics. He knew she was allowing everyone else to explain for her before she turned to the council members and gave her verdict. She would allow the council members to come to the conclusion as well.

"Am I missing anything?" Joanna asked.

No one spoke.

"After hearing the reports, ladies and gentlemen, have you come to a decision?" she asked.

The council members conferred for a few moments.

Herman spoke up. "It seems you have investigated everything. I am impressed. Forgive my skepticism. I served under your uncle. We will follow you and help lead the people here. This land is great land. I believe the people need to know as much as possible."

Joanna smiled. "Agreed. I understand your skepticism. My uncle betrayed many. Believe me, my only interest is protection and right rule of the people. We can let the people know of the camp, our steps taken to protect the people, and our reasons for remaining in this land. We will leave the rest to God. Thank you all very much for your help."

They continued talking over a few minor disputes between a few families then the meeting was adjourned.

After everyone had left, Liam turned to Joanna, "Great job, your honor. You have a wonderful way with the council members. They have a great respect for you. You don't lord your power over them. They know you are in charge, but they feel useful. You have done much to heal the hurts your uncle caused."

"Thank you, Liam," Joanna said. "I appreciate your service and kind words."

As they left the meeting, Ethan put his arm around his wife. "I am impressed as always at how you handle the people. You really are serving the Lord by serving his people."

Joanna blushed at his praise.

Chapter 3

"Your Honor, his sheep ruined my crops!"

"Quit overreacting. Not all of your crops are ruined."

"A good enough amount that it makes a difference."

"Your Honor, my fence was broken. Harem was supposed to fix it that day, and he got sick."

"Why can't you fix your own fence?"

"Why are your crops so close to my sheep pen?"

"Gentleman, please!" Joanna held her hand up to silence the quarreling. She had been listening to the men drive this argument in circles for a half hour. "I have heard your arguments and have come to a decision. Amos, the fence is your responsibility. Even if the man you hired to fix it is unable to do so, you still have a responsibility to keep your sheep contained. Samson, you know your crops are dangerously close to the sheep pen. There is always a possibility the sheep will break out of the pen. Now, there is still time to plant crops and have them ready for the harvest. Samson, you help Amos fix his fence. Amos, you help Samson plough the land on the other side of his field and plant new crops."

Both men grumbled but agreed that this was a fair judgment. They shook hands with each other and the judge and left to begin their tasks.

Joanna sighed and leaned back in the tent. It had been a long day of debate and it was not over. Since they had moved to the new land, everything had fallen into a normal routine complete with arguments and judgments. She had heard challenges from land and livestock disputes, problems with how a cabin was built, and robbery. She was glad to help the people, but the constant bickering was wearing on her.

The next dispute she was to settle was simpler. Two men came in arguing over how big to make a cabin. The answer came down simply to how much wood was available.

Sighing, Joanna folded the records she kept of every dispute she settled and left the council tent to head home.

The sun was setting and the villagers were beginning preparations for their evening meal. She loved this time. The smell of food cooking over open fires always warmed her. She knew Ethan would have the meal started by this time. He was a wonderful cook. She enjoyed it when he made the meal.

Joanna knew how lucky she was. In this time, few women were in positions of authority. Those that were, were usually unmarried. She not only held the highest position of authority in her tribe, but she was respected by nearly all of the people and had a wonderful, loving husband as well.

Slowing her steps, Joanna watched the villagers. For the most part, they all got along well. They enjoyed each other. They helped each other. She was surprised at how quickly the village was being built.

Though, she shouldn't be too surprised. This tribe had a reputation for being supportive of each other; protective of each other; helpful with each other. The widows and elderly had been taken care of first. Housing for some individual widows as well as group housing for some had been the first to be built. Any child without parents was taken in by other families. Many children had lost parents in the raids Corbin's army had done on the tribe. Those families were taken care of next. The housing currently in the process of being built was for other families. The single men would be the last to receive housing.

It was the beginning of summer and crops had been planted during the past several weeks. Everyone pitched in to help with the plowing and planting. It was well that everyone helped, for they all knew the crops were planted to feed the entire tribe. Livestock was penned in and taken care of as well as butchered as the need for meat arose. Next week would be time to sheer the sheep and gather the wool so more clothes and blankets could be made.

The scouts had reported no movement from the Gabon army camp. Joanna didn't want to take any chances, so she kept the scouts in place and had Liam continue with regular army training and drills. He reported that the men in the army were performing excellently. He had few discipline problems. Everyone remembered the horror of living in fear of Corbin's army. No one wanted to live that way again. Each man had made it his personal mission to train himself to protect the tribe.

Yes, Joanna was blessed. She had a wonderful husband, the respect of a fairly unified tribe, and an excellent military leader leading a motivated, strong army.

She picked up her pace and reached home quickly.

As she expected, Ethan had a mouth-watering stew cooking over the fire. "That smells outstanding!" she complimented as she walked up the path.

"I was thinking of you as I put it together," Ethan smiled.

"You sure know how to make a woman feel good." Joanna kissed him.

"Why don't you get washed up, and I'll have the stew on the table when you get back."

Joanna did as she was told, happy to have someone else making the decisions. When she returned, Ethan had the stew and cups of water on the table. They sat overlooking the village.

"You sure picked a nice place for a house," Ethan said smiling.

"I love watching the people," Joanna replied.

"Look beyond the village, Joanna."

"What?"

"Look beyond the village," Ethan repeated. "I know you like to watch the people. I know you picked this hill for our house so you could have a good view of them. But for one moment, look beyond the people, beyond the village. Look at the beauty that surrounds us."

Joanna did as her husband suggested and was awed by the beauty. Their valley was surrounded by gentle, sloping hills. One side was completely forested with beautiful pine trees. She watched birds soar high in the sky and land at the tops of the trees. She watched the river flow lazily over the rocks and heard the gurgling of the water. Just then, out of the trees, came a deer walking quietly to the river for a drink. Joanna watched the deer drink and walk stately back to its home in the forest.

Husband and wife sat in silence as they watched the sunset flame and hide behind the hills.

"Thank you, Ethan," Joanna whispered. "I never would have taken time for that had you not suggested it. I would have missed the beauty, lost as I was in the busyness of life. You are so good to me."

"I love you," he said simply.

"I love you, too.

The next day was hot and muggy. Children were allowed to finish chores quickly and take time to swim in the river. The owners of the sheep came to Joanna to gain permission to begin shearing early.

"It's too hot for the sheep. They'll be dropping like flies if they keep their coats too long." One shepherd explained.

"Is everything else on schedule?" she asked, not wanting to neglect anything.

"Everything else is fine. Anything not completed yet can wait. The sheep need to take precedence or we'll lose them."

"Alright," she agreed.

The shepherds left and gathered the sheep together to begin the long, laborious task of shearing.

———

The summer seemed to fly by. The crops grew well in the fertile valley. The crops were harvested and stored in the newly built storage sheds. All the housing was completed. No one lived in tents in the village anymore. Some of the shepherds and hunters lived in tents when they were away from the village, but everyone had permanent housing.

Joanna was so proud of her tribe. They had worked well together. Most had even put aside petty arguments to finish the harvest and complete the work needed to be done in their first summer in their new land. Many of the villagers seemed extremely peaceful and only minimally concerned about attacks. Liam was open with those who would ask about military training and scouting.

With the harvest in and stored, it was time for their annual harvest festival. Everyone was excited. The hard work was completed and this was the time to celebrate. Not a few engagements usually happened during this festival – the men feeling confident after having accomplished such a huge task.

Joanna herself had become engaged during a harvest festival. Ten years prior, during the festival, Ethan had proposed, sealing a three-year-long courtship. Joanna had been thrilled. Ethan was the most handsome man in their tribe. He wasn't particularly wealthy or of high status, but that hadn't mattered to Joanna. He was kind, loving, strong, and a hard worker. He made her feel special and never denied her respect.

"Thinking back ten years?" Ethan asked noticing the smile on her face.

"How did you know?" Joanna asked.

"I guessed," he said. "It was easy to guess, as my thoughts are the same."

"That was such a wonderful night. You certainly swept me off my feet. I thought you were never going to propose. A three-year courtship is a long time."

"Sure," he conceded, "unless you begin courting when you're fourteen. We were young."

"Yes we were," she laughed, remembering arguing with her father about being more mature than her age suggested. Looking back, she thanked him for having her wait to be married. She had been young.

"But we knew," Ethan said putting his arms around her. He didn't need to finish his sentence. They had known they were in love and wanted to be married soon after their courtship began. The length of their courtship only solidified their friendship and love for each other. She was grateful for the time they'd taken.

Ethan held his arm out to her. "Are you ready for the festival, my lady?"

"Absolutely," she answered taking his arm.

Together they left their new house – Joanna had insisted that theirs be the last one built – and walked down the path of their hill to the center of the village by the council building. Many of the villagers were already there setting tables up and bringing food. The musicians were getting set up and the dance area sectioned off.

The festival planners did not disappoint. They threw a wonderful party. Everyone stayed late into the night eating and dancing. Any arguments were set aside and everyone got along. Joanna watched carefully and saw many young men talk seriously with young women who ended the conversation with delighted squeals and throwing their arms around their man's neck. She counted seven such conversations and believed them all to be engagements. Knowing all of the villagers, she was pleased with most of the couples. One gave her a little concern, knowing the parents did not get along. She made a mental note to talk with each couple especially the one in question and counsel them before their marriage. That was her favorite part of her position.

"There's one more," Martha said as she sat down next to Joanna.

"One more what?" Joanna asked

Martha smiled. "I know you, Joanna. You're watching the young couples get engaged. I just saw another one behind you."

"That makes eight," Joanna said happily. She smiled. She enjoyed talking with her friend as friends. Martha was one of the best scouts they had. Most of their relationship consisted of giving orders and following them. Before Joanna became judge and leader of the tribe, she and Martha had been best friends. They still were, though more often than not, their friendship was overruled by the demands of Joanna's leadership role.

"It's nice to see you so happy," Martha said.

"Things had been rough in the old village," Joanna replied. "This new village has done wonders for the people. They've pulled together well. I haven't needed to preside over many disputes. I'm very pleased."

The two friends remained together for the rest of the festival. Their husbands joined them. Jonas and Ethan had been very close before their marriages as well. It was a bonus for the four that their spouses were such good friends.

The rest of the night went by quickly with dancing and eating. When the food ran out late in the night, the festival was over. Everyone was tired, but happy. They all returned to their homes looking forward to a day of rest the next day.

––––––

With the harvest over, everyone began preparing for winter. The new woolen blankets and clothes were distributed to the villagers by the shepherds' wives. The houses were made warmer by adding clay to the spaces between the wood slats that had been left open during the hot summer to let breezes in. Cook spaces were enclosed. Livestock pens were brought nearer to houses and some enclosed as well.

Winters in the land they had come from could be harsh. They did not know what the winter would be like in their new land, since they were closer to the ocean, but no one wanted to be caught off guard. They were glad for the caution.

Though, they were closer to the ocean than their old village, they were higher up in elevation, making for a quicker onset of winter. They were sheltered from much of the winds by the hills and trees, but the snow and ice still hit them hard.

Few people ventured out of their houses during this time. Joanna was glad for the comfort of her husband. The winters could be long and lonely times. Joanna's job was not as demanding during the winter, either, since people hardly left their houses to get into arguments.

The time came for the winter festival, but the weather was so harsh that it had to be canceled. It was a tough decision for Joanna, but she feared for the lives of the elderly and youngest.

In the end, those who did not need to leave their houses didn't. The hunters risked the cold for the sake of feeding the people. They passed the meat to their partners to distribute it to the villagers, but few others left their houses.

The winter seemed long to everyone. In fact, by the calendar, it lasted a full month longer than winters they were used to. But when the snow began to melt, no one could deny the beauty of the land they now called home.

Chapter 4

Joanna was awakened by a thunderous crack. She jumped out of bed and ran to the door, Ethan close behind her.

"What was that?" she asked.

"I'll go look," Ethan said as he dressed. He was stopped short by another loud crack. Then they heard some of the villagers screaming.

Joanna dressed quickly as well.

"Wait," Ethan said, grabbing his wife's arm before she ran out in the snow.

"What do you mean?" Joanna argued trying to break free. "The people are screaming. Something is wrong!"

Ethan held tight. "Listen," he urged.

Joanna paused just long enough to listen to the villagers. She relaxed a little.

"Those aren't cries of fear or pain," Ethan said. "Those are screams of excitement."

The couple went to the door to look out and listen more. Sure enough, the people were cheering and dancing in the village. Soon, someone came running up the path to their hill. It was Jonas.

"The ice on the river is breaking up!" he exclaimed. "It's thawing. Winter will soon be over!" Then he turned around and ran to tell others of the good news.

Joanna and Ethan turned to look at the river just as another loud crack thundered in the air. Sure enough, the river that had been frozen for three months was breaking up. The large sheets of ice were slowly but surely drifting down stream. They could see the water rushing underneath, finally free from its frozen prison.

Joanna and Ethan ran down the hill to celebrate with the villagers. Many of whom they had not seen in five months. There was much laughing, clapping, and dancing in the village.

Soon, spring came with a vengeance. The snow melted into muddy messes throughout the village. Flowers sprang up. Trees grew full with leaves. Birds began to sing. Smaller animals scampered out of their hiding places in the forest. New livestock was born, and the pens were again enlarged.

Soon planting could begin. The harvest had seen them through the winter, but now the people knew they needed to plant more since the winters here were longer and more harsh. Once the mud dried, the land could be ploughed and planted. Again, everyone worked together to accomplish what needed to be done to keep the village functioning.

Joanna spent more time in the council building, as people were out and about and arguing more now. They were more settled in their new homes and seemed to have more to disagree about, but she continued to judge fairly and no one left dissatisfied.

The canceled winter festival turned into an impromptu spring festival. Some council members gained Joanna's permission to have a banquet and dance while they waited for the mud to dry.

This was perfect. Everyone was restless, having spent so much time indoors during the winter. They wanted to get out and be with friends and family. It was a great way to begin the spring. The festival was planned around two weddings.

Joanna made sure to meet with the two couples before the ceremonies for congratulations and counseling. She had met with all eight couples who had become engaged at the harvest festival before winter set in. She wanted to make sure everything was alright after the winter before she married the couples.

The engaged couples were of the few people who ventured out of their houses during the winter; the grooms not wanting to go so long without seeing their brides. Joanna needn't have worried. The parents of each couple oversaw the engagement period and helped counsel each couple to the best of their ability.

Marriages were her favorite part of the job. She had such a wonderful, happy marriage herself. She wanted to pass along the joy to others.

The ceremonies were joint, since the brides were sisters. The older sister's ceremony was first, then as she left, the younger sister entered. Both brides looked beautiful in dresses they had worked hard on over the long winter.

After the ceremonies were finished, the whole village turned out to celebrate. Food was in abundance. Musicians were in excellent form. Everyone danced and heartily enjoyed themselves.

"You are an excellent dancer, my love," Ethan said breathlessly as he and Joanna sat down after a lively dance.

Joanna laughed, remembering her awkward dancing at their wedding. "You have taught me well!"

Ethan laughed also, remembering his sore feet after their celebration and his determination to teach his new bride to dance, lest his feet be bruised forever.

Chapter 5

"Your honor, may we speak with you, please?" Jonas and Martha entered the council tent after Joanna's last dispute of the day.

Pleased to see her friends, Joanna ushered them in. Noticing their somber faces, her face soon matched theirs. "Is everything alright?"

Martha deferred to Jonas who didn't waste time. "The latest patrol reported movement in the Gabonite army camp."

Joanna took a moment for the news to sink in. They had been living in relative comfort for almost a year. They thought the threat of their old enemy had lessened considerably if not vanished completely. Apparently their comfort was not to last long. "What kind of movement?"

"They're showing signs of packing up camp," Martha replied. "Some of their tents are down. They've brought in carts from the main Gabon village. All signs show these are mobile military stations."

"Can you tell which way they're headed?"

"Not yet, but our scouts are doing their best to learn all they can," Jonas answered.

"Please send word to the council members that we need to have an emergency meeting in two hours," Joanna instructed.

"Yes, your honor," the couple answered.

"Does Liam know yet?" Joanna asked.

"Not yet. He is out with the army on a training and is scheduled to return later this afternoon," Jonas said.

"Bring him to me as soon as he returns. We need to be as prepared as possible. That camp is only a day's ride away." A year ago, that day's ride seemed an eternity. Now it was closer than Joanna wanted to admit.

"Yes, your honor," the couple replied and turned to leave.

Martha turned back to her friend. "Joanna, we're with you in this. We all agreed this land was perfect, and the day's ride to the Gabon camp was far enough away. It's not on your shoulders alone. This land is worth fighting for." She stopped short of giving her commander military advice.

"I love it here too, Martha," Joanna replied. "I have the whole village to consider in this. Believe me, I will not make any hasty decisions."

Martha and Jonas nodded and left the tent.

Joanna sat down to pray. "God, I have tried to lead your people fairly as I believe you would want me to. I thought this land was right for us. Please give me wisdom to know how to handle this situation." She sat in silence for a moment, trying to listen to God. Feeling strength and courage from her time, she left to talk with Ethan.

She found Ethan returning from the fields. He was surprised to see her home early, but happy as always to have his wife with him. His happiness turned to trepidation when he saw her worried face. "What's the matter?"

She wasted no time in telling him everything Martha and Jonas had reported. They sat under a nearby tree before returning to the house.

"What do you want to do?" Ethan asked her.

"I want to fight!" she said forcefully. "I'm tired of running. These are good people. They have come through a lot. They are learning to work together. They enjoy one another. They are finding peace here like many of them have never known. This land is fertile. It has provided us excellent crops, animals for meat, wild berries, wood, everything we need. I don't want to give it up." She paused for a moment and then continued. "I prayed before I came here. I believe God will defend us."

"Then fight!" Ethan said urgently. "We have one of the best armies around. We only left the old village because we were frightened. The Gabonites fight dirty. We need to fight smart. Their leadership is evil and has poisoned the minds of the people. We have God on our side. Take him with you and go at them."

Joanna snuggled closer to her husband. He was strong. She was proud of him. She knew he wanted to be in the military. He had been before they were married, but he was wounded in battle and was no longer able to serve. She knew it bothered him, but she was glad to have him home.

"It's so easy to say I'll send the army into war, but it's hard when I think of each person in the army. It's not just a mass I'm sending out there. I will be sending someone's husband, someone's father, mother, sister, brother, son, daughter. These are people."

"They are people who have pledged their lives to protect other people," Ethan assured. "They knew what they were getting into when they volunteered."

Joanna sat quietly with her husband, thankful for his support. She sighed. "I have ordered an emergency council meeting. I'd better go."

"Would you like me there with you?"

"Please," Joanna answered, clearly relieved.

Ethan smiled and they walked to the meeting together.

When the entire council was gathered, Joanna began the meeting. "I have called you all together today because a report has come to me that there is movement in the Gabonite camp."

A grumble rose from the council members. "I knew this would happen!" "We told you we were too close!" "Let's go fight before they have a chance to come near us!"

Joanna held her hands up to quiet the council. It took several minutes, but finally they were quiet enough to listen to her.

"The scouts are not sure exactly what they are preparing for. I have asked for a report as soon as possible. They have seen tents being packed up, military carts being brought in. We have had no reports of other villages near this area, so we can only assume they are packing up to move back to the main camp or they are maneuvering here."

"What is our plan for this type of situation?" One member asked.

"I have asked Liam to meet us here to explain, but basically, we are prepared for war, should it come," Joanna explained. "Our military is at full strength. Our weaponry is top of the line. We have lines to protect the village. We have troops to go on the offensive. We are prepared, should it come to war."

"Where is Liam?" someone asked.

"He should be here soon. He has been with the military on a training." Joanna looked to Ethan for support. He nodded his head and smiled, indicating he thought she was doing well.

Joanna answered a few more questions as best as she could with the little information she had been given. Soon, the door opened and Liam walked in with Martha and Jonas.

Joanna sighed with relief. She was running out of answers. She called a brief recess while she conferred with her head scouts and military commander. No one left the room. She stepped into a back room with the other three.

"Liam, have they caught you up?" she asked.

"Yes, your honor."

She turned to her scouts. "Is there any more news beyond what you told me this afternoon?"

"Yes, your honor," Jonas answered. "The Gabonites are showing definite signs of coming this way."

"Oh no," Joanna groaned.

Jonas and Martha explained what their scouts had reported. The Gabon tents were coming down quick. The carts were being filled with military weapons and lined up facing the Thadon village.

"Also," Martha added hesitantly, "their military has grown. And, Corbin is there."

"How do they know we are here?" Joanna asked.

"Scouts, your honor, same as how we know they are there," Jonas answered, knowing she knew the answer.

"What do you think, your honor?" Liam asked.

Joanna turned to look at him, wondering why he was asking her and not interjecting his own opinion. He was the head of the military. It was his job to defend the people. She paused before answering.

Feeling a strength and peace she didn't know she possessed, Joanna looked each advisor in the eye and answered them. "We need to go to war. These people have been on the run far too long. They have lived in fear, and I won't have it any longer. Evil will not prevail. God is on our side, and he will fight for us."

"Are you sure?" Liam asked.

"Are you not?" Joanna countered.

"It's just that these people have been through so much. Is it wise to add war on top of it?"

Joanna looked at him incredulously. "Are you suggesting we stay here and let the Gabonite army inflict more atrocities on our people? Should we just let them have us to do with what they wish? Never again, Liam, never again. These people deserve to be defended."

"Do you want them living in fear of losing their family members in battle?" Liam countered.

Joanna answered, "I would rather they know we did something to defend our people then left them at the hands of evil. God is with us. He will defend us. I believe he will deliver Gabon into your hands. Now, gather the troops and go!"

"Joanna, I know what these men are capable of, both in military and against civilians." Liam said.

"Liam, you are the military commander!" Joanna said angrily. "Do your job and take the army out."

He looked her in the eye, as if to challenge her. "I will go, if you go with me. If you stay, I will not go."

Martha and Jonas remained quiet, disbelieving Liam would challenge his ruler.

Joanna smiled at Liam. "I will go. But because of your challenge and weakness, you will receive no honor in the victory. The Lord will hand Corbin over to a woman." She turned and left the room to tell the council of her decision.

Chapter 6

The council members were stunned at the turn of events. That Corbin had found them and was so near, brought a flood of fear among the people. Joanna could see the panic rising.

She shouted above the din. "People, people, listen to me!"

Soon the people quieted and turned to their leader.

"Yes, this is a fearsome plight we are in," she began. "However, I believe God is with us. He has protected us in this land so far, I believe he will continue to do so. I will ride out with the army to fight Corbin."

This last comment stunned the people. They were now in awe of their leader. That she, a woman not in the military, would risk her life for the people not only showed her bravery, but also her dedication to the people. This gave strength to the council members in the room.

"What can we do," Herman asked.

Joanna smiled in appreciation of the support he was showing. "First, we need to make sure the people are safe. We will place a guard close around the village. Make sure the people have packed only what they can carry, should they need to flee. They can take a few animals with them, should we need to run, but not all. Corbin's army is too close. Keep calm around them, though. Try to reassure them that the army is doing everything they can to fight Corbin back. We want to stay in this land. We don't want to run anymore."

She turned to the army commander. "Liam, assemble the troops. Get the guard in place. I will meet you at the formation site in thirty minutes."

"Yes, your honor," Liam said and turned to do as he was told.

Herman turned to the council members to assign their tasks.

Joanna turned away from the council and found Ethan at her side.

"I'm going with you," he said in a voice that allowed for no argument.

Joanna looked at him unsure.

"Don't worry. I know you're in charge. I am proud of you. You are amazing to listen to God like this. I won't get in the way. I just want to be with you and help if I can," Ethan said.

"I will gladly have you along," Joanna said, knowing she could use his military expertise. She had never been in a battle before.

The two left to gather their weapons. Ethan showed her what she would need. He had taught her how to use many weapons; she was glad of that.

They left their house and met Liam and the army. As they walked to the front, every soldier snapped to attention and saluted their commander.

As far as Joanna knew, Liam didn't mention his apprehension to the soldiers. She was glad of this. It would have shown weakness in the leader. She detected only strength and determination from each soldier, including Liam.

Joanna and Ethan marched to Liam's side. The military leader and tribal commander saluted each other.

Liam took her down the line of soldiers as he inspected each one. Joanna encouraged them as well. They still did not know that Joanna was riding with them, but they appreciated the tribal commander's support.

Liam and his officers inspected the weapons and supplies. All weapons were brought out. All food was packed together. No one knew how long they would be in battle. They wanted to be prepared.

As the officers made sure everything was in order, Liam took Joanna, Ethan, Martha, and Jonas to the commanding tent. He showed them the map of where they were and where they were going. He laid out battle plans.

"I believe we can reach this ridge tonight," he said, pointing to the map. "If everything the scouts have said holds true, Corbin's army will not reach this far yet. We can then, take them by surprise early in the morning, here." He pointed to an open plain of desert. "This will be good for us because we have the cover of the trees behind us here. They have wide open spaces behind them here and will have no cover. If we cannot reach this ridge tonight, the odds are in their favor."

"We need to move, then," Joanna said.

"Yes, your honor," Liam answered.

"Have there been any more reports from the scouts?" Joanna asked.

"No, your honor," Martha said. "Everything is still the same. They had been settled in that camp for a long time. They have quite a bit to pack up. It looks as if they're trying to erase signs of their existence in that area."

"This will be to our advantage," Liam said. "If they're worried so much about that, they're not battle ready, yet. They are strong and good fighters. As you said, they fight dirty. But if we can catch them off guard and surprise them, we will have the upper hand."

"What about their scouts?" Joanna asked. "If they had scouts that knew we were here, surely they're still watching us and will report back to Corbin that we're moving."

Martha and Jonas looked at each other. "Their scouts are not a problem, your honor," Jonas said.

Joanna didn't ask questions. She looked at the map again. "We need to move, then. I'd like to talk with the troops before we move out. Just a few minutes, and then we'll go."

"Yes, your honor," Liam said. He brought her horse around and led her to the front of the assembly.

Every soldier snapped to when they saw their leaders approaching. Joanna was pleased with the discipline they showed.

Joanna sat regally on her horse in front of the troops. She looked with pride at those who would defend her people.

"Soldiers of Thadon," she began, "today we march to fight a foe with whom we have a black history. The Gabon people have taken advantage of us for far too long. They have performed atrocities among our people that most could not dream up in their worst nightmares. They have chased us from our land in fear. Well, no more! No more will this evil torture us. No more will we live in fear. We have been deprived of our right to live in peace far too long. I say enough! Now it is our time to fight back. It is our time to take charge. Corbin has joined the army camp a day's ride from here. He is planning an attack on our peaceful village. We will not allow it! Tonight, we ride to protect our people and the life we have built here out of the ashes of our former existence. We have God on our side. He will go before us and defend us!"

The soldiers erupted in cheers.

At this, she raised her hand in triumph and turned her horse to lead the troops into battle.

Chapter 7

Joanna led the army out of the village. The villagers stood by waving and cheering in gratitude and support. The whole village seemed to be out. Every family had at least one member in the army. Joanna was glad for the show of support but worried they were wasting precious time in preparing for the possible need to flee. She took a deep breath and tried to rest in the assurance she had felt earlier while she prayed.

The road was nonexistent, so the army had to pick their way through the wilderness to reach the ridge at the edge of the desert. Thankfully, they did not have to climb the highest of the mountains surrounding their village. They followed the river as far as they could, using that water before the water in their canteens.

Liam explained more of his battle plans and talked about his training as he, Joanna, and Ethan led the troops out.

Martha and Jonas flanked the army to scout for enemies. They reported every half hour, not seeing anything yet. Soon, some of their other scouts found them and reported on the movement of Corbin's army. Thankfully, there seemed to be little change. They knew, however, that the reports were at least a half a day old since the scouts had to ride so far, but they were appreciative and encouraged by the reports.

They reached the desired ridge by nightfall. The army stayed there for the night, sleeping under the stars. The soldiers took turns for watch duty, so most could get rest for the next day's battle. No one made fires in case the enemy could see them.

Most everyone got some sleep that night, though they were all nervous about what they would encounter the next day. They hadn't been in battle for over a year. Joanna prayed they were in good shape. She and Ethan prayed for a long time together. Both felt reassured that God was on their side and would go ahead of them.

"I can't believe Liam's hesitance," Ethan finally said when they were alone.

"In a way, I can," Joanna replied. "Corbin's army is evil personified. We know what he's capable of. Many people just wanted to keep running and not face him."

"I'm proud of you, Joanna," Ethan said and kissed her forehead. "You have been in charge of this people under extreme circumstances. You have been strong for them. You have trusted God for them. I believe we will get to see the destruction of our enemies, what we have longed so much for."

"Thank you for being at my side every step of the way," Joanna said. "I believe with you here, they have accepted me more. Though our tribe allows for more opportunities for women than do other tribes, it still took them quite a while to accept me."

"But you have proven a fair and good leader. It's not because I'm your husband. It's because of you and what you have done for the people. God has blessed you for being faithful to him as well."

Joanna hugged her husband. They were silent and soon fell asleep.

Liam woke them before dawn the next day. He wanted them to be in on the scouting report first thing in the morning.

"Martha, Jonas, what do you have?" Joanna asked when they were all assembled.

"The report is still the same, your honor," Martha said. "They have packed more and seem to be ready to move out any minute, but they are still at their camp."

Liam thought for a moment then said, "Could we have misunderstood their movement? Could they be moving away instead of preparing for battle?"

"I don't think so, sir," Jonas said. "They are definitely preparing for battle and definitely pointed this way. I don't know what the hold-up is."

Liam wasn't as prepared for this scenario. He predicted they would meet up in the desert between the Gabon camp and the new Thadon village. "Tell me more about the surroundings of the Gabon camp."

Martha and Jonas described the camp and its surroundings. They drew a map of every tree and landmark they could remember from scouting.

All eyes turned to Liam. He studied the map then came up with a battle plan. Joanna was pleased with the quickness in his thinking, and the strength in his voice.

Soon, they assembled the troops and were on their way.

That afternoon they reached the trees on the edge of the Gabon camp. Everything was as Martha and Jonas and their scouts had described. The Gabon army was not in formation, though they had many weapons at the ready. It seemed as if they had no idea the Thadon army was coming. Joanna thought back to the remark Jonas had said about the Gabon scouts not being a problem. She wondered if her scouts had eliminated all of the Gabon scouts.

She looked back at her army. They were ready. She could see the determination on the faces of every soldier, including Liam.

Joanna and Ethan had decided that they would not enter the battle unless it was absolutely necessary. The tribe needed their leader. She would command from the back but leave everything up to Liam unless he showed signs of hesitation.

Glancing at Liam, Joanna saw there was no need for worry. His face was more determined than she had ever seen it. She could tell he remembered what Corbin's army had done to his family, just as she was remembering what had been done to hers. She had no hesitation about Liam's ability or desire to eliminate the Gabon army.

"Liam," she said. "Go! This is the day the Lord has given Corbin into your hands. Has not the Lord gone ahead of you?"

Liam nodded at his commander. Then he raised his hand to his people, gave the cry for advance and attacked the Gabon army.

Joanna, Ethan, Martha, and Jonas stayed in the ridge of trees watching the battle.

The Thadon army took the Gabon army completely by surprise. Liam had trained his soldiers well. They fought as a cohesive unit. Swords clashed. Spears flew. The line near Joanna held the catapults. She watched as the boulders flew beyond her army into the middle of the enemy. Archers drew their bows at the command of their leader and let the arrows fly. The Thadon solders seemed to move as one while the Gabon soldiers looked like ants scattered from their hill.

Joanna prayed as she stood transfixed watching the battle. She could tell her people were winning, though she could not tell how many soldiers might be lost.

After a few hours of fighting, the battle was over. Martha and Jonas went to the battlefield to get the report. They ordered their commander and her husband to stay where they were.

Soon, the scouts returned with the report. "All the troops of Gabon fell. Not a man is left!" Jonas said excitedly.

"Really?" Joanna exclaimed, matching his excitement.

"Yes! The Gabon army barely even put up a fight. They were scared to death."

"And our soldiers?" Joanna asked.

"Not a one was lost, your honor," Jonas said smiling.

"That's wonderful!" Joanna and Ethan exclaimed.

Martha came from a different part of the battlefield. Her face was not as excited at Jonas's. "Corbin got away," she said.

"Oh no!" Joanna groaned.

"He's the only one, though. Jonas was right. Everyone else is gone."

"Where did he go?" Joanna asked.

"He was seen heading in the direction of Jennel. It's a village about three day's ride from here; an ally of Gabon. Liam has followed him."

"Alone?" Joanna asked.

"Two of his officers followed him, but yes, the three are otherwise alone." Martha said.

"God help him!" Joanna prayed.

Chapter 8

He rode hard all night. He could tell his horse was getting tired, but he had to push on. He knew they were close behind him. If only he could find a place to hide for the night.

There it was!

Corbin pulled his horse to a trot. He'd come near a forest. Guiding his horse deep into the trees, he tried to find a pond or stream or something for his horse. He found a small spring and led his horse to it. Hopefully no one would find them in here. He got off his horse and drank some water himself.

He had to think. What had gone wrong? Where had the Thadon army come from? He had been planning the attack for months. As soon as he found out where their new village was, he sent word to his commander at the military camp, and they began training right away. Where were his scouts? Why had he not been informed of the Thadon army advance?

So many questions never to be answered. His whole army was gone. All for which he had worked so hard for so many years was now wiped away from him. He knew he was the only one left. He had snuck away at the end of the battle, after he saw his people were getting slaughtered.

He didn't understand it. His army was so much more advanced and prepared. The Thadon people were a people of peace, not of war, yet they had annihilated his army.

He had to put it behind him. What was he going to do now? King Maxim wasn't going to like this. As ruthless as Corbin could be, he was nothing compared to Maxim. Torture, he was sure of it. There was no way he could escape that. But what could he do to lessen the sentence? Remain alive? He'd have to think on that later. For now, he had to decide where to go.

He was headed in the direction of Jennel. They were allies of Gabon. They were not exactly enemies of Thadon, but they weren't allies, either. Surely he could hide there. He had no idea who, if anyone, knew he had left the battle. He had to assume someone was trailing him. He just needed to keep a few steps ahead.

Corbin decided to remain where he was for the night and then ride hard to Jennel the next day.

———

Liam and his two officers continued to ride.

"Do you see anything, sir?" Sharon asked.

"No," Liam said dejectedly. They had lost Corbin's track about five miles earlier. "He must have gone into that forest. I think we'd better stay here for the night and keep pushing toward Jennel in the morning."

"Yes, sir," Sharon and Joel said.

They dismounted and led their horses to a nearby stream. They were exhausted. A few hours of battle followed by several hours of tracking their foe took a toll on their bodies. They ate their small rations quickly and promptly fell asleep.

———

The next morning, Corbin woke with the sunrise. He didn't have any food with him, so he scrounged what he could find in the woods. Then, he mounted his horse and rode toward Jennel.

He decided to keep to the woods since it would hide his trail better, though it was much slower going and harder to pick his way through the brush. It took him all day to get through the woods. Finally, by nightfall, he left the woods and found an open space of desert. He recognized it as being near the village of Hashem, an independent village, not allied to anyone. He picked his way slowly around the village.

This tribe was known to be savage to any intruders. They especially did not like people from Gabon. It took him longer than he wanted to get by this village, but soon he was around it and on his way. It was completely dark by this time, and Corbin had difficulty finding a place for his horse.

Finally finding a small pond, he settled for the night.

Again, he woke with the sunrise, found a few meager bites to eat, and was on his way. He knew he was less than a day's ride from Jennel, so he urged his horse on.

By late afternoon, he reached Jennel.

Corbin was confident in the alliance between Jennel and Gabon, though he didn't want to parade down the main street of the village. He found a small house on the outskirts and got off his horse to slowly walk up to find shelter.

Walking back from the field was a woman. Corbin felt relieved. Surely the woman would give him shelter.

She saw him as she came closer to the house. She slowed down.

"Hello," Corbin said in a forced voice. He was near panic for wanting to hide, but didn't want this woman to know his fears.

"Good morning, sir," the woman said hesitantly. "Can I help you?"

"As a matter of fact, yes. I need shelter."

Without asking questions, the woman motioned for him to follow her to the house.

Relieved, he followed obediently.

She took him in to her small kitchen area. "Please sit down. I need to stoke the fire, and I'll boil some water for tea. Here is some bread left over from our midday meal." She passed him a basket which he took eagerly.

"Thank you for your kindness, ma'am," Corbin said.

"Our tribes are allies, sir," she said simply.

He stopped quickly. Hesitating, he put the bread down on the table. He wasn't sure how she knew. "Do you know who I am?"

"I know you are from the tribe of Gabon," she said. "You have a very distinct type of dress. I know you are in the military. Your dress is obviously a uniform."

"What is your name?" Corbin asked.

"I am Barbara," she said. "My husband is Andrew, the leader of the Jennel tribe."

Corbin relaxed. Surely she was an ally. He began eating the bread again.

"Why are you here?" she asked. "Why alone?"

He wasn't sure exactly how much to tell her, but figured it was safe since she was his ally's wife.

"I have just come from a battle with the Thadon army," he explained. "Most of my army was slaughtered. I escaped before the battle was over, so I don't know the fate of the rest of my army. I am on my way back to Gabon to ask King Maxim for reinforcements."

"Are you a leader in the army?"

"I am Corbin, the Gabon army commander."

Barbara smiled at him. "I thought perhaps you were. The way you carry yourself shows much confidence."

Corbin smiled proudly.

"The Thadon army, you say?" Barbara asked. "I haven't heard anything about them for many months. I thought you drove them away more than a year ago."

"I did," he said tersely. "They got away from me and found a new land. It's a beautiful land, very fertile with lots of game. My aim is to get reinforcements from Maxim, attack the tribe, make the people our slaves, and take over their land."

"Such ambitions, sir," Barbara said, as she brought the kettle over for his drink.

"Perhaps your husband is around and could help?" Corbin asked.

"My husband is out of town at present," Barbara answered. "You are welcome to stay here as long as you need. He should return tomorrow. I can hide you. You look very tired."

"I would appreciate that," Corbin said. "I am tired. I suppose reinforcements can wait a day."

"Of course, sir," Barbara said. Then she turned to show him where she would hide him. "Over here, sir, we have a corner that is well hidden. I will cover you with blankets. You will be both comfortable and hidden."

"Thank you for your kindness, ma'am. Your husband would be proud of your generosity."

"Thank you." Barbara turned to leave the house. "If you'll excuse me, sir, I have some more work to do in the field. When you are finished, please rest in the corner. I will return and make sure you are well hidden."

Corbin nodded and enjoyed the rest of the bread and tea. He watched the woman leave the house, comfortable in her allegiance, and glad for a rest before facing Maxim's wrath.

He knew Maxim would not be kind upon his return. He hesitated on what to say. How would he explain the slaughter? He had to put the blame on someone else. That was the only way to lessen the sentence he was sure to receive. He thought for a long time.

Finally, he had an idea. *I will tell him my horse went lame,* he thought. *The old thing is on it's last anyway. I will tell him I couldn't reach the camp in time. I was not able to warn of a possible attack. I will tell him I knew of the plans all along, but it was the horse's fault.*

It was feeble at best, but it was all his tired mind could come up with at the moment. He would have to get rid of the horse and tell Maxim that he killed the horse for its lameness.

Corbin was tired of thinking. He was satisfied at the moment and decided to lie down. He went to the corner Barbara showed him, covered himself with the blankets, and fell into a deep sleep.

An hour later, Barbara entered the house. She saw Corbin was not at the table and went to the corner. He was deep asleep. After covering him more with the blankets, she left the house again.

"This man has caused nothing but trouble for everyone in the surrounding lands," she said to herself. "I have heard my husband complain of him and how he treats the people."

Barbara's husband was currently meeting with the leader of another nearby tribe to form an alliance against the Gabon tribe. Andrew was a new leader of Jennel and did not agree with the alliance.

"God has delivered this man into my hands," Barbara said as she went to the small building where her husband kept his tools. She searched for something. Finding the tent which was their first house, she grabbed a spike and left the building.

Quietly entering her small house, she walked gingerly over to the pile of blankets where the man lay. She lifted up the blankets until she could see his face. He was still sleeping soundly. She raised the spike and quickly drove it into Corbin's temple.

Chapter 9

"Let's face it," Joel said almost whining. "We've lost him."

Liam was getting tired of his subordinate's whining. "No wonder you're not in the scouts," he mumbled. "We haven't lost him. His trail has gone cool for the moment, but we'll find him."

Sharon joined in. "He must have hidden in the woods last night and traveled through the woods to the other side. We have just a few miles more until we get to the end of the woods. I'm sure we'll find some trace of him then."

They had traveled into the wooded area trying to find Corbin. The trees were so thick they had almost gotten lost and had to find their way back out to the desert. This trek took most of the day, and they had to camp the next night near the same place. They were all discouraged now.

The three rode in silence for a few more miles.

"Look there!" Sharon said, and sped her horse up to the spot she was looking at. She jumped off her horse and examined the ground. "Tracks."

Liam jumped off and joined her. "You're right, Sharon. These are horse tracks. And not just any horse tracks. They are Gabon horse tracks. They shod their horses with very distinctive shoes. Good job, Sharon."

"It looks like they lead this way," Joel said, showing his commander the path he saw.

"You're right, Joel," Liam said, following the trail a few steps.

Joel relaxed, feeling as if he had redeemed himself in his commander's eyes.

Liam took some time examining the trail, making sure this was the trail they wanted to follow.

"This is strange," he said finally. "The trail seems to lead clearly in one direction. There was no attempt to disguise the trail or hide it."

"Perhaps Corbin was feeling cocky in his flight," Sharon offered.

"Or careless," Liam said, hoping for the latter. "It seems a clear path. Let's follow it."

The three mounted their horses again and followed the trail. They followed quickly yet carefully, wanting to gain on their enemy, yet not wanting to miss anything.

"Sir," Joel said nervously.

"Yes, Joel."

"That's Hashem ahead of us there." Joel pointed to the village in front of them. It was dark, so they had to strain to see, but there was no mistaking the lantern lit gate several yards down their path.

Liam motioned for them to slow and stop. "You're right. We can't go there. Those people are almost as bad as the Gabonites to intruders. Thank goodness they keep to themselves. We'll need to find another route."

He led the other two in a wide arc around the village. Apparently they were not far enough away from the village. Several dogs began to bark at them. At this sound and seeing signs of movement from houses, the three travelers picked up their pace and ran their horses as fast as they could away from the village.

"Someone's coming!" Joel said looking back.

Liam and Sharon took him at his word and sped their horses faster.

After several minutes of hard riding, Liam chanced a look behind them. He saw no one. He slowed his horse down, and the others did the same.

"No one is there," Sharon said.

"I'm sure I saw someone," Joel said, the whine returning to his voice.

"Let's just keep going until we find a place to water the horses," Liam said, trying to hide the irritation from his voice. He was unsure of whether Joel had actually seen anyone or if he was acting in fear. "That run took a lot out of them. Plus, it's extremely late now, and we need to rest."

They rode for a while longer in silence. Thankfully, the moon was full, and they had some light. The desert seemed to stretch out in front of them.

Soon, Sharon spotted a pond, and they camped for the night.

Waking with the sun, Liam took note of their surroundings. He noticed some of the grass on the side of the pond opposite where they slept had been mashed down. Near this grass, some of the plants had been eaten. It looked like a horse had been there. He continued looking and found a trail leaving the pond area. The trail was of a Gabon horse. He ran back to Sharon and Joel.

"He was here," Liam said when he returned.

"What? When?" Sharon asked, reaching for her knife.

"I think he was here the night before us," Liam said, and took them over to what he saw. He showed them the trail leaving the area.

"You're right, sir," Sharon said. "These are the same tracks we saw earlier. He was here."

"It looks like he's headed toward Jennel," Joel said.

"That's my guess, too," Liam said. "We need to be careful. Jennel is allied with Gabon, though not an enemy if ours. It's tricky ground there. They have a new leader as well, that I don't know. He could very well be more sympathetic to the Gabon people than the last leader. Let's ride carefully."

The three mounted their horses and followed the trail at a quick, yet cautious pace. Again, the trail was clear. No attempt had been made to cover or disguise it. Liam hoped Corbin was panicking. That would definitely be to his advantage. He wanted this man.

Corbin had tortured his people far too long. He himself had painful memories of family members lost. Liam was out for revenge. Personal revenge as well as revenge for his people. Corbin had killed Liam's fiancé three years ago.

Liam rode harder.

Soon, they reached the outskirts of the village of Jennel. Liam held up his hand to slow the others. He picked his way carefully, noting the trail they were following. It seemed to lead right to a house.

Liam got off his horse and motioned for the others to remain where they were. Leaving his horse with Joel, he crept up to the house. Then he stopped suddenly.

A woman came out of the house. The three riders were not hidden in any way. The woman saw them. She was headed right for Liam.

He grabbed his knife, in case the woman would try to attack, and walked to her.

She held her hand out for him to stop. He obeyed. She continued walking right up to him. "You are from Thadon," she said.

Liam said nothing.

"You are in pursuit of Corbin of Gabon," she continued.

"Are you friend or foe of my country?" Liam asked.

"I am neither," the woman answered. "However, I am an enemy of Gabon. Come, I will show you the man you're looking for."

The woman turned and walked back to her house. Liam followed, motioning for Sharon to follow discretely.

They entered the house. Liam held his knife ready in case she turned on him. She led him to a corner where many blankets were piled.

Pealing the blankets back, she revealed the body of Corbin of Gabon, a tent spike through his temple.

Liam stared at the body, then at the woman.

"I am Barbara," she said. "My husband is Andrew, leader of the Jennel tribe. Though our tribe may be allied to Gabon on paper, we are not in our hearts. My husband is at a meeting with other tribe leaders trying to sign new allegiances against Gabon."

Liam knelt down in front of Barbara. "My lady, we are forever in your debt."

Barbara touched Liam's head in a gesture of peace. Then the two wrapped Corbin's body, laid it on a cloth between two long sticks, and attached it to Joel's horse.

The three Thadonites then returned home.

Liam road harder than the other two in order to reach Joanna with the news. When he arrived back to the village three days later, he was met with a surprise.

Chapter 10

"What do you mean she's not here?" Liam asked Herman.

"When you didn't return for two days after the battle," Herman explained, "she felt the need to take the army to Gabon and attack Maxim's castle."

"She did what?" Liam nearly exploded. Then without another word, he mounted another horse and took off in the direction of Gabon.

After four days of hard riding, he finally caught up with Joanna and the army.

"What are you doing?" he asked.

"We need to finish them once and for all," Joanna explained. "Even with the desert army gone, Maxim still has his court army. He can build it up again and come after us. I believe God will deliver us. Are you with us?"

Liam paused for a moment. He was out of breath from riding so hard. His horse was nearly lame from the travel. Then he looked straight in his commander's eyes and smiled a sly smile. "Let's take him."

Joanna smiled happily. Ethan slapped him on the back with pride. The couple gladly let their military commander take over.

The army was still two days away from Gabon. Liam took advantage of this time to continue encouraging his troops. He shared the story of finding Corbin's body several times. Many cheers went up in excitement for the death of their enemy. Martha and Jonas came several times with reports from their scouts of events at the castle. It seemed as if confusion was the order now. No one had heard from the desert army. No one knew anything about Corbin. The Gabon scouts were too afraid to go looking.

The Gabonite people seemed to be afraid. Maxim seemed to be boiling over with anger, though not willing to go anywhere himself. The castle army was afraid and confused. Their leadership was faltering.

Liam made careful plans regarding this information. He didn't want to lose any of his soldiers though he knew in war, loss was inevitable. If the enemy was scared, they could do drastic things. He also knew what the Gabon people were capable of, especially King Maxim.

Joanna wanted Maxim alive. She wanted to try him in front of her people; at least in front of the soldiers. She considered taking him back to their village, though in the end decided that might be too traumatic for her people. Her plan was to capture him, charge him, and have him hanged in his own courtyard.

Liam sent Jonas and a few other scouts to stake out the layout of the castle. This was the most dangerous task of the operation. Joanna stayed with Martha during the night. Liam would not allow Martha to go with her husband.

Jonas and two other scouts crept to the castle in the dead of night, thankful for the darkness the walls offered.

It seemed that everyone was asleep which was odd, but helpful. It was odd because they thought someone should be up protecting the king. However, with everything else they had seen from the Gabon people, it wasn't as odd as normal circumstances.

They felt their way along the castle wall and entered a side door. As they made their way through the castle, they took note of the layout and every piece of furniture that might be in their way. A few times they had to hide quickly from a servant in the hallway and one time a soldier, but for the most part, they were alone.

After several hours in the castle, they left quietly and returned to the camp.

———

Martha hugged her husband upon his return. They had been scouts for many years, and the dangers were always present and real. However, this night it seemed more terrifying since they had never actually been in this enemy camp. No other tribe in the land had a castle. This added to the fear of the Gabon people. They were different from the other tribes, more terrible. Knowing her husband and the other scouts were home safe and had little to no resistance, was a blessing they were all thankful for.

Jonas and the others gave their report to Joanna and Liam, their scout training giving them excellent memories of the layout of the castle.

"We are extremely grateful to you for this information," Joanna said. "I know it was dangerous. You all are very brave and are to be commended for your work."

For the next several hours, Liam and the scouts worked together to form a plan of attack. Each guard station would be taken out. "Though, I don't think that will be too difficult," Jonas said. "No one was there."

"We want to be prepared," Liam said.

After each guard station was taken care of, they would move to the castle's inner chambers and find the king's guard and then the king.

The officers were brought in after the plan was formed. Each was given their assignment. The officers then went to their troops and explained each assignment to the soldiers.

The time was planned for nightfall the next day. The soldiers and officers were ordered to rest as much as they could. No one knew what the battle would be like the next day.

Joanna and Ethan sat together in their tent.

"I can't believe it's finally here," Joanna said excitedly. "We've never been this close before. This man has tortured our people for almost two decades, and now we are here to be part of our people fighting back."

"It's a testament to your good leadership," Ethan said.

"It's a testament to obedience to God," Joanna corrected with a smile.

The two sat together for a while longer, talking and praying.

"You know," Ethan said, "I think you're absolutely right. You have been obedient to God in all of this in a way I never have seen anyone be before. The former leaders of our people, especially, had turned away from him. They led our people down wrong paths and allowed them to worship false gods and do things directly against God's laws. I think God got fed up with the old leaders and people and just let our people be taken advantage of. Then you come along and are obedient, and God has given us victory. And, it seems he has subdued the Gabon people and their leader and will give us victory in the future."

Joanna smiled at her husband's praise and snuggled closer to him. "I pray you are right."

The next day, everyone was ready. No one seemed nervous. Each soldier took careful check of his weapons, cleaning and sharpening each blade and spearhead. Again, they packed provisions, not knowing how long they would be in the enemy camp. They packed everything up and left no one behind, for no one wanted to be left behind.

Each soldier had trained hard for this day. Each wanted to see their hard work come to fruition. No one wanted to be left out of the victory.

After everyone was assembled and ready to go, Joanna again addressed her army.

"Soldiers of Thadon," she said proudly, "you have served your tribe well. You have made your mothers, fathers, sisters, brothers, wives, and husbands proud. You have made me proud. You are about to embark on a most historical attack. It will be remembered throughout the history of Thadon. Your attack on the Gabon army camp several days ago will be remembered as well. You will be remembered throughout our history as a great army; the army who subdued a terrible foe and brought honor once again to our great tribe. God went before us with the army camp. He goes before us now. He has smiled upon our tribe and is giving us back the great name that was taken from us with former leaders. You are bringing back the great name of Thadon to this land. Great victory to you all!"

Cheers erupted from the soldiers.

Liam allowed their cheers for a few moments then silenced them with a raised hand. Immediately, they snapped to attention in front of their military commander. It was now time for battle.

Liam led the line of soldiers to the gates of Gabon. All was dark. He motioned for the first group to attack the front guard. They were virtually unopposed. There were two guards at the gate, but they were sleeping. The first group of Thadon soldiers tied the guard so they were unable to move, then set their own guard while the rest of the army advanced into the compound.

Each set of troops found their objective and took it out with relative ease. A few guards tried to fight, but were easily subdued.

"This is too easy," Liam whispered to the officer next to him as they awaited the next group.

"Don't ruin our good luck, sir," the officer said almost laughing.

"But don't you agree that this is too easy?" Liam said cautiously. His eyes darted around to make sure he wasn't missing anything.

They were taking over this once mighty city in less than an hour. This was supposed to be the fiercest enemy they had and hardly anyone was coming out to fight them.

Just then, they heard a scream and scuffle. "That's more like it," Liam said as he sent a man to see what was happening and help, if needed.

They had found one pocket of resisters. A group of the castle guard had hidden in an alcove and come out to attack the invaders. However, their attempt at resistance seemed minimal.

The man came back and reported on the dead and injured enemy, and the post that was now manned by the Thadon army.

Finally, with each guard restrained or dead, Liam and his group entered the inner chambers of the castle where King Maxim was sleeping.

Restraining himself from killing the madman outright, Liam gagged him, tied him up, and carried him out of the castle, through the front gates, and back to Joanna.

Chapter 11

Joanna, Ethan, Martha, and Joel again stood together trying to watch the battle. This was more difficult to see than the first, since it was night and most of the battle took place in the castle. They were pacing in nervousness, since they couldn't tell what was going on.

"It's too quiet," Joanna said. "Aren't battles supposed to be noisier than this?"

"You're right," Ethan said. "I don't understand."

"I think it's what you said earlier," Jonas said. "I think God has subdued the enemy and given us victory. There's no other explanation for all we have seen.

"Jonas is right," Martha said. "What we saw in there, was nothing more than utter confusion. It seemed as if their minds had been turned off, and they were mere babies again, unsure of what to do. The guard was almost nowhere to be found, and Maxim was plain crazy. And when Jonas and the others went in last night, hardly anyone was around."

They watched for a while longer and finally saw someone coming.

"Kael, what's going on in there?" Jonas asked his scout.

"Sir, it's just like last night," Kael said. "Hardly anyone is around to fight and those that are seem so confused, as if they've completely forgotten how to fight. It's a miracle, sir. This once fearsome foe has become a sad group of imbeciles. I almost feel sorry for them. Then I remember the past."

They all stood silent for a while, remembering the past.

Kael left to get another report.

"No mercy on them, Joanna," Ethan said as he saw his wife's face soften. "You know what they are capable of."

She smiled at him. "Oh, I wasn't thinking of showing mercy. I was just remembering my father and wishing he could be here to see this day."

They all agreed. Each one had someone they wished could be there that day to see this enemy surrender.

Soon, Kael came riding back. "It's over, your honor," he said excitedly. "They're on their way back. Commander Liam has Maxim wrapped in a sheet."

"It's over?" Joanna asked unbelieving.

"Yes, your honor," Kael said, then turned to rejoin the army.

The four friends watched as the Thadon army paraded to them; everyone smiling; everyone returning. Joanna saw minor cuts, but no casualties beyond that. Then she saw Liam. He had what looked like a large sack thrown over his shoulder. He was smiling broader than she had ever seen him smile.

"Your honor," Liam said as he approached. Then he dropped the bundle in front of her unceremoniously. "Your charge."

Joanna was almost too excited to look. She took a deep breath and began to unwrap the bundle. There, wrapped in a sheet was the once great Maxim, King of Gabon. He had a gag in his mouth tied around his head. His hands and feet were tied together. Joanna started laughing. The others around her began to laugh as well. This man who had afflicted terrible atrocities on so many people was now in front of her, bound and completely helpless.

Maxim narrowed his eyes and began to grumble. This only made the others laugh more. He grumbled more and started kicking his legs which made him look like a worm. Finally, Joanna ordered the gag to be untied.

"You despicable people," Maxim spat. "I should have gotten rid of you all long ago. My father had the right idea. You aren't worth anything. You're the lowest scum on the earth. I'll get rid of you all!"

"Maxim," Joanna said patronizingly, "do you realize that you are utterly alone now? Your words are empty threats. Corbin is dead. He was killed by a woman from Jennel."

At this, Maxim quieted his tirade a little. Jennel was supposed to be his ally.

"Your people are all either subdued or dead," Joanna continued. "My army just took them all out with little to no resistance. My army annihilated your army several days ago. Nothing is left.

Now, Maxim was quiet. He hadn't realized his people were gone. Then he became angry all over again and began hurling insults at Joanna personally. "You're nothing but a weak woman," he said menacingly. "I wish I'd had my way with you before Corbin drove you off your land."

At this, Ethan struck him over the head. "You will not talk about my wife that way."

Maxim glared at him, though feeling the blood begin to ooze down his neck, decided on a different tactic. "I remember your father," he said. "I certainly enjoyed slitting his throat."

Joanna seethed. She had never known how her father died. The army commander at the time kept the information from her. Now, any sympathy for the man lying before her was gone.

"Maxim of Gabon," she said evenly, "you are hereby charged with atrocities against the people of Thadon. As judge of the people of Thadon, I sentence you to death by hanging."

It was done. Simply said, but done.

Joanna turned and walked away.

Liam picked Maxim up again, but not after giving him a swift kick to the side. He took him to a nearby tree which they had already tied the hangman's noose to. Sitting Maxim on a horse, one of the officers tied the noose around his neck then slapped the horse's rump sending the horse skittering away. The army stood watching their fallen enemy hang.

Ethan hugged Joanna and turned her away from the sight. "It's finished, my dear. You don't need that image in your head."

"Thank you, Ethan," Joanna said, as she hugged him back. "Thank you for defending me earlier."

"You're welcome," Ethan said simply.

Chapter 12

Upon returning to the Thadon camp, Joanna and Liam received a hero's welcome. The scouts had ridden before them and told the people of the good news. The two commanders rode in on horses in front of the marching army. Ethan was by his wife's side as always. The people lined the village cheering and throwing flowers.

Joanna basked in the joy and peace she saw on her peoples' faces. This was what she had longed for since childhood. Her family and the families of so many others were now vindicated. Their enemy was gone, and they could now live in the peace their long dead ancestors had planned for them.

Joanna thanked God for going before them and protecting them.

A victory festival was planned for the next week. Everyone wanted it to be special. New decorations were made. The musicians practiced new music. Copious amounts of food were made.

Joanna was in her element. She loved the festivals. She loved seeing the people so happy together.

"Well, your honor," Liam said as he came to where his commander and friend was sitting, "I'd say this was a big success."

"You did a good job, Liam," Joanna complimented.

"So did you," he said. "And you were right. I was wrong in my hesitation to go after the army camp, and you got all the credit. The people are singing your praises right now."

"They should be singing God's praises," she said. "He's the one who went before us. He's the one who subdued our enemy and gave us victory. I'm convinced that he blessed us, because I decided to follow him when our ancestors drifted away from him."

Liam thought for a while. "You know, Joanna, I think you're right. So many leaders before you turned farther and farther away from God. You turned to him. You sought his advice and direction and protection. You gave me the example I needed. I pray we never forget the righteous acts of the Lord."

"I pray that, too," Joanna said. She turned to Martha. "Did the thank offering get sent to Barbara?"

"Yes, she and her husband are due here in three days," Martha said.

"I hope for an alliance with their tribe," Joanna said. "We owe a lot to her. May God bless her."

The festival lasted through the night, and the next two days. Everyone had a wonderful time and celebrated their new peace.

When the festival was finally over, Joanna and Ethan retired to their house. She was happy to be with her husband, alone again.

"You know, this is my favorite place to be," she said. "As much as I like governing the people, I always like coming home to you."

"I'm glad," Ethan said. "I like having you home. I want to say it again, my dear, I am so proud of you. You followed God, something your ancestors didn't do. Against many odds, you followed him and brought long sought victory to our people."

"I pray we never stray from him again," Joanna said. "I pray that all of God's enemies may perish. But may they who love him be like the sun when it rises in its strength."

"Amen," the couple said together.

———

Joanna followed the Lord the rest of her life, and the Thadon people had peace under her rule.

The Willing Widow

"…Where you go, I will go and where you stay, I will stay. Your people will be my people and your God my God."

Ruth 1:16 (NIV)

To: Mom, Dad, Tacy, and Jay; the best family during the worst of times.

Chapter 1

"Mrs. Elliott!" Jake shouted as he yanked his sweat flecked horse to a stop in front of the ranch house. He and his horse were panting from the hard ride and panic of the situation.

Kit Elliott glanced out the kitchen window as she was making dinner. She saw Jake, one of the ranch hands, galloping to the house. The horse was foaming with sweat. Dropping the knife in the sink, she ran to the door to see what was the matter.

"Mrs. Elliott!" Jake shouted again, as he jumped off the horse.

"What is it, Jake?" Kit asked fearfully. Jake was usually a stoic man, not given to emotional outbursts. The panic on his face made the adrenaline pump in her ears.

Gulping for breath, Jake said, "I tried to call you, but couldn't get your cell phone."

"Sorry, it must be in another room," Kit said. "What's happening?"

"There's been a stampede, ma'am."

Kit's heart seemed to stop. It was happening again. Five years ago, her younger brother had been caught in a stampede on their family's ranch. He died instantly as the cattle ran over him without notice. Now, there was only one reason Jake would be coming to her with news of a stampede: Gavin, her husband.

They'd only been married for two years. Gavin and his family had moved from Kansas City to Montana for adventure and peace from the city six years earlier. They had fallen in love the first night they met at a local dance club. They'd dated for four years and finally married.

Three years ago, Gavin's father, Jonathan, had died in a car accident when a drunk driver hit him on the highway. Gavin's mother, Sue, had remained on the ranch to be near her sons, though she still kept the family apartment in Kansas City. Carter, Gavin's younger brother had married Carmen a year after Gavin and Kit were married. Sue had always missed the city, but remained at the ranch so as not be alone as well as have memories of her husband and his love for the wilds of Montana.

Kit grabbed hold of the banister for support. She tried to gulp in air as everything seemed to spin around her, and the air seemed to grow thin.

Jake could see she was fighting for control. He went to her side to steady her.

"What happened?" she whispered.

"Something scared the cattle, and there was a stampede," Jake tried to sound gentle. "Gavin and Carter were out there by themselves to begin with. They did everything they could. Adam and I got there soon after, but the cattle were in a major panic. Gavin and Carter both were knocked off their horses. The other hands made it to the valley and were able to help calm the herd down. The men are working on Gavin and Carter now."

Kit took a breath. "Are they alright?"

Jake looked down. "I can't lie to you, ma'am. It doesn't look good. I've come to get you to see if you want to go to the valley."

Kit knew this meant that it might be her last chance to see Gavin alive. She immediately agreed, and Jake let her take his horse. She jumped on the horse and took off toward the valley. Although the horse had already been through a lot, in desperation she pushed him on faster and faster.

When she reached the valley, she had trouble seeing where Gavin and Carter were. She quickly scanned the area as she guided the horse down the hill. Finally finding where the men were huddled together, she urged the horse toward them.

The men looked up as they heard the hoof beats nearing. Seeing the owner's wife coming, they parted.

Kit jumped off the horse as he slid to a stop. Running to the men, she scanned their faces. Each one was grim. She looked down and saw her beloved husband lying beaten on the ground. Not knowing what gave her the strength to move to the gruesome sight, Kit rushed to her husband. He was bruised, bloody, and broken. She could tell he couldn't move, but his eyes met hers. They were a mixture of pain and love.

"I'm sorry," he whispered.

Kit leaned down and stroked his face, not caring about the blood on her shirt. She couldn't say anything. The tears fell freely.

"I love you," Gavin said.

"I love you, too," Kit whispered. She held him for a few more minutes. He took a few staggering breaths, then his body went limp. Kit let out one agonizing wail then cried uncontrollably.

Nearby, Carmen's horse slid to a stop. She jumped off and ran to her husband. Carter had died before either woman arrived to the valley.

The ranch hands moved away, knowing nothing they could say would comfort the grieving wives.

———

The joint funeral was almost more than she could bear. She thought her experience with her brother and father-in-law might prepare her for how to handle this moment, but she was wrong. Nothing could prepare her for seeing her beloved husband devoid of life, lying in a coffin. What would she do now?

Kit sat in the pew at the back of the sanctuary. She couldn't look in the coffin again. All the guests had gone and now family was gathered at the front of the sanctuary, each one wanting one last look at the departed.

Carmen wailed over her loss. Her mother tried to guide her out of the room, away from her husband's coffin.

Kit's parents had come to the funeral but left with the guests. The pain of the loss of her brother had left them bitter and angry. They couldn't handle funerals and just came as a courtesy to their daughter.

Kit's parents separated themselves more from their daughter as her faith in God grew along with her relationship with her husband's family. The Elliott's were Christians who took their faith seriously. They enjoyed life in God's grace. Kit's parents couldn't understand their faith and had come to be angry and bitter toward God, therefore growing farther apart from their only surviving child.

Sitting alone in the back of the sanctuary, Kit simply stared ahead. She had looked at the body in the coffin, but, as good as the morticians were, the body lying in the box did not look like her husband. She knew it was just a body and that Gavin was with God. But she still could not look again.

She felt numb. Five days ago, she was happily married. They owned a prospering cattle ranch. They were happy.

Now, she was alone. She was a widow. How awkward it felt to realize that. She had always associated that word with eighty-year-old women. She was twenty-four. She didn't know what to do with the ranch. She couldn't sell it on her own; she and Gavin had co-owned it with Carmen and Carter. It would be a long time before Carmen was able to think about practical things.

Kit didn't want to think about practical things. She wanted to grieve the loss of her husband; her best friend. They had been through so much together. Gavin had helped her through her brother's death. In turn, she had helped him through his father's death. She had nursed him through many broken bones and other injuries due to cattle ranching. He had helped her through emotional injuries due to her estranged relationship with her parents.

Now, she was alone. Anything else that came along, she was alone to deal with. She didn't know if she could do it. She had always been so dependent on someone. Gavin was her rock. No, God was her rock, she knew that, but Gavin was her human rock.

Why, God! She wanted to scream. No, she wouldn't ask that question. There was no answer to it. This side of heaven, there was no answer to that question. Things just happened. God didn't cause it, but he allowed it, and it happened. Now, it was her time to pick up the pieces and try to make a life out of the new normal.

Kit felt the pew move. Someone had sat near her. She didn't look up. She didn't need to. It was Mama Sue. Her mother-in-law always wore the same perfume, lavender. It had been Jonathan's favorite. Kit felt comforted by the silent support Sue gave. A widow herself, now grieving the loss of her two only sons, Mama Sue knew words would not comfort. Kit was grateful. So many people had tried to say comforting things to her the past few days. They had tried to say, "I know how you feel." Well, they didn't know how she felt! It was all she could do to keep from saying that. The most comfort came from those that simply hugged her and didn't say a word.

The two widows sat in silence together. Each lost in their own thoughts; an island of quiet mourning in a sea of turmoil. No one could comfort them. Wisely, no one tried.

Soon, the final family members coaxed Carmen out of the sanctuary. Kit and Sue were alone.

Finally, Kit spoke. "God is our strength."

"Always and forever," Sue replied.

Chapter 2

The months following the funeral were tough for all three widows. They tried to band together in their grief while continuing with the work of the ranch. It was busy with selling the beef cattle. Kit was thankful that Gavin had shown her how to do the books and had even had her talk with some of the companies they worked with. The others looked to her for leadership with this.

Soon winter settled over the land. Snows came and covered the ground seeming to give a clean slate. Sharing the ranch house, Kit and Sue enjoyed each other's company during the cold days. Carmen stayed in her parents' house a few miles away, therefore Kit and Sue did not see much of her during this time. Kit was grateful that Sue had agreed to stay in the big house when she and Gavin had married. She was glad for the company after his death.

The two women busied themselves with tasks that had been neglected during the ranching season while they tried to oversee the winter duties with the cattle and ranch hands. By the end of each day, they were exhausted.

"What are you thinking, dear?" Sue asked one night that Kit was especially quiet.

Kit paused a moment and said a quick prayer of thanks that she was so comfortable with this woman. "Just thinking that it's hard to get much motivation to do anything with Gavin gone. There was so much around the house that I would do for him. Now that he's gone, everything I do is just another reminder that he's not here."

"I understand," Sue said. Then, sensing that Kit had more to say, she remained quiet.

"I feel cheated," Kit finally said. "I never got to say everything I wanted to. He was taken so quickly. I keep thinking of so many things I want to tell him or ask him, and I will never get the chance."

"Why not write him a letter?" Sue asked.

Kit gave a short, bitter laugh.

"I'm serious," Sue said.

"But he still won't ever know what I'm thinking," Kit protested.

"How do you know?" Sue asked.

"I don't know anymore," Kit sighed. "I always thought and said to other people who'd lost someone, even when my brother died, I would say something about him watching us from Heaven or riding horses in Heaven. I just don't know now."

"What has changed your mind?" Sue asked.

"I really don't know. I've just found myself thinking negatively when people have made comments about Gavin seeing me from Heaven or doing something he enjoys in Heaven. I wonder why would he want to see me down here depressed and upset when he's in Heaven and there is no sadness? Can he even see me? Is he really up there yet or is he just asleep, and we all get there at the same time? I just don't know anymore."

Sue thought for a long time. "I understand your thinking," she said finally. "I've never really thought about it that way before. That must be very hard and confusing for you."

Kit remained silent, thankful that Sue didn't demean her thoughts.

"If nothing else, writing your thoughts down would help to get them out of your head," Sue said. "This way you're not brooding over it. Just a thought." Sue kissed her daughter-in-law on the forehead then went to bed.

Kit sat at the kitchen table thinking. Finally she went to her room for bed. As she got in to bed, she had a nagging feeling that

Sue might be right. Throwing the covers off, she went to the writing desk and turned on her laptop. Sitting down, she began to type.

Dear Gavin,

This seems really silly to write to you since you're gone. However, Mama Sue suggested it might be a good idea, so I'll give it a try. Here goes…

Well, first off, I miss you terribly. You were my best friend. I miss being able to talk to you. I miss being able to sit in silence with you. I miss your encouragement. You always were supportive of me, no matter what. When my parents basically disowned me, you were right there to hold me. You were so encouraging when I wanted to learn more about the ranch business. Thank you for teaching me so much. It has truly helped since you've been gone. I miss your strength. You were the strongest person I knew. I know now where you got it from. Your mother is amazing. She's grieving herself, yet she always takes time to help me through my grief, Carmen also, when she's around. Physically, you were strong as well. I don't know how you did so much around the ranch. I've gained a new appreciation for you since I've started doing more with the cattle. Thank you for believing in me. Thank you for leading me. You helped give me a good foundation with Christ that I feel able to learn more about him and get to know him more on my own now…

Kit wrote and wrote and wrote. She was hardly aware of time. When she finished her letter, it was well past midnight. She had been writing, thinking, crying, laughing for over three hours.

"Mama Sue was right," she thought. "I do feel a lot better."

When Kit woke the next morning, she felt more refreshed than she had since Gavin's death.

"You were right, Mama Sue," she said at the breakfast table. "I wrote Gavin a letter last night, and I feel so much better. Whether

Gavin will ever know of this or not, I do. It's so nice not to carry that burden anymore. I truly feel as if it has been lifted from me. I'm sorry I doubted you."

Sue just smiled and said, "I'm glad you feel better, dear."

"Now that I've expressed what I wanted to Gavin, how do I express what I feel to God?" Kit asked. "I don't question his goodness. I know he's good. I don't question why this happened. I know I will never know this side of Heaven. Am I just supposed to accept it, move on, and be okay with it? I don't think I can do that."

Sue took her coffee cup out of the microwave and sat down at the table. "I struggled with that as well, when Jonathan died. I think there is a difference between accepting and being okay with it. I don't think we need to be okay with it. God made us human with human feelings. Jesus even wept when his best friend died."

"Yeah, but he brought his best friend back to life," Kit countered. "We're not getting any of that."

Sue smiled. "True, but I believe that story was showing the human side of Jesus. God never wanted death to happen. He knew it would because he knew the choice Adam and Eve would make, but death saddens him as well, I believe. So, it's alright for us to be sad and grieve the loss of our loved ones. So, I don't think we need to be okay with it.

"Now, accepting is a different story. I believe acceptance means acknowledging that it happened, letting God know we don't like it, but being willing to do what he wants us to with it. Does that make sense?"

Kit thought for a moment. "Yes, it actually makes a lot of sense. It takes a lot of burden off us as well."

"That's what God wants," Sue said. "He didn't create us to be alone. Whether or not we marry again, or someone marries at all, God wants to commune with us. He created us to be with him. He wants to love us. He gave us the choice to choose him or not, but he wants us to choose him. He doesn't want us to go through life alone and miserable. He wants to take the burden for us. It doesn't mean that life will be happy all the time, or ever. But he does guarantee us his joy and life with him in Heaven."

"Thank you, Mama Sue. God sure has blessed me with you."

"And me with you, dear."

―――

"Christmas will be hard this year," Kit said one evening as she and Sue were cleaning up from dinner. They had both thought this, but neither had made the comment yet.

They had celebrated Thanksgiving with the ranch hands as usual. It was difficult, but they had busied themselves enough that neither thought much about it during the day. Christmas would be a different affair. They usually spent this holiday with just their family. They gave the ranch hands the two days off to spend with their families. This year, it would just be Sue and Kit.

"Yes it will," Sue agreed.

"How did you handle your first Christmas without Jonathan?" Kit asked.

"It was hard," Sue answered, "but I had my boys to help me through." Sue wiped a tear from her cheek.

After a long pause Kit said, "We'll be here to help each other through this year."

"You don't want to do Christmas with your family?" Sue asked cautiously.

Kit suppressed a bitter laugh. "No, Mama Sue, I don't. My parents have all but disowned me. They didn't call for Thanksgiving or for Gavin's birthday. They haven't offered any help with the ranch, though they have much more experience than I do. You're closer family than they are. I want to stay here with you."

"I would love to spend the Lord's Day with you, dear," Sue said, placing a reassuring hand on her arm.

Kit laid down the towel she was using to dry the dishes and sighed. "This is really hard."

"I know, dear," Sue answered.

"I mean it's hard enough to have lost my husband, but to have my own parents not show any support…" Kit let her voice trail off. Sighing, she continued, "I'm just so grateful for you, Mama Sue."

Kit gave her mother-in-law a hug.

"As I am for you," Sue said through tears.

They let each other cry as much as they each needed to, both grateful for the comfort in doing so.

After several minutes of tears, the two wiped their eyes.

Kit said, "Why don't we do something special this year for Christmas?"

"Like what?" Sue asked.

"I don't know," Kit said thoughtfully. "I know we can't leave the ranch since the hands will all be gone. Perhaps we could try new recipes for the Christmas feast."

"We could make handmade decorations for the house," Sue said.

"That would be fun," Kit said.

They finished cleaning the kitchen as they began to make plans for Christmas, two weeks away. Looking online, they found new recipes and fun decorations to make.

The next two weeks they tried to ease their grief by putting their energy into Christmas. They planned the Christmas dinner for the evening of Christmas Day, so Carmen could join them since she would spend Christmas morning with her family.

As the day came around, Kit actually felt herself getting excited. Christmas had always been her favorite holiday. She and Gavin had loved buying gifts for each other and their families as well as cooking for the family feast and decorating the house. She tried to honor his memory by putting energy into the preparations. She and Sue actually found themselves smiling and laughing more often than not.

"This was a great idea," Sue said the night before Christmas Eve. "I think it really helped us both through part of our grief this season."

"I agree," Kit said.

The next evening, the two women dressed up for their church's Christmas Eve service. Bundled in their warmest coats, they headed to church. They were greeted by friends and candle light as they entered the sanctuary.

Each shed a few tears at the knowledge they were spending their first Christmas without Gavin and Carter, but they both enjoyed the service.

"That really was beautiful," Sue said on the way home.

"It was," Kit agreed. "I love how they decorate the sanctuary with candles instead of turning the lights on. It makes it feel more intimate and comfortable."

"And the music was beautiful," Sue continued. "I love the acoustic piano and guitar for this service."

Kit agreed.

When they reached home, each said good night and went to sleep, praying for a peaceful sleep.

The next morning, Kit slept in. She woke up to the smell of bacon and eggs. After cleaning up and dressing, she headed to the kitchen. "How early did you get up?" she asked smiling, knowing Mama Sue never slept in. "And why didn't you wake me?"

"I got up at my usual time," Sue answered returning the smile. "And I wanted you to sleep as long as you needed to. I checked the cattle and fed them, so there's not much to do now."

"You shouldn't have done that alone," Kit chastised, noting the steady snow falling outside.

"I was fine," Sue said. "I took my phone with me and would have called you if I needed to, but I didn't, so don't worry about it, and come and eat."

Kit smiled at her mother-in-law. This woman had been more of a mother to her than her own mother ever had. Sue accepted her for who she was, but wasn't above giving her opinion when she felt it needed to be shared. She was loving and kind. Kit did as she was told.

"Wonderful breakfast, as usual," Kit said, as she buttered a biscuit.

"I love cooking and thought I'd just get started for the day," Sue answered.

"Well, we have a lot of cooking to do for today," Kit said.

They finished their breakfast and cleaned up while talking cheerily. Each shared memories as they came, and neither requested the other to stop. They felt comfortable sharing memories and thoughts about their departed loved ones.

The rest of the day, they cooked and cleaned and set out their home made decorations.

"It seems silly to go through all this work when it's just the three of us here tonight," Sue said.

"I agree, but I think it's helpful," Kit replied.

When Carmen arrived, she made excited comments about the food and the decorations. She also brought food to share as well as gifts.

The three enjoyed the others' company and had a peaceful, comfortable meal. After dinner was finished and cleaned up, they all went to the living room and sat near the fire place.

"I have something I would like to talk with you both about," Sue said.

"What is it?" Carmen asked.

Sue took a deep breath and looked in the fire. Kit and Carmen looked at each other. It wasn't like Sue to not look them in the eye when she talked. They each sensed something was wrong.

"Are you alright?" Kit asked when Sue didn't speak for several moments.

Sue took a deep breath. "Yes, dear, I'm fine. It's just not an easy thing to tell you."

Kit and Carmen waited as Sue gathered her strength to speak.

"I have decided to move back to Kansas City," Sue said finally.

No one spoke for several minutes.

Finally, Sue spoke again. "I'm sorry I made this decision without you both. I still have the apartment in the city. I don't foresee myself remarrying again. I have some family and friends still in Kansas City, so I will have a support network there. Though you might not want to think about it now, I'm sure the two of you will remarry someday. Your families and friends are here. I'm sure you will be fine. You're doing fine with the ranch. You don't need me."

Kit and Carmen were stunned. First they lost their husbands, now they were losing a woman who had been like a mother to them both.

"I will go with you," Kit said.

"I will, too," Carmen said, though with less conviction than her sister-in-law.

Sue smiled. "That's very kind, but your lives are here. It would be silly."

"Are you sure?" Carmen asked. "I will go if you need me to."

"Thank you, dear, but no. You stay here. In fact, it's starting to snow harder, you'd better get heading home now. I won't be leaving for a month, so we'll see each other before then."

"Are you sure?" Carmen asked again.

"Yes, dear," Sue said.

Sue got Carmen's coat from the closet and gave her a hug. Kit hugged her as well, and they watched her walk through the snow to her car. They stayed at the window until they could no longer see her tail lights.

Sue turned worried eyes on her daughter-in-law. "You've not said much."

"I want to go with you," Kit said determinedly.

"Your life is here," Sue said weakly.

"You know it's not," Kit said. "I'm basically estranged from my family. I can't run the ranch on my own. It wouldn't be safe for me here with a bunch of ranch hands anyway; no matter how nice they are. I'll sell my part of the ranch to Carmen and come with you to Kansas City."

"Are you sure?" Sue asked.

"You are my family," Kit answered. "Where you go, I will go. Your people will be my people. You've already taught me about your God. No one in my family believes in God. It would be so difficult to be here without you. I want to go with you. Please don't tell me no."

Sue smiled at her daughter-in-law. Never having daughters of her own, Kit had always felt like a true daughter. She pulled Kit in to a hug. "I would love it if you came with me."

Chapter 3

One month turned into six as Kit and Carmen convinced their mother-in-law to stay through calving season and to help sell their husbands' ranch. "After all," Kit had reasoned, "it first belonged to your husband."

Finally, after the last calf was born and the prospective buyer in place, Kit and Sue packed up their belongings, said tear-filled good-byes to Carmen, and headed for Kansas City. They had decided to drive Kit's SUV and have Jake, who was driving the moving van, tow Sue's sedan. This way the move seemed to go easier on the two women.

They stopped in Denver for a night and resumed their travels the next day. Kit was unimpressed with her first views of Kansas. "Flat," was how she described it. "At least Montana has some hills."

Sue laughed, "Don't worry, dear, it gets better."

Kit felt easier as they drove through the Flint Hills. Sue took them on a detour off I-70 through Lawrence, which Kit thoroughly enjoyed, then they headed to Kansas City.

Sue and Jonathan had kept their apartment on the Plaza and had vacationed there often. Kit was impressed when she first set foot in the spacious place. Though, not as spacious as her former ranch home, she thought it cozy and comfortable.

"Well, what do you think?" Sue asked.

"I love it!" Kit answered.

"I know it doesn't have the spacious country that you're used to," Sue began.

Kit put a hand on her arm. "I'm fine, Mama Sue. It's lovely."

Sue smiled a thankful smile at her daughter-in-law.

———

Two months later, Sue came home from lunch to find Kit in her usual spot by the front bay window looking out over the Plaza.

"Good afternoon, dear," Sue said.

"Hello, Mama Sue," Kit answered.

"Are you feeling well?"

"Oh yes, just thinking."

"What about?"

"Well," Kit began, "I'm actually feeling a little bored."

"Really?" Sue asked.

"Yes," Kit answered. "I'm used to helping out on the ranch, whether it be out in the field with the cattle or with the books. I'm feeling a little useless here."

"You know you don't have to work, though," Sue said. "Our financial advisor invested our money in the stocks, and it's looking well. Plus the sale of the ranch will soon bring more money in."

"I know, I just want to do something to feel useful. All I do now is just sit around here and miss Gavin." Kit said.

"It's interesting you should say that, dear," Sue said, coming to sit by Kit.

"How so?" Kit asked.

"Well, I was talking with my cousin, Jane, at lunch today and she said that her son, Emmett, just lost his assistant. Apparently, she was supposed to just take maternity leave, but decided a week before it was over that she didn't want to come back. So, he's without an assistant for his catering business. I mentioned to Jane that you had quite a bit of experience with books and things and might be interested in the job. She gave me Emmett's card, if you'd like to call."

Kit's face lit up. "Oh thank you, Mama Sue! I should have known you'd know what I was thinking."

Sue handed Kit the business card, and Kit ran to the phone to make the call.

"Hello?" the voice answered.

"Hello," Kit said. "My name is Kit Elliott. My mother-in-law is Sue Elliott-"

"Yes, of course!" the voice interrupted excitedly. "Mrs. Elliott, I'm so glad you called. This is Emmett Williams. My mother, Jane, is Sue's cousin. She told me of their conversation at lunch. I must tell you, you are a godsend for calling, if you want the job. When can you start?"

"I'm sorry?" Kit stammered. "What did you say?"

"Forgive me, I hurried too fast, I do that often," Emmett said. "Let me back up, and slow down. My assistant was on maternity leave and decided to remain home with her daughter instead of returning to work. I just found this out two days ago. I have three major parties coming up in the span of two weeks, plus interviewing new clients. I need an assistant. Mom told me about your background with your ranch and how your late husband, so sorry for your loss, by the way, had you learn the books and everything. I don't have time right now for an interview. Would you be interested in trying the job for a few days to see if it's a match for you?"

Kit felt speechless, but she cleared her throat to answer him. "Yes, sir, I would very much like to try the job. I could start tomorrow, if you'd like."

"Wonderful! Do you know where my office is?"

"I believe you're near the Plaza, is that correct?" Kit asked.

"Yes, just south. Perfect! I hate to run, but I'm late for a meeting with a client. I'll see you tomorrow morning at nine o'clock sharp!"

With that, he hung up the phone. Kit slowly pushed the off button on the phone and stared at Sue.

"Well," she said, "I have a job."

"Wonderful!" Sue said. "I think you will enjoy it. Emmett's a nice man, and his catering business does very well. It will be fun for you."

"Thanks, Mama Sue."

The next day, Kit rose early and took her time getting ready. It was a crisp October day, so she thought she'd walk to the E.W. Catering office. She breathed in the fall air and enjoyed looking at the trees just beginning to turn colors.

At five minutes till nine, she opened the door and stepped into the office. It was nicely decorated displaying pictures of the city. The receptionist at the desk took her name and asked her to wait for Mr. Williams.

A few minutes later, a tall, casually-dressed man with dark, mussed hair entered the waiting area, said a few words to the receptionist, and turned to Kit.

"Good morning, Mrs. Elliott. I'm Emmett Williams. Thank you so much for coming in. Please follow me, and we'll get started."

Kit immediately liked this man. He seemed genuinely kind and happy. He walked fast and talked faster. He seemed organized yet frazzled. He talked as he led her through the hall to her new office. She did her best to keep up with him.

"Well, here we are," he said. "This will be your office. The files for our customers are in that file cabinet. I don't know how Olivia had them. I'm sorry, but I believe she was a little disorganized. Feel free to organize them however you can access them best. I'm often needing former files for ideas of similar menus. These three files here," he pointed to three files on her desk, "are the upcoming events. We have the Goldberg bar mitzvah, the Lyndon wedding, and the Gray family reunion. They are all happening within two weeks of each other. I need you to go over the requests, and make sure we have everything needed for the menus. Order what we don't have. Here's the rolodex of our vendors. Then, make sure we have all of the correct place settings. Contact the event sites to make sure staffing is available."

He continued to list out what he wanted Kit to do. Kit wrote as quickly as she could.

"Any questions?" He asked, when he finally finished.

Kit had a few, which he answered easily.

"I think I've got it," Kit said confidently.

"If you have any questions, I'm just next door," he shook her hand and left.

Kit looked around her new office feeling a little overwhelmed. "Well," she said to herself, "I'd better get to it."

She looked at the upcoming event files and saw many notes saying see another file for menu options. Looking in the file drawer gave her no help. The filing system was completely unorganized. Taking out a pen and paper from the desk drawer, she quickly wrote out a "to do" list. Then, starting at the top, she got to work. After finally locating the menu files, she made a trip to the kitchen and, with the head chef, checked off all of the ingredients in stock. Then, she made phone calls to the vendors to order the remaining ingredients. Next, she went to the supply room and talked with the head of that department about what utensils they had for each event. Then, she called the event sites and made arrangements with them for staffing and other necessities. She also called the florists to make sure everything matched E.W. Catering for the decorations.

By the end of this, she was exhausted. It was almost five o'clock, and she still wanted to tackle the filing cabinet. At six o'clock, a knock sounded on her door. She was sitting in the middle of the office with files in a circle around her. Not able to get up without stepping on files, she called, "Come in!"

Emmett Williams opened the door and laughed. "I'm thinking I liked the old filing system better."

Kit smiled nervously. "I'm just trying to figure out where everything is and what to do with it all."

Emmett smiled at her nervousness. "You know, I do the same thing. Only I usually do it after everyone's left, so they don't see the mess my office gets in."

Kit relaxed and laughed with him.

"You've done a great job today, Mrs. Elliott," he said when their laughter died down. "I'm really impressed. Everyone I've talked with has nothing but good things to say about you. Thank you very much."

"You're welcome, sir," Kit said.

"Please, call me Emmett, everyone else does."

"Alright, please call me Kit."

"I will. Are you leaving soon? You don't have to stay past five," Emmett gestured toward the clock.

"Oh, no!" Kit exclaimed as she jumped up in the middle of her circle of files. "Is it really six? Mama Sue will wonder where I am. I'm sorry. I'll have to finish these tomorrow."

"Not a problem," Emmett said. "Have a good evening. See you tomorrow." Then he left her office.

Kit smiled. She liked this man. He seemed to be a good boss. Sue was right. She also liked this job. "I think I can do this well," she said to herself as she gingerly stepped over the files. Turning off her computer and gathering up her purse and jacket, she left the office.

Chapter 4

"Kit, I need those files immediately!" Emmett snapped as he walked past her office door.

Kit's head jerked up. She was not used to her boss talking like that. Usually he was in a very happy mood. She gathered the files he needed and quickly went to his office.

"Those people will pay me for services!" he said, snatching the files out of her hand. "See? I did do it!" He pointed to the invoice of a party he catered two months prior to her hiring. "These people are trying to swindle me out of my money. Well, I won't hear of it."

He snatched up the phone and began to dial.

"Excuse me, sir," Kit jumped in.

"What?" he snapped.

"Might I help?" Kit offered. "I could call them and request the payment.

Emmett smiled almost patronizingly. "If you think you can deal with them, go for it." He shoved the file back at her. Sitting down behind his desk, he watched her leave his office.

Kit hurriedly went to her office. She had checked over these files many times and knew exactly what to say to the client.

"Hello, Mr. Farber?" she said when the man answered the phone.

"My name is Kit Elliott. I am calling in reference to an unpaid bill to E.W. Catering. I believe we did you a service and were not paid in full for that service."

"The service was not done to my satisfaction," the man said haughtily.

"That was not stated at the time of service, sir. In fact, I have a note here from you saying exactly that you believed the service to be excellent and that you would even recommend our business to anyone else," Kit replied. "Now, do you wish to retract your written statement?"

"Written statement?" the man asked.

"The thank you card you wrote from your daughter's wedding," Kit replied.

"I, uh," he stammered.

"We will be requiring that payment, in full, in cash, by the end of the day, sir."

"Today?"

"Yes, sir," Kit replied. "I really hate dealing with creditors, and I can't imagine you would like it, either. The end of the day, please. Thank you." She hung up the phone before he could say anything else.

"Impressive."

Kit looked up at her office door. Emmett was standing there smiling.

"How long have you been standing there?" Kit asked embarrassed.

"Since, 'hello, Mr. Farber,'" he said smiling. "I thought I ought to listen in and see how you did it. You seemed quite confident. I appreciate you taking this from me. I was not in the right state of mind to be talking to the man. Thank you."

"You're welcome."

"I'm impressed. You seem quite level headed and didn't squirm away from the confrontation either with him or possibly with me. Well done."

"I've had to deal with beef merchants often. Trust me, you and Mr. Farber are easy," Kit laughed.

"Thanks again," Emmett said. "How are things coming for the Goldberg bar mitzvah?"

"Everything is on track," Kit answered. "Jason has done an outstanding job with the menu. The dishes and flatware are already at the site. We have sixteen wait staff. I will be there two hours before."

"Again, I'm impressed," Emmett said, then turned and left for his office.

Kit smiled at the praise from her boss.

———

"What a wedding!" Sydney said.

"You've done an excellent job with the menu," Kit complimented. "They're going to be knocked off their feet!"

"You're good for my ego," Sydney replied.

The two had become friends working the Goldberg bar mitzvah for E.W. Catering. Kit enjoyed the pastry chef.

They stood at the entrance from the kitchen to the ball room as they watched the guests from the Lyndon wedding file in. Kit had never seen such finery and fancy clothes.

"It's almost like a fairy tale," she said.

"I know," Sydney replied. "These high society people really know how to do it right."

The back door to the kitchen opened and in a loud, hissed whisper they heard their boss. "We're short a waiter! I knew something like this would happen. This is our biggest client of the year, and we're short a waiter!"

"Don't worry, sir," Kit said. "I'll handle it." She rushed to the group of wait staff and stood with them awaiting orders from the head waiter.

Emmett just stared after her. "What's she doing?"

"Being a waitress," Sydney answered.

"Does she know how?" Emmett asked.

"We'll find out," Sydney said, then she returned to put the final preparations on the desserts.

Emmett watched as Kit effortlessly fit in with the wait staff. She took orders and flawlessly executed them. He couldn't help but be impressed with this young woman.

———

Kit thoroughly enjoyed waiting on the tables at the wedding. She chatted with the guests when they wanted to talk. She nearly invisibly refilled their glasses and removed their empty plates as they continued their conversations.

The wait staff seemed to improve upon their jobs as they saw their second-in-command working alongside them. The cook staff took note as well. She didn't question them as other waiters did. She took orders in a refined, dignified manner and executed perfection.

Emmett enjoyed watching her work, though he didn't have as much time as he would have liked since he needed to oversee the entire operation. He did notice, though, that the whole event went smoother than events with his previous assistant had.

When the reception was over and the ballroom cleaned up, Kit drove home exhausted. It was well past midnight. She hoped to sneak into the apartment without waking Sue. Gently, she turned the key. She was surprised to see a light on and Sue sitting in the living room.

"Is everything alright, Mama Sue?" Kit asked anxiously.

"Oh, everything's fine, dear," Sue assured. "I just got reading this book and couldn't put it down. Then I finished it about a half hour ago and figured you'd be home within the hour, so I thought I'd wait up for you and see how it went."

Kit smiled. "It was a lot of fun, actually. I got to be a waitress."

"Really? You've never done that before, have you?" Sue asked.

"Nope, but I sure fooled them," Kit laughed. "They all thought I'd waited professionally. I kept telling them I'd just waited on my family and the ranch hands, but they didn't believe me."

"And Emmett?" Sue asked. "What did he think?"

"Well, he was surprised when I filled in for the absent waiter, but he was too busy to take note, I'm sure. I just hope he's not mad that I wasn't helping him otherwise. He didn't say anything about it."

"I'm sure he was fine," Sue said smiling.

"Well, I'm exhausted," Kit said yawning. "I'm going to bed. Good night. Thanks for waiting up."

"Good night, dear."

Chapter 5

"Mrs. Elliott, may I see you in my office, please?"

Kit looked up from her computer and saw Emmett standing in her doorway.

"Yes, sir. I'll be right there." Kit saved the document she was working on and went to Emmett's office.

"I wanted to talk with you about the Lyndon wedding," Emmett said.

Kit was unsure of what he would say. Had she overstepped her bounds by helping the wait staff? Had she missed something she was supposed to help Emmett with? She waited for him to continue.

"I'm very impressed with how you handled it," he said. "Everything went very smoothly. Parts of the event were better than ever before. You have done an exemplary job with everything you've done."

"Thank you," Kit said with a sigh of relief.

"When I hired you last week, we said we would try it for a week and see how you fit. Well, I think you fit amazingly well. I'm very impressed with everything. I would like to make your hire official and give you more responsibilities," Emmett said.

"I accept, sir," Kit said smiling. "I've really enjoyed working with you and your staff."

"Wonderful," Emmett exclaimed. "Here's the paperwork you need to fill out to make your hire official." He handed her a pen and the paperwork and helped her fill it out.

"Now, we have several events coming up," Emmett said. "Here's a list of what I need done. Please let me know when you have contacted the vendors and finalized the menus. Welcome aboard."

"Thank you," Kit said. She took the list and turned to her office, smiling.

Kit thoroughly enjoyed the tasks she was given. The vendors were pleasant to work with, and she liked the chefs as well. At the end of the day, she walked home with a smile on her face.

"It's so good to see you happy again, dear," Sue said when Kit arrived home.

"I'm really enjoying what I do," Kit answered. "It's nice to work again. The people I work with are great. I'm enjoying the city much more than I thought I would."

"Wonderful!" Sue exclaimed and hugged her daughter-in-law.

———

A month later, Kit was working in her office when Emmett appeared in her doorway.

"Kit," he said as he sat down in the chair opposite her desk. Kit had become used to the informality around the office. She was glad her employer felt comfortable talking in her office instead of the formality of his. "We have a new account that I believe I have you to thank for."

"What is it?" Kit asked, curious.

"It's a wedding," Emmett said. "The client is Mr. Edward Waggoner. He's a well-known art dealer in town. He's the biggest client we've ever had."

"That's wonderful!" Kit exclaimed. "But what do I have to do with it? I've never met or even heard of this man."

"Oh, but you have," Emmett said. "Remember the Lyndon wedding? Your first wedding with us?"

"Yes," Kit remembered well the wedding she helped the wait staff with a month prior.

"One of the tables you helped was this man's family," Emmett explained. "He was so impressed with your service and the food that he wants us to cater his daughter's wedding."

"That's wonderful!" Kit said again. "But it's not entirely due to me. Your menu and kitchen staff, and all you did to put the whole event together, was incredible."

"You are modest," Emmett said with a smile. "When he called, he talked mostly about you. When I told him you were my second-in-command, he was even more impressed."

"Thank you," Kit said shyly.

"Thank you," Emmett said smiling. "Now, here's a list of everything I need you to do for this wedding. If you need anything, just ask."

Kit thanked him again and watched as he left for his office.

———

Walking home that evening, Kit found herself whistling in the crisp November air. She smiled to herself as she approached the apartment complex.

"You're in an especially good mood today," Sue said as Kit entered the kitchen.

"It's been a wonderful day!" Kit exclaimed. "Emmett came to my office today and assigned me a lot of duties for his biggest client ever! I'm so excited to begin working with this family. They seem so nice on the phone."

"Who is the family?" Sue asked.

"The Edward Waggoner family," Kit answered. "I've never heard of them, but apparently they are well-to-do."

"He's an art dealer in town," Sue said. "He's very influential with the arts and other aspects of the town. Well done, dear."

"Thank you," Kit said modestly.

"So you really are enjoying it here?" Sue asked hopefully.

"I am," Kit said. "I was unsure when we first moved, but since I've really felt that I've found my place here with work and church, I really do like it here."

"No regrets?"

"No regrets," Kit smiled. Then her smile faded. "I do wonder if I did the right thing, though, since the sale of the ranch is still pending. It's been a long time."

"I know," Sue agreed. "I'm a bit concerned as well, but God will provide."

"But how long can we still make payments on both the ranch and the apartment?" Kit asked.

"We're fine, dear," Sue answered. "We can always take money out of our stocks, if we need to. We might need to do that sooner rather than later, but we still have some time."

Kit eased a bit at her mother-in-law's encouragement and reassurance.

The two continued chatting as they prepared dinner.

———

The next few weeks flew by quickly. Kit and Sue were invited to Jane's house for Thanksgiving. Emmett was present for the holiday gathering. Kit enjoyed watching her employer care for his aging parents and play with his growing nieces and nephews.

After Thanksgiving dinner, Emmett invited Kit to view the lighting of the Plaza Christmas lights. They stood out in the cold with the crowds for hours waiting for the event to happen.

"You're not too cold, are you?" Emmett asked.

Kit smiled. "I'm from Montana. This isn't cold!"

Emmett smiled through his chattering teeth.

Kit laughed.

When the announcer came over the loud speaker, a hush fell over the crowd. He announced the special guest who would be flipping the switch to begin the Plaza holiday season. All of a sudden, the lights were on.

Kit stood in awe as the crowd cheered.

"Do you like it?" Emmett asked.

"This is incredible," she said. "I'm used to wide open spaces, and this is just amazing. It's so beautiful."

"I'm glad you like it," Emmett said.

The two decided to find a coffee shop to warm Emmett's freezing fingers. They stayed out late just talking.

"So, tell me about Gavin," Emmett said.

"Really?"

"I'd like to know about him."

"Thank you for asking," Kit said sincerely. "He was a great man. He was fun. He loved to joke around, yet he could be intensely serious when the need arose. He was a very godly man, though he had his faults. He was a hard worker, yet always had time for me. He was my best friend. He and Mama Sue led me to Jesus, and I'm forever grateful to them."

"He sounds like a wonderful man," Emmett said. "You're lucky to have found him."

"I know," Kit said.

"Thank you for telling me."

"Thank you for asking. Many people don't know if they should bring him up or say anything. I like to talk about him. Sometimes it feels as if people want to forget him, but I don't. I know I'll move on someday, but he will always be a part of my life."

Emmett reached across the table and squeezed her hand. "I'm glad you had him."

Kit smiled back at him.

Chapter 6

December flew by in a flurry of activity along with drifts of snow. Kit tromped her way through the snow to the office the week before Christmas. Stomping the snow off her boots, she smiled at the familiar sight of Emmett shoveling the snow along the sidewalk in front of the building.

"Can I help you with that?" Kit asked, knowing his distaste for cold weather.

"I'm f-f-fine, th-th-thanks," Emmett chattered.

Kit laughed and took the shovel from him. "Go get some coffee and get warmed up."

Emmett knew better than to argue. They'd had the same conversation for the past week.

"It really doesn't snow like this every year," he said. "I can't remember a winter like this one."

"I must have brought it with me," Kit said. "You really ought to wait for me to get here to start the shoveling. I know you hate it. You know I enjoy it. Why bother with it?"

"I feel it my manly duty to at least try," Emmett tried to sound gallant in his explanation.

Kit only laughed in her response.

"I guess it just makes me look silly, huh?"

"I love to laugh," Kit replied with a smile. "It's a great way to start the day."

Emmett laughed with her, then turned and went inside to get warmed up.

Later that day, Emmett stopped by Kit's office. "You're coming to the Christmas party, right?"

"I wouldn't miss it," Kit said enthusiastically. "I've heard it's a blast!"

"It usually is," Emmett smiled. He loved throwing parties, especially for his staff. The Christmas party was a big ordeal within the company. "Don't forget your wine for the wine exchange."

"I've already got mine," Kit said. "Mama Sue and I went wine tasting at a few little wineries around the area last weekend. I found some great stuff. I made sure to get double so I'd get some, too."

"Good idea," Emmett said laughing.

"By the way," Kit said, "I've been meaning to tell you how impressed and thankful I am that you give the staff the Christmas week off."

"Christmas is such a special time for me and most people," Emmett explained. "I just didn't think it was fair to make my staff work so others could play."

"That's very generous of you. But don't you lose some big business that way?"

"Some, but not much. We really have a good reputation around town, that people still call us for other bigger events. That makes up for any loss we might have had over Christmas."

"Good," Kit said. "Is your family still coming over for Christmas dinner?"

"Wouldn't miss it," Emmett said. "Sue says you're an excellent cook. I'm excited to check it out."

"Well, I'm nothing like the chefs you have here," Kit said modestly. "I do alright."

"I'm looking forward to it," Emmett said and smiled.

———

The Christmas party was everything everyone had said about it. Emmett had rented out a ballroom in a nearby hotel. He catered the event himself. The music was lively and everyone had a great time.

Kit danced most of the night until her feet hurt. Finally she had to sit down. Emmett came and sat next to her.

"Tired already?" he asked.

"Well, it is nearly midnight," Kit answered. "My carriage is about to turn into a pumpkin, you know."

They laughed and enjoyed watching the staff loosen up and have fun.

"You really do a wonderful job with the staff," Kit complimented.

"They're a great staff to work with," Emmett replied.

"They are," Kit agreed, "but you really do a wonderful job with them. They respect you. It's hard to find that nowadays."

"Thank you," Emmett answered.

They talked some more and were joined by other staff members. Finally, about two hours later, the staff began to thin out and go home.

"Well, about time to clean up," Emmett said.

"You didn't even hire someone to help with the clean up?" Kit asked.

"Don't usually," Emmett said.

Kit didn't reply. She admired this man. Most bosses were not this willing to get on the level of their employees. She stayed and helped clean as well.

"You don't have to stay, if you don't want to," Emmett said.

"If you don't mind the company, I'd like to stay," Kit answered.

"I'd love your company," Emmett said.

Kit just smiled, not missing his words.

Emmett kept the music playing as they cleaned up.

"I love Christmas music," Kit said. "It's so peaceful and joyful."

"'Tis the season," Emmett said.

"You know," Kit said hesitantly, "in a way, you remind me of Gavin."

"I'll take that as a compliment," Emmett said.

"It is. You're not a whole lot like him, but he did the same with the ranch hands for Christmas as you do with the staff. He let them have a few days off at Christmas, even though it meant that he had to take care of the whole herd himself. Mama Sue and I helped out."

"What about his brother?" Emmett asked.

"Carter helped some too," Kit said.

They continued cleaning in silence for a while. Soon, "O Holy Night" came over the speakers. Without thinking, Kit began singing. Her rich soprano voice filled the ballroom. On the second verse, Emmett joined her. Kit was amazed at his full baritone voice, but kept singing. The two sang in perfect harmony until the song ended.

When the music was over, they remained silent for a few moments.

"That was beautiful," Emmett said. "You really have a lovely voice."

"Thank you," Kit said shyly. "I used to sing at church, but just haven't had the heart to sing since Gavin died." Then she added hesitantly, "Until now."

"Thank you for sharing it with me," Emmett said.

"My pleasure," Kit said. "Thank you for sharing your voice with me."

"My pleasure," Emmett smiled.

"Merry Christmas!"

"Merry Christmas!"

Kit watched happily from the kitchen as Sue greeted her cousin and family for the holiday meal. Though their small gathering of five – Kit, Sue, Jane, Jane's husband Sam, and Emmett—seemed happy, Kit couldn't help but remember Christmas past. She smiled as she thought of the ranch and their small family. Gavin would get up early to tend to the cattle. Kit and Sue would make the dinner. Gifts would abound. Everyone would eat too much and laugh until their sides hurt. After cleaning up, they would light the fire and each claim a place on the couch or a chair and take a nap.

Until last year…

"Merry Christmas, Kit," Emmett's voice broke into her thoughts and rescued her from the sadness that would inevitably flood her emotions.

"Merry Christmas, Emmett," Kit smiled back with mixed emotions. She didn't want to forget Gavin. She wanted to grieve appropriately. However, she didn't want to wallow in her sorrow and become depressed. She decided not to analyze it this time and thank God for the day.

"Can I help with anything?" Emmett offered.

"I've really got it under control, unless you're looking for something to do," Kit answered.

"Well, it's either sit here and watch you work, or help you," Emmett said smiling.

"If that's the choices, here," she handed him a stack of plates, "you can start setting the table."

Emmett smiled and took the plates.

For the next half hour, Kit and Emmett chatted and got everything set up for the Christmas dinner.

"Everything looks lovely, dear," Sue said as she, Jane, and Sam came in to eat.

"Thanks," Kit answered. "Emmett did the decorating."

"Wonderful!" Sam said, patting his son on the back.

The small gathering of family and friends sat down together.

"Emmett," Sue said, "would you give the blessing?"

"Sure," Emmett said.

Everyone held hands.

"God," Emmett began, "thank you so much for this day. Thank you for all it means with your Son coming to earth to bridge the gap between us and you. Thank you for his example of humility through the birth in the manger. Thank you for bringing us together with family and good friends. Thank you for this food. Thank you for your saving and continuing grace. Please be with us today as we celebrate you. Amen."

Everyone chorused, "Amen."

"Thank you, Emmett," Sue said.

Emmett nodded.

Kit smiled. She was impressed with her boss and friend. He didn't put on airs with his prayer. It was simple and meaningful. She thanked God for the friendship he had given her with Emmett.

The meal passed happily with laughter and much food. Some memories of past Christmas were shared. Some stories of the past year were told. Everyone enjoyed each others company thoroughly.

When everyone agreed each had had their fill, Emmett announced that he would clean the dishes and sent the others to rest in the living room.

Kit stood up with her plate in hand and followed him to the kitchen.

"I said I would clean up," Emmett said.

"I know, but I will either sit here and watch you or help," Kit said smiling.

Emmett smiled back then threw a dish towel at her. "Well, if that's my choice, you dry."

Kit caught the dish towel and laughed.

The two worked together to get the kitchen put back in order. After a few moments of silence, Emmett spoke up.

"Sue looks well," he said.

"She is well, thanks," Kit answered.

"I mean emotionally," Emmett clarified. "She seems so happy. Is that a front for the guests or is she genuinely happy? I mean she's been through a lot."

Kit thought for a minute. "I believe it's genuine. She's had pain, but she's given it all to God. She trusts him and it shows."

Emmett was silent for a moment. "What about you?" he finally asked.

"What do you mean?"

"Is your peaceful demeanor genuine or a front?"

Again, Kit thought before answering. She didn't think about her answer, but about how she admired this man and appreciated his genuine interest in her and her family. She had seen it with others in the staff as well. "It's genuine," she finally answered.

"How does it happen?" Emmett asked wanting to know. "I've seen other people deal with less than you've had to and they're a wreck. I know you're a Christian, so I can assume its God with you, too. But I've seen Christians fall apart at the drop of a hat. You're not doing that. Why?"

"I don't have any other choice," Kit said simply. "I could go downhill as I see others do. Even my sister-in-law is still deep in depression. To me, that's not a choice. God doesn't want that. He allowed Gavin to die and me to live for a reason. I don't know what the reason is, but I have to trust him. I have others to think about besides myself, so I won't allow myself to drift away from God. I've found the most incredible peace with God and amazing understanding of his grace, that I wouldn't trade it for anything. And if losing my husband is what had to happen to get me there, well… God knows best."

"Do you think that's why Gavin died?" Emmett asked.

"No, I didn't mean that," Kit explained. "I have no idea why Gavin died. I just try to see the positives in all that has happened. I don't want you to think this has been easy, or that I don't miss Gavin. It's been the worst thing ever. I couldn't wish this on my worst enemy. I just try to see what blessings God has for me through this and how I can bless others with my experiences. I believe that God allows things to happen to people who he knows can handle it with his help. So, if it had to happen to someone, well, I guess in a way I should feel blessed God allowed it for me. Sorry, I feel like I'm rambling. These are just thoughts that run through my head when I think about the questions you've asked."

"Thank you for sharing with me," Emmett said sincerely.

"Thank you for asking. I do appreciate it," Kit said.

"What were Christmases like with Gavin?" Emmett asked.

Kit smiled contentedly. She liked the fact that, not only was Emmett not hesitant to ask about Gavin, but he genuinely seemed interested. "Christmases were very nice and relaxed. We had four together before we were married and only two after. As I said before, he would give the ranch hands the day off. He would go out early to take care of the cattle. While his dad was alive, they would work together. Mama Sue and I would get breakfast ready. We would make a light breakfast and begin working on the mid-day feast. The men would run in and out of the kitchen saying they were helping, but really grabbing bites to take back to the living room as they watched football. Dinner was always fun and full of laughter and stories. After dinner, Gavin, Jonathan, and Carter would clean up the kitchen and Mama Sue and I would get the gifts ready. We would sneak a few peaks at some football games as well. Then we'd open gifts and play a game or two, then crash watching more football."

"Sounds a lot like mine growing up," Emmett said. "In fact, it sounds like they are planning what game to play right now."

"Do you like to play games?" Kit asked.

"I do," Emmett answered. "Dad and I get a little competitive, but we'll try to hold it back today."

"Oh don't hold back on my account," Kit said. "I get pretty competitive, myself."

"Really?"

"Oh yeah."

Emmett laughed. "Alright, then, it's on!"

Kit laughed back. She enjoyed the easy laughter that came with her boss. Sometimes she even forgot he was her boss.

"Before we do gifts and games with the others, I'd like to give you your gift," Emmett said.

Kit was taken aback, not expecting a gift. "Only if I can give you yours," she said.

Emmett looked surprised that he would receive one from her, but agreed.

They both left the room to get their respective gifts.

"Oh, how fun!" Kit exclaimed as she took out the contents of the gift basket Emmett handed her. "A Royals hat."

"Which you must wear to opening day," Emmett said. "I always take the staff to opening day every year."

"I can't wait," Kit said. "And a Chiefs scarf."

"Which you can wear proudly this year since it looks like they'll be going to the playoffs."

"A bottle of Gates Bar-B-Que sauce."

"The best in town," Emmett said. "Don't let anyone tell you different."

"Jazz CDs, I love jazz," Kit said.

"These are musicians from Kansas City," Emmett said. "This one is my favorite, Claude 'Fiddler' Williams. He's amazing. You don't think about the violin much when you think about jazz. This man will change your mind."

"Great! And Boulevard beer. Thank you so much!" Kit said excitedly.

"It's all stuff from Kansas City. I wanted you to feel at home here," Emmett said.

"I really appreciate it. I'll fit in now," Kit said as she put the Royals cap and Chiefs scarf on.

"Looks great," Emmett said.

"Now yours," Kit handed him a wrapped package.

"This is heavy," Emmett said. Opening the wrapping, his mouth dropped open and his eyes widened. "You remembered," he said in almost a whisper.

"I did," Kit said.

"How did you remember?"

"I just did," she said. "You told me that some of your favorite memories were travelling south with your father and looking at the Southern architecture. You also said you didn't have a camera then and wished you had. I saw this book in one of the stores on the Plaza and thought it was perfect for you."

"It is," Emmett said excitedly. "Just look at these houses. Oh, and here's Rainbow Row in Charleston! I love it. Thank you so much."

"You're welcome," Kit said.

"Okay kids," Sam called from the living room. "We can't decide, games or gifts? What do you want to do?"

"Let's start with games," Emmett said. "Kit says she gets competitive, too. I want to see this."

"Are you sure?" Sue asked. "You may regret that."

They all laughed and began with a game of hearts.

They played games for the next three hours before deciding to take a break.

"Well, Emmett," Sue asked, "what do you think?"

"You were right. She is competitive."

"Told you," Kit said smugly after winning more than half of the games.

"Next time, you're on my team," Emmett claimed.

"Okay, time for gifts," Jane said.

Everyone oohed and ahhed over the gifts as they were unwrapped for the next hour. Finally time came for the Williams' to go home.

"Thank you for a wonderful Christmas Day," Emmett said. "Have a great week off and we'll see you back after the New Year."

"Thanks," Kit said. "You have a great week as well. Thanks again for the gift basket."

"You're welcome. Good night."

After everyone left, Sue lay down on the recliner and motioned for Kit to have the couch. Kit lay down as well, thankful for the quiet.

"It was a nice day," Sue said.

"Yes it was," Kit answered.

"How are you doing, really?" Sue asked.

Kit paused for a moment. "Better than I thought. This year is a little easier than last year. I think I knew a bit more of what to expect. It helped to be in a different place with a different routine as well. It's almost as if I'm a different person and that part of my life is far behind. I still get sad. I've had my moments today, but it has been easier."

"And having Emmett here didn't hurt either, I'm sure," Sue said.

Kit blushed and turned the question on her mother-in-law. "How about you? You seemed to be enjoying yourself."

"I did, thank you. I really like the Williams'. They kept everything lively. I almost didn't have any chance to think about the boys or Jonathan."

"It was a nice day," Kit repeated.

"Yes it was," Sue replied.

Chapter 7

"Kit, what in the world is this?" Emmett stormed into her office and dropped a box on the chair next to her desk. "Are you kidding me with this?"

Kit had only once before heard Emmett this angry. He had never been angry at her. Her hand started shaking as she moved to open the box. Taking out the teal colored cloth napkin, her face registered shock.

"That's not right, is it?" Emmett said, angrily.

The Waggoner wedding was three days away. They had been working feverishly for the two months after Christmas to get E.W. Catering's biggest event ever exactly perfect for the clients.

"Oh no!" was all Kit could say.

"Oh no is right," Emmett said. "The wedding is only three days away, Kit. How long have you had this box?"

"A week," Kit said, crestfallen.

"A week?" Emmett practically shouted. "You've had this for a week and you haven't opened it?"

"No, sir," Kit said. "They've been our best vendor and we've never had a problem with them before, I didn't think it a high priority."

"What do you think now?"

"Look," Kit said defensively. She was getting tired of her boss's tirade and demeaning comments. "I will fix it."

"How, Kit? We have three days. It will take that long just to get this mess straightened out."

"I said I'll fix it," Kit snapped.

"You have until three o'clock today to fix it," Emmett said, "or you are calling the mother of the bride to explain why the napkins don't match the table cloths that her daughter picked out four months ago!" He stormed back out of the office.

Kit sank down in her chair and put her head in her hands. "Lord," she prayed, "I don't know what happened. I don't know why I didn't check the box. I'm sorry. Please show me what to do. What do you want with this?"

Kit sat in silence. Not hearing anything, she began to cry.

A knock sounded on her door. Grabbing a tissue, she quickly wiped her eyes and nose. "Come in."

Sydney stepped through the door and quickly shut it behind her. "What happened?"

Kit began to cry again. She pointed to the box of napkins. "These are the napkins for the Waggoner wedding. They're teal. They're supposed to be hunter green. I had the box for a week and didn't open it. Emmett is seething. If I don't get this fixed, I'm afraid I'll lose my job."

"You won't lose your job," Sydney said. "We've all messed things up around here more than once. It's just your turn now."

"That's not helpful," Kit said, stifling a laugh between tears.

"We can fix this," Sydney said. "Hunter green, right?"

"Yes," Kit said.

"Follow me."

Kit rose to follow her friend. They went down the hallway to a rarely used part of the building. Sydney opened a closet and began rifling through several boxes. "Here, look through these," she said.

Kit did as she was told. They looked through ten boxes before finding what Sydney was looking for.

"Here!" she exclaimed. "Is this the right color?"

"Oh my goodness, yes it is!" Kit said excitedly. "How many boxes of these are there?"

"Just the one," Sydney said. "Do you need more?"

Kit's heart sank. "Yes, we need three. There will be five hundred guests at this wedding."

The two friends sat on the floor in the middle of boxes and napkins as they thought what to do next.

"Is hunter green the only color for the wedding?" Sydney asked.

"No, white as well," Kit answered.

"Do you have all the white linens you need?"

"I think so."

"Let's go look."

They put the boxes back in the closet and took the hunter green napkins back to Kit's office. Sydney went and picked up the white linens as well. For the next two hours, Kit and Sydney poured over the reception set up to see how they could make work what they had.

"I think you did it," Sydney said happily.

"We did it," Kit said, as she looked again at the drawing. "It's definitely more white than they wanted, but I think it will look elegant. I just hope it will pass Emmett's inspection."

"I wish I could go in there with you," Sydney said supportively.

"If he likes it, I'll give you credit. If not, I'll leave you out of it," Kit said.

Sydney smiled. "If he doesn't like it, I'll go give him what for!"

Kit smiled back. "Thank you so much for your help. I would have been lost without you."

"Any time," Sydney said.

"Well, here I go," Kit said, picking up the drawing and heading to Emmett's office.

Sending up a quick prayer for strength, she knocked purposefully on the door.

"Come in," Emmett said, still sounding angry.

Kit took a deep breath and walked confidently in.

"Do you have it, or are you ready to call Mrs. Waggoner?" Emmett said.

"I think I have it," Kit said, placing the drawing on his desk.

Emmett scoured every detail of the table layout with the descriptions of the napkins, place settings, center pieces, and name tags. "And you have the right colors?"

"Yes, sir," Kit said.

"Where did you find them?"

"Spare closet."

Emmett scanned the drawing again. Leaning back in his chair, he gave a sigh of relief. "You really came through, Kit."

"Sydney was a huge help," Kit said.

"I must admit, I had my doubts on this one," Emmett said. I know you have come through in other situations, I'm sorry I doubted you with this one. Still, you know the importance of checking the inventory the minute it arrives?"

"Yes, sir," Kit said. "It won't happen again."

"This is more white than they originally wanted, you know," Emmett said. Scanning the picture again he added, "I like it this way better. It's more elegant. Nice work."

"Thank you. Again, though, I didn't do it alone. Sydney helped."

Emmett smiled at her desire to give credit where it was due. "She did a nice job, too. What are you working on the rest of the day?"

"Just checking everything else for the Waggoner wedding. Anything else you'd like me to do?"

"That's perfect," Emmett said. "Thank you."

Kit smiled and left for her office. Once behind the closed door, she slid to the floor and her hand began to shake.

"Everything okay?" Sydney asked.

"Yes," Kit said relieved. "He said you did a nice job, too."

"Thanks," Sydney said and lay down on the floor. "How silly it seems that something like the wrong color of napkins should be such a big deal."

"I know," Kit said, "but that's the world we live in with this business."

"Well, if I ever get that uptight about napkin color, just slap me," Sydney laughed.

"Can I do that if the icing color doesn't come out perfect?" Kit said laughing back.

———

"Mr. Williams, this is not the layout we had discussed."

"I know, Mrs. Waggoner," Emmett said.

"The wedding is tomorrow, Mr. Williams, why are you changing things on us now? You are not holding up to your reputation."

"I'm sorry, Mrs. Waggoner."

"The mix-up was my fault, Mrs. Waggoner," Kit said, knowing she needed to take the blame for her mistake and not let Emmett suffer for it. "I received the wrong color linens and needed to make a few changes."

"This is more than a few changes, Mrs. Elliott," Mrs. Waggoner said disappointedly.

"I know, I am sorry. I-"

"I think it's lovely, Mother," Elaine Waggoner jumped in. "It's so much more elegant than what I had picked out."

"You really don't mind, dear?"

"Not at all, Mother."

Mrs. Waggoner seemed to be debating within herself.

Elaine put a hand on her mother's shoulder. "It's my wedding, Mother. I like it. I really think it will be fine. No one will even notice. You and I are the only ones who know the original design. I really like this one better."

"Alright, if you like it, I like it."

"Thank you, Mother."

The two women left the ballroom in search of the florist.

"You didn't have to do that," Emmett said.

"Yes I did," Kit answered. "It was my fault. Your name is on the business. You have a reputation to uphold. You don't need to suffer for my mistake."

"Thank you," Emmett said sincerely. "I'm glad she liked it."

"Me too," Kit said emphatically.

"You wouldn't have lost your job, you know," Emmett assured.

"Really?"

"Really," Emmett said. "We've all made mistakes. It was just your turn."

Kit groaned. "That's what Sydney said."

"She was right. You know, once, when I was just starting out, I booked two weddings in the same hotel on the same day. I royally mixed them up. I had the food for one wedding with the place settings for the other and vice versa. Fortunately, an hour before the weddings, the brother of the groom came in for one wedding to sneak a taste of the food and kindly questioned me on my thought process for serving ham at his brother's Jewish wedding. Needless to say, we were sweating by the time the receptions started. I have vowed never again to take more than one event on the same day."

"Oh no!" Kit laughed. "That's awful! I'm glad to know why we've turned down multiple events on the same day."

Emmett laughed with her.

The rest of the reception went off without a hitch. The mother of the bride even came up to Kit and Emmett afterward to thank them for a beautiful job well done.

Chapter 8

"Do you want a hot dog? I'm headed up," Emmett asked Kit.

"No thanks, I'm still working on this," Kit pointed to her concessions. Opening Day had finally arrived. Kit and the staff were grateful. Not only did they get a day off to just enjoy each other, but their boss would finally stop talking about it.

After the Waggoner wedding, their other events were much smaller and easier, thus giving Emmett time to check up on his favorite baseball team. Every day he would come in with some new statistic or news report about the Royals.

"This is going to be their year! I can feel it!" he would say.

Kit had to laugh. If she thought he was like a kid in a candy store leading up to Opening Day, he was like a kid having just eaten the candy store at the game. He drove her to the game two hours early so they could watch batting practice. He took her all over the stadium explaining the history and updates added just a few years prior.

He was most excited in the Hall of Fame built in the outfield. He showed her all of the pictures and related many memories of past players he'd seen and even met.

Kit especially enjoyed the fountains. They were a beautiful display in between innings and during Royals home runs, which they had already scored two by the sixth inning.

"So, is it worth putting up with his antics for the month leading up to this?" Sydney asked, as she moved into Emmett's seat next to Kit.

"It really is," Kit said excitedly. "This is fun. I've never been to a real baseball game before. I've watched them on TV, but we weren't close to any professional teams in Montana. This is great."

"I'm glad you enjoy it," Sydney said. "This is one of the highlights of our spring quarter. Emmett usually tries to do something each quarter or season to keep the staff close together and relaxed."

"I've already experienced the Christmas party and this. What's next?" Kit asked.

"In the summer, we go to a lake and have a cook out. Some people stay and camp. In the fall, he takes us all to a University of Kansas football game. Not everyone is a fan of KU here, but we enjoy the tailgate and the game anyway."

"That's really great that he does so much for the staff," Kit said with admiration for her boss. She had always liked him, but knowing what he did to help the staff feel close together and relax, made her appreciate him more. It was another thing that reminded her of Gavin. He always tried to keep the ranch hands close together and enjoying each other's company. He would have loved this game.

Kit shook her head to remove the feeling of sadness that waved over her at the thought of her late husband. The thoughts were still there daily, but sometimes the grief was more intense than others, and she never knew when it would hit.

"You okay?" Sydney asked.

"Yeah, thanks," Kit answered.

"Comin' through," Emmett called. Sydney moved over, and he sat down. "Here, try this." He handed her a cold container.

"What's this?" Kit asked.

"Chocolate malt. Every stadium has their trademark concessions. You've already tasted the Gates BBQ. Now it's time for ice cream."

"I eat it with this? What is it, a piece of bark?"

Emmett laughed. "It's a flat wooden spoon. I don't know why it's not a regular spoon. Just eat."

"It's a bit chilly for ice cream, don't you think?" Kit asked.

"You're chilly now?" Emmett teased. "Are you getting used to our weather, Miss Montana?"

Kit gave him a defiant look and devoured the chocolate malt. When she was finished, her teeth were chattering and Emmett was laughing.

———

"What do you want to do now?" The game was over, the Royals had won, and Emmett was literally bouncing in excitement.

"I've never seen you like this before," Kit exclaimed.

"I love baseball," Emmett explained. "I get excited."

"I can tell," Kit laughed.

They were walking to Emmett's car. Kit was walking forward and Emmett was walking backward since, in his excitement, he was walking faster than Kit.

"So," he said. "What do you want to do now?"

"What is there to do?" Kit asked.

"Let's go to the Power and Light district."

"Okay, and do what?"

"I don't know, just walk around. Maybe have dinner."

"Alright, I'm game," Kit said as they reached the car. Emmett opened her door for her then got in on his side.

As they reached the Power and Light district, finding a parking spot was harder than they expected.

"Looks like everyone else at the game had the same idea," Kit said.

"Don't worry, we'll find something," Emmett said undaunted.

Soon, he did find a place right in front of a restaurant. "Let's walk around and then eat here."

"Sounds good," Kit said.

They walked around, and he pointed out some of the landmarks downtown. "There's the Sprint Center. Sometime I'll take you there when a really good concert is coming."

"I'd love that," Kit said.

After a few more moments, Emmett slowed down. "Are you okay," Kit asked.

"I'm fine," he answered. "Are you alright with this?"

"What do you mean?" Kit asked confused.

"I mean walking around here just the two of us and going to dinner. Is that too weird?"

"Not for me. Is it for you?"

He visibly relaxed. "No, I'm really enjoying spending time with you."

"Me too," Kit said.

"I hope this doesn't make things weird at the office," Emmett said.

"I don't think it should," Kit said.

"Okay, good," Emmett said. They finished the tour of the Power and Light district and ended up back at the restaurant by the car.

After dinner, Emmett drove Kit back to her apartment.

"Thanks for a great day," Kit said. "I really enjoyed it all."

"I'm glad you liked it. I did too."

"See you tomorrow."

"Bye."

Emmett watched Kit walk to her apartment and wave to show she had gotten inside. "Okay, Lord," he prayed. "What now? I really like this woman. Please show me what you want."

Chapter 9

"Mama Sue?" Kit called as she returned from work one day in May. "Are you home?"

Sue came from her room with eyes swollen from crying.

Kit dropped her purse and ran to her mother-in-law. "What's the matter?" she asked, as she lead Sue to the kitchen table and fixed her a cup of tea.

Sue sniffled a few times and took a deep breath. "I have some bad news, dear."

"I can tell that," Kit said. "What is it?"

"Do you remember on the news last week when the stock market dropped so low?" Sue asked.

"Yes," Kit answered. "I know you've been on the phone trying to get hold of our broker since then. What happened?" Kit sat down in the chair opposite Sue, anticipating the blow this news could bring.

"Well, we lost everything," Sue said as fresh tears fell.

"Everything?" Kit asked in disbelief.

"Everything," Sue said. "Jonathan and the boys invested most of our savings in the stock market. They anticipated growth, and I just didn't see it any differently, so I left it in when they died."

"We still have some in savings, though, don't we?" Kit asked.

"A little, but not enough to keep this apartment."

"But, what about my salary with the catering company? Surely that will help." Kit offered. Sue had not asked her to pay anything for rent in the apartment yet. Kit hoped she would now allow it.

"I'm saddened to have to ask for your help, dear," Sue said lowering her head.

"Don't be sad about it, Mama Sue. I want to help. Plus, when the house finally sells, we can put that money in savings to help, too."

"That's the other thing, dear," Sue continued. "You know how we've been waiting for months for Mr. Conner to buy the ranch?"

"Yes," Kit said cautiously.

"His money was lost in the stock market as well. He's backed out of the sale. Real Estate is plummeting and will go further down. I'm afraid we will need a miracle to sell the ranch now."

Kit sank back in the chair letting the information settle in. "What are we going to do?" she finally asked. "I barely make enough to keep payments on this apartment. We don't have enough to keep the ranch. I can't move back to the ranch with no money to pay for it, and I wouldn't leave you anyway."

"I don't know, dear," Sue said defeatedly.

Kit sat for a minute then squared her shoulders and said through tears, "We pray. You said we need a miracle, we'll pray for a miracle. We've weathered tougher storms together before. We'll get through this together as well."

They bowed their heads together and prayed for the next hour.

After they exhausted their prayers, Sue said, "Let's not do anything rash right now. We'll wait a few days and see what God says."

"I agree," Kit answered. "For now, would you like chicken or pasta for dinner?"

"How about both?" Sue answered.

They got up and began cooking dinner, both silently agreeing not to talk about the elephant in the room for the rest of the evening.

After dinner, they relaxed in the living room and watched a baseball game.

"You know Gavin would have loved this," Sue said. "He loved baseball."

"He watched it whenever he could," Kit agreed. "He got me started enjoying it. I know he wanted to take me to a live game."

"He really loved you, dear," Sue said, as tears came again.

"I know," Kit answered with tears of her own. "I loved him so much."

"I know," Sue said.

"He was a good man. He and I both attribute a lot of that to you and Jonathan. You were both great parents to both boys. He really cared for you."

"Thank you, dear," Sue said. "I know you miss him."

"I do," Kit said softly.

"He wouldn't want you to mourn him forever, you know."

Kit didn't answer.

"You're young. He's in Heaven. He's having a party. He would want you to as well. Don't mourn him forever, dear. It's alright if you want to move on, whenever you're ready."

Sue got up and left the room for bed leaving Kit in the living room to ponder her mother-in-law's words.

"Lord," she prayed. "You know my heart. You know why you have me in the situation I'm in. I don't understand it. I don't like it, but I trust you. I am lonely, but I have come to settle in my new life. I would love a husband, but only the right one. I don't want to always compare him to Gavin. I want him to be his own man. I want him to love you and me and accept the past and present you have allowed for me.

"I don't understand why things seem to be getting worse instead of better," she continued. "I thought it was getting better, but now this. I won't ask you why. I know I probably won't know the answer to that this side of heaven. I will say that I don't like it. But I do trust in you. Please take everything you've allowed and work it for your good. Work through me to your good end. Amen."

———

The next day, Kit got up and went to work with a heavy heart. She didn't feel anything moving from the Lord. She was disappointed but still trusting. She sat down in her office and buried herself in work, trying not to think about her own problems.

A knock on the door made her jump.

"Not going to lunch?" Emmett asked.

"You scared me," Kit said testily.

"I'm sorry. Is everything okay?"

"No – yes, I'm fine," Kit stammered.

"Really? It's nearly two o'clock and you've not moved from your desk since nine." He sat down in the chair opposite her desk. "What's wrong?"

Kit looked at her hands. "Emmett, you know I usually appreciate your questions about my family and myself. Right now, though, I don't know if I'm ready to share."

Emmett looked concerned. He stood up from the chair. "Alright, but when you're ready to share, you know where I am." He left her office without another word.

Kit laid her head down on her desk and cried. Here she had a wonderful friend who always showed an interest in her, and she was shutting him out when she needed a friend the most. When the tears stopped flowing, she grabbed a tissue, wiped her eyes and nose, and went to Emmett's office.

"You're right," she said, when he motioned for her to sit. "There is something wrong. It's big. You've always been so kind to me and interested in me. I'm sorry I shut you out."

"It's alright," he said reassuringly. "If you don't want to talk, you don't have to. I just wanted you to know I'm here."

"I appreciate it so much. I do need to talk," she said. Then she told him everything Sue had told her the night before. When she finished, they both sat in silence for a while.

"I'll help in any way I can," Emmett said finally. "The company has a little bit of money that I could give you a raise, but I'm afraid it might not help as much as you need it."

"I'm sure the others are hurting as well, I don't want special treatment," Kit interjected.

"I was wanting to give you a raise, anyway. You've done excellent work since you've been here. I was holding out until you'd been here a year, but I can bump it up to now. In fact, consider it done." He wrote a note on his paper and sent an e-mail to his accountant.

Kit tried to hold back the tears. "Thank you. But what about you and the company with the stock market crash? Are you alright? Can the company really afford to do this?"

"Don't worry about that. The company and I are truly fine."

"Thank you," Kit said again. "Well, I'd better get back to work. Thanks again for listening."

"Any time," Emmett said. "Thanks for trusting me."

Kit smiled and went back to her office with her heart a little lighter.

That night she told Sue what Emmett had done. "Praise God," was all Sue could say.

"Good morning, Amber," Kit said to the receptionist the next day as she entered the office. "Is Emmett in his office already?"

"Good morning, Kit. No, he's not in today. He had to go out of town on some emergency business this morning and said he'd return in a few days. He said to give you this file to begin working on."

Confused, Kit took the file and went back to her office. She couldn't think of any out of town business that was far enough away that Emmett might not be back for a few days. Looking at the file Amber handed her, she realized she wouldn't have much time to think about it. This was their next event and several of the vendors had not shipped their items. She was going to be on the phone all day.

Chapter 10

A few days later, Kit arrived home frazzled from a rough day at work. She still hadn't heard from Emmett. No one in the office had heard from him. She was in charge and not sure she was doing it right. She was beginning to get frustrated. "If this is what the raise entails, I don't know if I want it."

"Kit! Is that you?" Sue called from the kitchen.

"Yes, Mama Sue, it's me," Kit called back.

"Come here quickly, dear. Jake's on the phone with some news!"

Kit hurried to the kitchen. Jake would have news about the ranch. Judging from Sue's voice, it was good news at that. "Jake? How are you?"

"I'm fine, Mrs. Elliott," Jake said on the other end of the receiver. "I have some good news about the ranch."

"Really? What is it?" Kit asked excitedly.

"Someone wants to buy it."

"Are you serious?" Kit asked. "What's their terms?"

"The buyer wants to pay what you're asking," Jake said.

"That's wonderful," Kit said relieved. "What about you and the rest of the hands?"

"Well, there's more good news with that," Jake said. "The man isn't from around here and doesn't know much about ranching. In fact, he said he probably wouldn't be here much either. He wants to keep us all on and give us raises to take care of the ranch for him."

"Oh, Jake that's wonderful!" Kit exclaimed. "Who is the buyer?"

"I don't know. He wanted to remain anonymous and is working through a financial advisor. That's the one I've talked to."

"Interesting," Kit said. "Do you think he's legitimate?"

"Definitely. He said he'd pay cash whenever we're ready to sign."

"Cash?" Kit asked in unbelief.

"Yes, ma'am."

Kit put her hand over the receiver. "What do you think, Mama Sue?"

"I'd say this is our miracle," Sue answered.

Kit smiled. "Jake, tell him we'll sell. Send us the papers as soon as you can. Thank you so much."

After a little more small talk about the ranch, Kit hung up the phone. She and Sue simply stared at each other in unbelief.

Finally, Sue jumped in the air and shouted, "Praise God!"

"Amen to that!" Kit said.

The next day the papers came through the fax machine at the catering company as Kit had instructed. She searched through the papers for a clue as to who the buyer might be. All it said was that the sale was in the name of Andrew Harmon's estate. Kit had no idea who Andrew Harmon was. She thanked God, took the papers home to show Sue and sign it next to Carmen's signature, then faxed them back to Montana. Within the next hour, she got a call from her bank saying the money had been deposited in her savings account.

That night, Kit took Sue out to dinner on the Plaza.

———

The next day was Saturday, and Kit enjoyed sleeping in. It had been an emotional week. Not only with the sale of the ranch, but also with the running of the company. She had no idea where Emmett was and was a little miffed that at least as his second in command he didn't tell her. She decided to brush it off and head in to the kitchen for a leisurely breakfast.

Sue was already there making French toast.

"Smells wonderful," Kit said, as she sat at the table and took the mug of tea Sue offered her.

"We have much to celebrate today," Sue said.

"Yes we do," Kit agreed.

A knock sounded on the door. "Are you expecting anyone?" both women asked the other. They laughed.

"I'll get it," Sue said, noting Kit's robe and her hair piled on her head in a messy bun.

"Emmett," Sue said, "do come in."

Kit tried to jump up from the table to run to her room and freshen up, but ended up knocking over the tea and orange juice on to her robe and the floor.

"Need some help in there?" Emmett called from the entryway.

"I'm fine," Kit laughed. "The kitchen's a mess, and so am I, but come on in."

Emmett smiled at the scene when he entered the kitchen.

"Please, have a seat," Kit said. "That chair's clean."

"Thanks," Emmett said laughing.

"Where's Sue?" Kit asked.

"I asked if I could talk with you alone, first," Emmett said. "I owe you an apology. I should not have left you alone in charge of the company with no instructions and no word as to where I was. I heard you did a great job, though."

"Thank you," Kit said. "I appreciate that. I admit I was miffed, but we've had some great news to over shadow that."

"I know," Emmett said.

"You know?" Kit asked.

"I do. You sold the ranch. Congratulations!"

"Thank you, but how can you know? You just got here. Sue didn't have enough time to tell you."

"I have a confession," Emmett said. "Andrew Harmon was my grandfather, Mom's father."

"What?" Kit said.

"He left us a sizeable amount when he died many years ago. I invested my portion of it and bought the ranch."

"You invested it?" Kit asked. "But the stock market crashed last week. How could you still have money?"

"I didn't invest in the stock market. I invested in life insurance. That's a story for another time, though."

"Okay, so you were the one who bought the ranch?" Kit asked.

"Yes, I did."

"Why?"

"Kit," Emmett began shakily, "I've come to grow very fond of you these past few months. I've thoroughly enjoyed every moment we've spent together. I was so happy when I first thought of you as my friend instead of my second in command. Then, I was confused and scared when I thought of the possibility of more than just friendship with you. I've prayed so much about this and just feel like I need to trust God and tell you how I feel."

Kit was silent.

"I think I'm falling in love with you," Emmett said simply. "Now, I didn't buy your ranch to make you fall in love with me. I really thought it might be fun to own a ranch and have a place to go for vacations. If it happens that you would like to spend vacations there with me in the future, all the better. What do you think? Could I be more than a boss, more than your friend?"

Kit couldn't help the smile that spread across her face, nor the tears that filled her eyes. "I have prayed for God to send me a good man. I was shocked and scared when I thought I heard him say that you were that good man. I pushed aside those thoughts, but I will gladly let them come to the forefront again. Yes, Emmett, I would love for you to be more than just my friend."

Emmett stood up and took Kit's hand. He helped her up and hugged her.

"Oh, no!" Kit jumped back. "You'll get orange juice and tea all over you!"

"Gladly," Emmett pulled her close again and kissed her this time. Kit felt herself melt in his arms.

Finally, they pulled apart and started laughing.

"So, how do you want to do this?" Emmett said.

"What do you mean?" Kit asked.

"I'm willing to wait as long as you want, but I want you to know that I want you to be my wife."

Fresh tears fell down Kit's cheeks again. She sat down in the chair.

"Did I say something wrong?" Emmett asked, concerned.

"No, not at all," Kit said. "It's just that, well, Gavin and I dated for four years waiting for the right time to get married. We were married for only two years and now the only regret that I have is that we didn't get married sooner. Life is short. I think when you've found the one God wants you to be with, there's no point in wasting time."

Emmett laughed. "I'll drink to that! Well, let's tell Sue and my parents before we make a date anyway. Oh, what about your parents? Do you want me to ask them?"

Kit's face fell at the thought of her parents. "No, I'll call them. I think I'd want Mama Sue to walk me down anyway. Let's go tell her."

Sue was overjoyed at the news. Then all three went to Emmett's parents' house to share the good news. Everyone was excited. Sam and Jane took all five out to dinner that night. Food and laughter flowed. It was the happiest they had been in a long time.

Chapter 11

The next five months flew by with wedding preparations mixed with work. The staff was elated at the news of their bosses getting married. Kit had become part of the E.W. Catering family as well as the Williams family.

Finally, the day of the rehearsal came. Carmen and her family as well as Kit's parents flew down the day before. Kit had a wonderful time reconnecting with her sister-in-law and meeting her new boyfriend. Time with her own parents was tense, but Kit refused to let that ruin her day.

Emmett hired a different catering company for the rehearsal and reception, wanting to give their staff/family the chance to celebrate with them.

The rehearsal went by easily. Everyone enjoyed the dinner. When the last bottle of champagne had been drunk, everyone parted ways looking forward to what the next day would bring.

Kit and Sue went back to their apartment. "Care for some tea?" Kit asked as they arrived.

"I'd love some," Sue answered.

They sat down at the kitchen table for the last time together. "I'm going to miss this," Kit said.

"Me, too," Sue replied. "You'll always be welcome to come any time, dear"

"Thank you," Kit said. "I would love that."

"I'm so happy for you, Kit," Sue said as a single tear rolled down her cheek. "You deserve this happiness. You'll still be my daughter, though, no matter if Jane claims you as well."

"I will always think of you as my mother, Mama Sue," Kit said. "We've been through a lot together. You can't discount that. You've been wonderful to me. Thank you for leading me to Jesus."

"It's all been my pleasure, dear."

"I love you."

"I love you, too."

The next day was a beautiful October day. The leaves were turning vibrant colors. The air was crisp. Kit woke up in an extremely good mood.

Sue had made French toast for breakfast. The two shared their last meal together while living under the same roof. Then Sydney came to pick Kit up for their hair appointment. The two spent the next hour laughing with the stylists as their hair was curled, pinned, and sprayed.

Next, they went to the church to get dressed and have pictures taken.

The photographer set up a room for Kit and Emmett to see each other for the first time alone before pictures were taken.

As Kit entered the room, Emmett just stared. "You look amazing," he whispered. Then he kissed her.

"You clean up well, too," Kit teased, loving how he looked in a tuxedo.

After pictures were taken, the coordinator placed everyone to get the wedding started.

Everything was perfect. Kit stood tall and strong as she gazed into her new husband's eyes. Emmett gazed tenderly at his new bride. The kiss lingered when the pastor told Emmett to kiss his new bride. Everyone cheered as the couple turned around and was pronounced Mr. and Mrs. Emmett Williams.

The couple couldn't stop grinning as they proceeded back down the aisle.

The reception was beautiful and fun. The band played lively music for everyone to dance to. The dinner was wonderful, though Emmett told his chef it didn't compare to his own cuisine.

Before the reception was over, the announcement came that the couple was ready to leave for their honeymoon. The guests formed two columns as the couple came in between showered with bubbles. At the end of the columns stood Sue, smiling through happy tears.

"I'm so happy for you, dear," She said as she gave her daughter-in-law a hug. "Bless you, my dear. You have been more than a daughter to me. May God bless you in your new life."

"I'm not leaving you, Mama Sue," Kit smiled. "Just think of it as acquiring another son."

"If that's alright with you," Emmett said.

"It's more than alright, Emmett," Sue smiled. "May God bless you both, my children."

They each hugged Sue and then set off for their honeymoon.

————

A week later as Kit and Emmett were driving by the Plaza back to their apartment, Emmett drove by the office building.

"Did you get a new sign?" Kit said as they approached it.

"What do you mean?" Emmett asked, trying to hide a smile.

"The sign was blue, now it's green. When did you put it up? Was I so occupied with our wedding that I didn't notice it?" Kit said.

"Nope, it just went up this week," Emmett said. He slowed down in front of the office.

"Oh, Emmett," Kit said, as she saw the sign in full.

The sign now read "E.K.W. Catering."

"Thank you," Kit said happily.

"It's yours now, too," Emmett said as he squeezed her hand.

"I love you, Emmett."

"I love you, too, Kit."